FLIGHT OF THE KING

The Phoenix's Ashes, Book Three
A Circus of Shifters Reverse Harem

By
Rebecca Ethington

Published by Imdalind Press

Production Management by Imdalind Press

ISBN (print) **978-1-949725-19-3**

ISBN (e-book) **978-1-949725-16-2**

Printed in USA

This Edition, November 2018

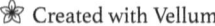 Created with Vellum

CONTENTS

To My Little Ones

1

ELLIOT

"I am leaving to rescue Jarron from Rydaim tonight. There is no question. There is no discussion. I am going, and I will be going alone."

If I ever had a question that Killian would be a superb king, I think he had just answered that. Not only was he doomed to be a superb king. He was also going to be a stubborn, arrogant, and bossy king.

And I sure as shit hoped that my face told him as much. Because all the stubborn arrogance was really getting on my nerves.

My nose was wrinkled, an intense glare set on him that was accentuated by the red-gold flame beaming behind my eyes. I tapped my fingers on my forearm impatiently, arms crossed over my chest as I sat back on the couch. If I had nails I would probably look as elegant and bossy as he did. Of course, the fact that I was mostly naked, still covered in ash from the fire, and quickly staining the bathrobe Killian had wrapped me in, took away any hope of anyone taking me seriously.

Killian was still streaked with ash, but at least he had taken a minute to pull on some deep grey joggers.

Deep grey joggers and nothing else.

I hadn't truly been able to see him from where I was sitting on his lap in the bathroom a few minutes before. I had seen the deep moss-green of his eyes, I had felt the strong lines of his muscles throb beneath my fingers. But little else.

Now I saw him. I saw the muscular lines of his hips as they angled past the waist of his sweatpants. I saw the full breadth of his tattoo as it stretched over his sun-kissed skin. The tail of the creature dipped over his side, closer to that alluring waistband and over those abs, each one defined and shaded as though he had been painted by a master.

I would write that master painter a thank you letter, if I wasn't so freaking irate right now.

Sitting here, the heat of my anger or magic or whatever the hell was inside of me, rippled and roared like a monster waiting to come out. At least my skin wasn't bulging with little dragon spawn like I had seen Killian's do, not that it helped the rumble of an explosion that was threatening to escape. One sneeze and the whole hotel would go up in flames.

I really couldn't put anything past my very angry phoenix, anymore. Of course, it wasn't the phoenix that I was worried about. I seem to have more power than stopping time and farting fire.

I had seen someone that was in Rydaim. Which, I now

learned, was in Spain. A whole ocean away. Trapped in what Killian recognized as the enchanted dungeon in the middle of Rydaim. Shackles, rocks, bars, everything around him was made to restrict his shifter. To keep his dragon locked inside.

I didn't need Killian to tell me how bad that was, both in that he was stuck there and that I was seeing him stuck there with my own special breed of voodoo.

Which is why I sure as shit didn't need Killian to try to keep me here. I couldn't stay here. I needed to be there, I needed to save him.

That weird burning, twisting power that had showed me Jarron was also pulling me there. I wasn't about to deny that after what had happened.

Nothing was going to keep me from Jarron. Killian could try, but I would find a way. Even if I had to shrink myself down to an ant and stow away, I was coming.

And yes, I recognized that creating ant-me may not be possible, but I was a freak of nature. I was pretty sure the mythical Phoenix-Fae-thing inside of me would pull-out something amazing.

Xi had warned me not to drink the Kool-Aid, but as she predicted, I did. Two tiny drops and everything inside of me had changed.

I wished I knew what, or even how to explain it. It was as though a light had been turned on inside of me. Well, a light if it was confusing and foggy as hell.

Which brings me back to the buzzing twisting power of doom. Well, not doom, but pretty darn close anyway.

"You can't just barge into Rydaim and pull him out, Killian. Father will catch you, there is no way that he will sit back and let that happen," Drake said, following Killian around the makeshift map that he had been hovering over for the last few minutes.

Well, we all had, Zoe, Drake and I all staring at it with different levels of confusion. I had given up a few minutes ago and resorted to scowling from the couch.

"There are other ways in beside the main entrances," Killian began, his irritatingly smug smile stretching over his face. "This is a duplicate of the schematics of the original construction of Rydaim, well at least as much as I can recall."

"And where the hell did you see an original schematic?" Zoe's confusion was fading into skeptical awe. "Especially enough to memorize it."

"Callay." Killian provided, his voice framed with a weird warning, his eyes not deviating from the map, which was good because if he saw the look that Zoe was giving him, that warning may have turned into a full-on threat.

That warning was suddenly making sense. Zoe clearly didn't like the slave, or didn't like that she was a slave.

But that one I understood.

The tension hadn't left Killian's back, and muscles were pulling and pulsing in a way that I would lie if I said it wasn't distracting.

I wanted to run my hands over those tight muscles and soothe it away, or even just feel them pulse and pull.

Woah. I forced a swallow, now was not the time for this.

I didn't know how someone could be both horny and scared shitless simultaneously - but I had somehow managed it.

"Where did she get it?" Zoe asked incredulously, her hands on her hips as she stared down Killian, who was still looking at the map, and not at her.

"She got it from a friend."

Zoe scoffed at that, and I didn't blame her. I wasn't on anyone's side in this, but that answer sure seemed like a weird excuse to me.

"Is this friend Ceres?" This time Zoe earned herself a look from Killian; whose normally green eyes were so dark that they could have easily been confused for Jarron's.

Ugh. Even thinking his name was a stab in the heart.

There went the hormones. Thank god. Not that they would have been able to stick around with the tension that was starting to stink up the room.

The look Drake was giving me screamed that they had done it all before, sibling rivalry at its worst. And I thought Jarron prodding his brothers was bad... Jarron.

Jarron in a freaking prison with freaking vampires. Who cared about the king?

We really needed to get back on track.

"No, Zoe," Killian's angry snap sliced through my pain, pulling my focus back to them.

"And you're sure she's not setting you up for disaster?" Drake said, obviously trying to keep a calm amidst Zoe and Killian's eye-dagger competition.

Panic rumpled through the air, the tension and anger very quickly hitting a boil, and making the weird warmth that was rolling under my skin pick up.

Thankfully, there were no flames on my arms, but that didn't mean I wasn't about to burp bubbles or summon demons, or whatever I could do.

"Callay is trustworthy--"

"Who cares where the freakin' map came from," I shrieked jumping up from the couch and barging through them, cutting off from their escalating fight. "If it's gets us to Jarron that's all that matters."

"Gets me to Jarron," Killian corrected, fixing me with a dark-eyed scowl. His eyes were firm, his jaw tight and I was having a hard time deciding if I wanted to kiss him or smack the smug authority off his face.

If only either of those would get me the outcome that I was hoping for. Killian may not want to hear about why I needed to be there with them. But he was going to.

"The members of the rescue party hardly matters if you can't get in, or if you can't get Jarron out," I said, choosing my words carefully. "So how do you plan on getting him out?"

"The ways in and out are much more prevalent than anyone knew. I doubt even The Forgotten know the depth of it."

"If The Forgotten didn't know about it then how..." Zoe interrupted Killian, but I cut her off with a look, doing my best not to slam my fist into table, or thigh, or air, or anything I could come in contact with on the way.

"I don't care about the map." I was giving her my best warning glance, which she only smiled at. "I care about Jarron. How are you going to get him out?"

Killian's lip twitched, the frustration in his eyes shivering before I clicked my tongue impatiently. I would not let his manly charm do me in, I was mad dammit, and I was going to keep them on task.

"Thanks to the map, I will be able to get in, and retrieve not only Jarron but any Fae I find along the way."

"So, you are getting Jarron and any other people you bump into?" I asked. He nodded, leaving all of us looking at him, waiting for him to continue. He didn't.

Ugh. Arrogant Dragon!

"Could you be a little more vague? I didn't get it the first time." The snark snapped out of me no matter how I tried to restrain it.

Which of course would mean that I tried.

Which I didn't.

I stood there, hands on hips, wearing a fluffy robe, hair in a messy bun on top of my head, staring at Killian with all the dignity I could muster.

Zoe popped a hole in that real quick, chuckling darkly at me.

"I used this path to get out so I could reach you," Killian continued over Zoe's snickers, she was now kneeling next to the table as though she was worshiping it. "No one saw me. I am sure I can use it to get back in, and then get everyone out another way. Perhaps following this path."

He traced his finger along yet another of the large black lines, a trail of ash dragging down the papers, past what I was sure were buildings and roads.

The more he dragged, the more the map made sense, until it was more than a large round fountain, more than squiggles and lines.

Trails. Caves. Each winding pathway. It all hit me like a lightning bolt, everything making sense. Everything but where Rydaim was.

Luckily, that little tidbit wasn't going to be a problem, though. If Killian wasn't going to let me come along, and creating a tiny ant version of me didn't work, I was sure I could find him anyway.

Activate the power of the heart strings... or something. Whatever was connecting me to all of them was already pulling on me like a dog with a sharing problem. My connection to Jarron could easily lead me right there. I just had to take advantage of that. I was sure no one would notice a flaming phoenix flying into their underground city, anyway.

Totally fucking doable.

Well, if I wanted to be butchered in the first five minutes.

Yeah, I needed to be with him.

"If you can get in undetected, then I see no reason why we all can't go. I was still staring at the map, my mind twisting and turning as that same buzzing pulled at my spine.

Speaking of the line in my heart that connected me to Jarron, it was already pulling me towards him. Well, maybe not him, but that place in the map where I was sure he was.

This time, instead of pulling me toward the black ring that denoted a fountain, it yanked me towards a large box, a massive square that moved besides roads and who knew what else.

Just a boring box, drawn into the map.

Well, a boring box where I was sure Jarron was.

Right there, beyond the paper. Like I could reach through the sheets of hotel stamped stationery and grab him.

Damn it all. That wasn't possible, I knew that wasn't possible. One sip of Killian's magic juice and I was thinking I could move through tables.

That sounded wrong. So wrong.

"It's not safe for you to be there," both Killian and Drake said together, their joined pronouncement making me jump.

Of course, now would be the time that Drake would join in, choosing to agree with Killian for the first time in probably years, on the one thing that I was ready to fight to the death on.

"It's not safe for me to be here alone, either," I countered.

I really didn't want to pull out Drake's broken dragon thing again, but it was kind of a huge problem in this scenario.

And that was without my soul needing us all to be together.

My phoenix bristled in agreement, not that anyone could see it, but it was all the confirmation I needed.

I needed to be there, right there. In that dark box in the corner of the map where that tight little string was pulling me.

No, not pulling. Dragging. In fact, it would rip my heart out in attempt to get there if I didn't help it along.

That damn box! It was a sirens call, and I turned to it, but whatever darkness had been there a minute ago had gone. It was just a square on a map. Nothing special, and I still wasn't sure it was anything besides an intersection of a few roads.

"You won't be alone," Zoe began, her eyes shimmering in that warning flame I had seen too many times. "You will have Drake--"

"And Zoe," Killian cut in.

Zoe looked about ready to explode. "I'm going with you."

I really didn't want to see the look she was giving Killian right then.

"You can't leave her here alone," Killian's voice was raising in both octave and volume, the man nearly hovering over Zoe as he roared.

The two of them were officially going at it again, and Drake was having none of it.

His eyes were hard little daggers as he stared at his siblings, his arms tight coils of muscles crossed over his chest. He looked pissed, and I almost would have believed it, if his eyes weren't glistening.

"We need to stay together," I whispered to him, placing my hand on his arm as Zoe and Killian continued to rant over each other.

A warm wave of energy moved through me, his muscles flexing beneath my fingers as his jaw tightened. There wasn't a hint of a dimple, and the melted honey in his eyes had been dissolved by angry tears, but the intensity of his stare still made my insides cartwheel.

"I wish I could protect you," He whispered as Killian kicked a chair over something Zoe had said, sending it tumbling over the beige carpet, and right into the beige wall.

We both jumped, Drake stepping toward me as Killian heaved.

"You can. You already are. But we need to stay together," I promised, the warmth of his hand as it lifted to cover my own sending even more spirals through me.

"Trust me on this," I finished, thankfully keeping my voice from shaking.

Although, you never would have known with the way Zoe was now screaming at her brother. No wonder he had kicked a chair.

"You can't change the past Killian!"

"You're right," They were right up against each other now, the two tall powerful dragons looking like one of those cartoons that stretched their necks for the higher spot.

I had a feeling this was more of a power struggle than a fight over battle rights.

I did not want to see their dragons fight, and I really didn't want to see them fight over the crown.

I was half expecting hotel security to have shown up by now, although what they would do with two raging dragons I wasn't too sure.

"I will always trust you on anything," he said, before planting a kiss on my temple and stepping away.

Right into the dragon's pit.

Concern washed over me as he rushed right between them, hands held out like a barricade. A very hot, very angry barricade.

I think I had only seen Drake stand up to his brothers like this once before, and even then it was with Jarron, who was kind of a push-over, if I was being honest.

I mean, an absolute panty melting, sex god push-over. But still, a push-over.

Seeing Drake now, however, my panties were melting in a completely different way.

"Knock it off, will ya?" Drake bellowed pushing the two away from him and sending them stumbling. Zoe was knocked right out of her rage, Killian however rose to his feet with all the strength of a freight train. Everything about him was pulsing with strength as he faced his brother, even his forearm looked all pulsey and dangerous as he brushed his hair off his hard, little dagger eyes.

Phoenix screaming inside my head, I was ready to vault over the table and push the guy out the window, kick him in the balls again if I had to.

"Do you really wish to fight me," Killian's voice rumbled the ugly vases full of fake flowers, the strength of his pseudo warning rattling the gaudy paintings that lined the walls. "I will teach you what it is to fight a king."

And Killian rushed Drake.

And I completely lost it.

"That's it!" I yelled, nearly as loud, although it didn't pull anyone's attention. I sprinted around the table, placing myself in between Drake and Killian and looked up at the massive stretch of muscle, tattoo, and perfectly carved skin that was now barreling toward me.

Ugh. What I wouldn't give to be another foot taller right then.

Didn't matter, here I was, and I was going to solve this with one solid poke in Killian's sternum, lucky it forced him to take a step back so I could see his face. Not that the smirk that was now taking over his features was helping.

"You guys need to knock it the fuck off!" I continued with all the strength I had in me. Facing Killian was much easier than facing his dragon after all. "You aren't king yet. We need to get Jarron before Dabria turns into an executioner, and I am going with you."

"We've been over this, Elliot," Killian groaned, dragging his hand through his hair as he took a step back.

"You're right, we have, right after I saw Jarron in the bathroom, in a prison. My stance has not changed." He raged even more. Let it come. I was ready to take it.

"It's not safe for you..."

"I don't know, Kills," Zoe said, her tone thankfully soft enough that she wasn't going to send them back into a battle royal. "With this, it might be doable."

She gestured towards the map, towards the lines and squiggles and the damn box that kept pulling me in, like a fish with a line.

The damn thing was beckoning me to it again, and whatever conversation Zoe had struck up behind me fell away. I knew it was important, Zoe was suddenly on my side and all that. But that box... I wanted to go there. I wanted to step through the map and grab Jarron and pull him out.

Well, that made it sound like I was crazy, which up until a few minutes ago I was decidedly not.

But then I had a vision of Jarron in a dungeon I had never seen, located a million miles away and everything had gone to shift.

No power was apparently outside of my ability. Nothing was sacred, hell, nothing was safe. And the more I stared at that black box, the more everything felt like this disgusting bubble of doom.

But not doom in the way the world-ending-alien-invasion doom, but in the way that if I didn't make it to him there was gonna be a whole lot more trouble than any of these guys were ready for.

Fire farts were just the beginning.

Staring at the black box made all the energy that was rumbling under my skin zoom to life. It bubbled and pricked as that weird energy began to heat. I was used to heat, but this was different, and beyond weird. Like little bugs eating away at me.

Their feet scurried over my skin like a thousand needles, a thousand ropes that were pulling me closer to the map, pulling me closer to that square where I knew Jaron was. He was a million miles away. I had to get to him.

I had to move through the map to reach him.

There I go sounding like a loon again. A few weeks ago, the craziest thing I had done was jumped off cliffs and buildings and turned into a giant flaming bird. I had done that, so why couldn't I move through a map? This was just the next step, right?

Killian, Drake, and Zoe were still arguing, their voices buzzing through the tunnel that was pulling at me, all the little feet dragging me right to that black box. It was just a black square on a piece of hotel letterhead, my logic knew that. It didn't stop it from sucking me into it as though it was a black hole in the middle of the universe.

"Jarron," I whispered, the angry buzz of the siblings' conversation was scratching the back of my mind as I leaned closer, towards the map, towards the black box.

My spine had wrapped itself into a tight coil, my fingers shaking as I stretched towards the square, towards the paper and the portal that would take me to Jarron. The little bugs picked up, pulling me in. I was ready to grab it, to pull myself through paper and table and universe and whatever else is in my way to reach him.

I was sure it would work, everything else had worked. Yes,

something in the back of my mind was sure that I was bat-shit crazy and maybe I was.

But as they bickered, and I reached my hand towards it, my fingers millimeters from that square, I was sure I was going to fall right through it.

Instead, I fell into the table.

2

ELLIOT

My hand gave way, unable to support my weight, and my head hit the hard surface with a thwack that echoed around the room and stopped their conversation as though someone had run a truck through it.

That truck was clearly me.

"What the fuck!" I wasn't sure if it was Zoe or Drake that had screeched, for all I know it could've been me with the waves of pain that were rippling over my skull.

Who knew that coffee tables could be so goddamn hard?

"Ow." The low moan echoed from my throat as I slid off the table taking the pieces of the map along with me and scattering them over the floor like little paper snowflakes.

"Are you okay?" Drake asked, dropping to his knees and prodding at my neck and ears before carefully turning to stare at the back of my head as though I was sprouting an eyeball back there.

I wasn't sure if he was looking for an injury or some sign

that I had completely lost it. With the way I was acting there had to be something stamped on my forehead that promised of my insanity.

Danger, Insanity. Released on Impact.

I was obviously past that.

The look Killian gave me as he hovered over me, splayed out on the floor, was only adding to that.

"You okay Ellie girl?"

"Oh, you know," I said with a flippant wave. "Just passing out, having visions, and then trying to make out with a coffee table."

"Well, save your next kiss for me," Killian said, his smile not quite hitting his eyes. "And you're not crazy."

"I'm starting to doubt that."

"I saw him, too, Ellie girl," he whispered, leaning down to run his finger over my cheek. Yep, I totally shivered.

Shit. I needed tea, and I had no idea where the blue Smurf-drugs had ended up.

He smiled before dodging away to pick up the papers that my fall from grace, and mental instability, had scattered.

"Next time you pass out, you might try angling yourself away from the table," Zoe snickered, giving me a look before she joined Killian in the map retrieval.

"Well, I'm sorry I don't have better aim when I'm passing out. Which I wasn't by the way," I grumbled, earning myself a very fiery scowl from an already fired up Zoe.

You would think that hitting the coffee table so hard would shove some good old-fashioned logic back into my mind. Nope, I was still going to snap at a Dragon. Because we all knew that was the safest thing.

I already knew what would happen if I kicked a dragon, I wasn't interested to find out the rest of it. Zoe was not a good one to try that out on.

"You can't move through the table, you know," Killian said, beginning to shuffle the papers and placing them back on the table.

"That's actually what I was trying to do." The words burned my tongue, the insanity dripping from them as the little bugs scuttled over my skin again.

All aboard the crazy train!

Everyone around me froze, wide eyes staring at me as they looked from me to the table.

"Yeah, I know I have clearly lost it," I grumbled as I pulled myself to sitting, thankful when my head didn't go into full on spin mode. "But in my defense, I was pretty sure it could be done..."

I was really not helping my case, and the way their wide eyes were staring at the table I was starting to wonder if Killian and Zoe were frozen in time.

Maybe I could do that too. Because, clearly no one had heard my gripe, which was probably for the best.

"What is that?" Drake's voice shuddered as he slowly stood, the same wide-eyed stare that Zoe and Killian had fixed me with tracing over his face as though it had been slapped there.

"What is what?" I was officially starting to freak out.

I mean I expected some kind of reaction for admitting that I wanted to move through a table but the wide-eyed horrified stares that were still moving between me and the table was starting to make me question my sanity.

"Did you do this?" Zoe's voice quivering, like, full on quivering. Forget the time loop, maybe I had pushed us into another dimension.

That should've been my first clue that something was horribly, awfully, and completely wrong. Even when her father had been flying his way toward us after Drake had shifted Zoe hadn't had a drop of fear, well, not compared to this.

This look was terrifying if only because the light from her dragon had disappeared.

Patting my arms and legs to make sure that I still existed, I jumped to standing, muscles and heart tight as I looked toward the coffee table that had held their attention so thoroughly.

Half of the map was still there, although it was scattered and jumbled so much that the entire thing looked like a toddler's art project. The pieces that had held the black box were gone. The black box, however, was still there.

Burned into the wood.

A large black square of the wood was being eaten away by a smoldering char that burned in little embers of the brightest red, but it was burning funny, as though the fire had tried to eat the table from the inside out.

It was a perfect, black, burning box. Well, all except for a shape that shimmered, untouched, in the center of the glittering embers. A near perfect carving that was too detailed to be accidental.

A dragon stood out against the smoldering wood, the sparks of flame making the wings of the creature glitter as though they were gold.

"What the holy priest with a hand grenade is that?" I thought I had been losing it before, but that was before I came face-to-face with some sort of emulated miracle.

"How did you do that?" Zoe's eyes drifted to me for the first time in the last few minutes, shock dripping from the little sparks of fire that tried to swallow her pupils.

"Unless I somehow have the power to create magical artwork by slamming my forehead into a coffee table, I am pretty sure I didn't do that," I rubbed my hand over the what I was sure would be a bruise as if to emphasize the point, Zoe didn't seem too convinced and neither did Killian who was looking as frightened as she was.

I would love to say that my Phoenix had created that, that my power had jumped out of me and burned away this little square and a little dragon that was going to make everything perfect so I could go and rescue Jarron. But I hadn't.

Well, I was pretty sure I hadn't.

I was getting used to the super powerful flame weapons. Creating immaculate table art just didn't seem to be my forte.

"That's the dungeon," Killian said, shifting through the papers in his hands as he put the map back together, dropping one page after another and connecting the dark lines until the black square returned, covering the burn on the table with perfect symmetry.

Symmetry and a haunting dose of what-the-fuck.

The papers perfectly covered the scorch marks, but instead of the bright white paper and clunky black lines, the papers were scorched.

This time, it wasn't a Dragon. A Phoenix blackened the white sheets, its wings spread wide, a line of fire shooting from its open mouth. The fire of its attack burned into the paper as though it was real, quickly eating through the surrounding sheet of white.

"I'm there too," I gasped as the paper curled and dissolved, sending flakes of burning embers into the air.

Killian looked genuinely scared, now, his eyes were shaking, his jaw was tight. He wasn't the only one; Zoe stepped back from the table as if I had some sort of witchcraft voodoo. Which was ridiculous because I had legitimately grown up around a witch!

"That's the dungeon," Killian responded, "you're in the dungeon."

The paper continued to burn and curl until it was gone, leaving only the shimmering gold of Jarron's dragon. I had never seen the beast, but I had seen the fire, I had seen his skin shimmer. I knew it was him.

Right where I thought he was.

"Well, if you needed more proof that I needed to come with you, there you go," I gestured towards the table in what I was sure was a calm reaction, even though everything inside of me was twisting uncomfortably.

I wanted to say that this was some kind of good omen, but it only felt like step one to a very ugly funeral.

"You can't be serious, Ellie, I know you want to be there but this... this is..." Killian's growls came to a halt as he ran his hands through his hair, turning away from the table with a swear that I wasn't sure was meant for me.

"Freaky beyond reason?" I provided earning myself a chuckle from Zoe.

"I could say that covers it," Zoe said through her laugh.

"I need to be there. And obviously whatever super mega power is inside of me needs me to be there too," I said carefully pleading my case and causing Killian to turn towards me so fast that his hair flipped around him.

Normally the look would incite a million butterflies and send me into a twitterpated pole-jumping event.

But without the poles, and without the jumping.

Oh, lord, I tried to focus on the angry part of the angry super model.

No jumping poles, not yet.

Damn it, it was getting worse.

"Don't say it Killian," I said, heart tensing as Drake came up beside me, his hand soft as it ran down my spine. I didn't have the guts to look away from Killian. Hell, I didn't have the guts to look at Drake. For all I knew he was going to be giving me that same horrified 'oh hell no are you coming with us' look that I was getting from Killian. I plowed on before anyone could stop me.

"I know you want me to be safe, I know you would give anything for me to stay here, but I can't. You saw Jarron, Killian. I did that! I don't know how, but somehow, I did that. I drank that thing and everything has gone to pot. But the one thing that's buzzing through my head and apparently imprinting him on coffee tables is that I need to be there and that we need to stay together. All of us," I was firm, my eyes hard little specks and I looked from Zoe to Drake and back to Killian as if driving my point home, or at least begging for a tiny bit of leniency.

The man in question, however, was still fuming. It was very clear that no matter how eloquent my speeches were he was going to be a very tough sell.

"You are bonded to my dragon, and because of that it is my place to protect you," Killian said, the grind in his jaw swallowing half of his words. "Protecting you does not mean taking you into Rydaim so that I can lose you forever."

"It also doesn't mean hiding me from the world. Yes, I'm unreliable, my super crazy magic powers do the weirdest fucking things at the weirdest fucking times. I don't know if I'm gonna stop time, burn vampires, explode into flames, or create holy freaking lightning towers."

"I haven't seen that one yet," Drake said with a chuckle.

"You're not helping," I whirled on him, cursing the fact he looked so calm and agreeable. He was really putting a cool-down on my rampaging.

It really didn't help that he didn't back down either, he just stepped closer, his hand weaving around my waist. Drake's warmth leached through the fluffy fabric of the robe, his fingers pressing into my waist, and cupping around my hip bone.

Dagnabbit that wasn't helping either.

I swallowed, pushing away the rush of heat and narrowed my eyes at Killian, forcing my determination to rumble back to life.

"I'm going. And don't make me kick you in the balls again to make that happen."

I mean, I wasn't one to threaten violence, but in this instance it seemed completely justified. Thankfully, Killian's stony façade faded a bit.

"Protect me Killian. Don't smother me."

I was calm, but firm. A calm firm boulder that wasn't going to take no for an answer. If I could make puppy dog eyes without looking constipated I probably would have done that too. His facade was cracking and I was ready to break it down.

I did not get the glorious win that I was hoping for, however. Killian nodded, growled, and walked away, slamming the door to his part of the suite behind him.

"I'm going to take that as a yes," I said loudly enough that he could hear me.

Don't prod the dragon. Don't prod the dragon.

With the way my phoenix was rumbling in my chest she was ready to do just that, there couldn't have been worse timing.

If there ever was better. It was clearly a lesson that was having trouble taking hold.

"We leave in at dawn," Killian said through the door. "And if you get killed…" His voice choked, and my heart tensed as Drake pulled me closer to him, his own fearful tension feeling like coiling rope through my robe.

I had wanted to be there I knew I needed to be there. But suddenly it was all way too real.

"At dawn!" he screamed, another door slamming as the entire room shook and the growl of his Dragon ripped through the air.

I cringed, taking a step back. I half expected to hear the walls rip apart as his Dragon emerged. I waited to hear screaming and chattering and furniture being torn apart but it was only the faint tinkling of water as he turned the shower back on.

"Well that went better than expected," Zoe said, shifting the papers around to reveal the mark again, her eyes narrowing as she tried to figure it out as if it had some secret that she was going to steal from it.

I really hoped she didn't find anything, not that I was sure there was anything to find. It was all another little creepy part of whatever creepy thing I was.

I was starting to feel like the less I knew about it the better.

"And what was expected?" I said, the nervous lump in my throat making me sound like I was croaking instead of asking a question. I was already dreading the answer, it really didn't help that Drake had now begun to snicker.

"You really aren't helping to boost my confidence," I grumbled, giving him a look that only sent him laughing more.

"He didn't get his way. Let's just say that kicking his pride is almost as bad as kicking him in the balls," Drake said unable to hold his laugh any longer.

"Oh."

"But Ellie," Drake said his touch soft as he pulled me to face him, his fingertips drifting up the back of my arms and sending a shiver down my spine. "Take it from a guy who's already dead, if they catch us there won't be any pretend after this. No circus to hide in. Everything will be gone. I hope you're ready for that."

"I'm ready for anything. For Jarron," I said, pretty sure my heart was lodged in my throat. "I will do anything for all of you."

Damn it all, I knew it was true. And even though it was scary as shit, I was also very aware that this *anything* could easily end my life.

3

DRAKE

"Elliot?"

Drake's voice shook as he pushed past the door. He knew he shouldn't be inviting himself in here. Walking into a girl's room was never a great idea, especially when said girl has an affinity for shooting fire or lightning or other mysterious magic when scared.

Yet, here he was, walking around the piles of clothes and tattered suitcases towards the sound of running water that was drifting from her massive bathroom. He was sure he had heard crying, which on its own seemed pretty out of character for Ellie, but if it was true he wouldn't let her suffer alone.

Which is why he had come in here, or at least that was what he was trying to tell himself.

"Elliot?" He asked again, this time right outside the door to her bathroom, his palm flat against the door. With the amount of steam that was drifting through the crack in the door it was amazing that the door itself didn't feel like it was on fire.

"Drake?" She was alarmed, and instant regret slammed against his gut. It was almost enough to make him turn away. He would have if his dragon hadn't perked up, an awkward combination of worry and need pushing him forward.

"Yeah." Thank god his voice stayed strong. "I heard crying, are you okay?"

Saying it like that may have been a little odd, but considering she had face-planted into a coffee table twice and was having visions of Jarron, he didn't want to leave her alone. Killian and Zoe were off figuring out some way for them to get him to Spain without use of a commercial airliner, which would be way too slow in this situation, which left him, standing here, right outside her door.

"Umm, Hi! Yeah, I'm fine... just taking a shower." Even with the mumbles being drowned by the sound of running water he didn't believe her.

"You really are a terrible liar," he mumbled, sure that she couldn't hear.

Considering the loud growl that came from the room, she heard.

He was trapped between a chuckle and an eye roll. Instead he smiled and pressed his forehead against the heavy wooden door. Leave it to Ellie to be perfectly stubborn.

The line that always pulled him to her tightened, the thing coiling against his heart like a lasso. The tight little pricks of need that came with it made it feel like barbed wire. He would give anything to step into the room, to pull her out of the shower and into his arms, even though just thinking of the action cranked his need for her up to eleven, heating through his cheeks in a flush. He may not normally be the type to turn a tender shade of red at such instances, but thinking about her, and thinking about her in that way, was very easily doing him in.

His hand was dragging down the side of the door, inching toward the handle, ready to pull it open, when it opened anyway, swinging wide and thanks to his precarious forehead lean, sending him stumbling right into the steam filled room.

Drake was barely able to catch himself, which was good because even with powerfully strong dragon bones he was sure that falling head first into the sink would not end very well. Either sink or skull would end up broken, and either way he would end up with a wicked headache.

"I would call you a stalker, but I know you better than that."

"Not stalking, just worried," Drake said, still staring into the dewy porcelain sink as Ellie closed the door behind him with a click, trapping them in with the heat.

"No need, I'm not crying." Drake straightened to look at her, his heart pounding in expectation of what he would see. He had barely been able to handle the lacy underwear she had been wearing when they peeled off her clothes before, and his mind had been swimming with the image ever since.

It was probably good that Killian had sat with her then. Not that he trusted his brother's self-control. But he really didn't trust his. Coming here may have been a mistake in that, he was obviously putting himself to the test.

His pulse was already heightening before he turned from the sink, heart pounding, stomach throbbing as he turned and finally saw her, standing in swirls of steam.

THE TOWEL WAS ALMOST AS BAD AS THE UNDERWEAR, COVERED more, left less to the imagination.

"I'm fairly certain I heard at least a sniffle," Drake teased, stepping closer and singing the praises to every deity when she didn't step back.

"Maybe one," she tried to force a smile, it only made her look more pained. "But thanks to the scalding hot water it has melted it all away."

"That and the ash, I see." How Drake's mouth had gone dry in a steamy room he could not fathom, but it had. Dry as a bone, while every other bone pulsed and pulled him forward.

"Yes, clean it all off only to put it back on. Logic." She gave him a wink, lifted a finger as though pointing to a light bulb and stepped back towards the still-running shower with a "I have to finish rinsing my conditioner."

The normally bouncing curls of her tomato red hair sagged down her back as she turned from him, the long strands stretching over her bare skin, covering the pink tinged flesh as it darted towards her waist. Drake swallowed. Yes, this was much worse than that lacy black underwear. It got even worse as she dropped the towel, the white fluffy fabric falling to wrap around her ankles as she darted back into the shower, and behind the thin white shower curtain that revealed each of her perfect curves.

Drake stepped back, trying to imprint the image of her perfectly round bottom into memory, while simultaneously trying to forget he had seen it. If only to help himself calm down, and the pressure of both abdomen and groin to ease. At least enough that he could breathe and think straight.

Thank god there was a place to sit down, toilet or not, one deep breath was all he needed to stop the blood from rushing away from his head. Or at least he hoped so.

"I don't know what my phoenix will do if I try to shift with too much gunk in my hair," Ellie said from behind the curtain, giving Drake enough cover for his deep inhale. Thank god the steam was helping. "Maybe I'll turn into a fireball."

"Or perhaps you won't be able to get off the ground," Drake tried to joke along with her, even though the humor was lost. The truth of the words were a little too close to home for him.

His burgeoning need for the girl evaporated into the steam as pain blossomed over his chest. Ellie was now peeking around the shower curtain, her eyes hooded and sad.

"Now, who's crying?" Even her prod was deflated by worry.

"I'm not crying." Yes, he was a bit too sharp, but he didn't need her thinking him a crier along with the rest.

"Did Zoe and Killian leave?"

He nodded, "They went to go find a way to carry me like a defenseless baby is carried by a stork."

Bitterness rolled off his tongue, painting the air and tarnishing it with a malice he didn't realize he was holding. Crying was bad enough. He dropped his head, content to look at the slick tiles and at his fingers as they twisted one over another. To look anywhere but at his beautiful, capable, strong mate. She was everything that he was not. Not right now.

"They aren't going to carry you like a stork-baby," Ellie said. It was clear she was trying not to laugh, which was really not helping.

"Considering they left talking about making a sheet and blanket basket, I'm not one hundred percent convinced of that."

"Won't Killian let you ride on his back or something?"

"That would be worse." The gnawing ache in his heart was starting to feel like a glaring hole. "Dragons do not let people ride on their backs, let alone their pathetic baby brother."

The hole was ripping all the way through him now, his vision shaking as his fingers turned one over the other, and he knew that Ellie was right.

She may not have been crying, but his soul had, his dragon had whimpered at the disgrace of being carried, and pulled him to where he needed to be.

"Drake?" Her voice was right in front of him, her perfectly painted toenails stepping into view. Slowly, he lifted his head, dragging his eyes up her slender body, and the towel that she hung in front of her, not around her. Lacy black underwear be damned. The drape of the towel did little to hide the curve of her hips, the way her muscles arched under the skin, angling toward the part of her that was thankfully hidden by a damn lucky fluffy white towel.

Thank god for fluffy white towels, or he knew he would be in a lot of trouble.

She held her hand out to him, palm up as she asked for his, as she pulled him to his feet. He did his best to keep a good amount of steamy air between them.

"Drake," she repeated, holding his hand between them while the other clutched the towel. "First, you aren't pathetic and if I hear you say anything like that about yourself again I will slug you. Straight up fist to the face, and I am sure I will do it wrong and break my hand, but it is still going to happen."

He couldn't help but crack the smile. "I deserve that, I probably deserve that fist to the face right now. Killian always has a way of making me feel more broken than I really am."

"Killian is arrogant," She sighed, rolled her eyes and looked to the door, the expression holding more longing than Drake expected and his stomach flipped, right before dropping even lower. "And you better believe I will whack him between the legs again if he keeps that up, too."

"Where is this sudden streak of violence coming from?"

"I've been pushed too far the last few days. I am ready to fight back. I ain't afraid of no dragon," She paused and squeezed his hand, the sound of water picking up as if someone had turned it up. "Not Killian's. Not yours. You aren't broken, and I'll fight you to prove it if I have to. Besides, I'm not enough of a pompous ass to not let you ride me."

She smiled, proud of her proclamation, but Drake felt all the blood rush from his head, everything spinning as he tried to find his breath and instead started coughing. It took her a second to realize what she had said, and when she did her face went as red as her hair.

"Oh my fucking god!" She gasped, her voice a shriek as her hand flew to her mouth, and the towel fell right to the floor.

She stood before him, completely exposed. Her perfect breasts, tight abs and everything in between was glittering in the steam of the bathroom. So much for keeping space between them, the space had exposed her, and he could see every amazing piece that made up *her*. Drake's hormones had hit a high, his dragon rumbling with a need so loud that if the shower hadn't been on the room would have been full of his growl, of the feral call of both beast and man in their desire to claim her.

Oh shit, he was in trouble and he knew it. Thankfully, he wasn't as out of control as he had assumed. Her body, her words, everything about her was drawing him in. What she had said before that, however, had expunged his feral need to claim her, and made him love her all the more.

"Well crap," she said with a sigh, exhaling with a heave as she looked down at the towel clearly debating on if she should pick it up or not, and if it was worth it.

Drake stopped her before she could come to her decision and stepped closer to her, letting his fingers drag around her waist, caress her side, her back and drift over the top of her bottom, around the dimples that pinched just above them.

Oh, he wanted to kiss those dimples. And he would get the chance, even if it was not right then. She gasped at the touch, the sound igniting his dragon further. His free hand traced up her waist, skimming over each rib, over each muscle before trailing up her spine and to the nape of her neck, guiding her against him. It was only flesh, her flesh, against him.

What he wouldn't give to remove his clothes, to press his skin against hers, to feel the heat of her phoenix, to let her feel the fire of his dragon. He could already feel her shiver underneath his touch. That would have to be good enough for now.

"You are going to make me explode," she moaned, throwing her head back as he held her against him, exposing her neck, revealing the soft skin of her breasts.

He was amazed he wasn't already ravaging her. But damn it all, he was already playing with fire. Nothing good would come of this.

But he couldn't help himself either.

"In a good way or a bad way," Drake whispered, his voice a low rumble as he leaned closer to her, desperate to let his lips drag over her neck. To taste the sweat that was dripping over the skin there.

"I really like this hotel room, Drake, and I am very close to destroying it."

Well, damn.

At least she had the strength to put on the brakes.

Drake stepped away, although not enough that she tumbled out of his grasp. The way she was wobbling she would have crumpled to the ground like a feather, and he was sure she had had enough of that for one day.

"Sorry, honey," he whispered, carefully holding her up while he retrieved the towel and wrapped it around her. "Seeing you like that..."

He couldn't get another word out if he tried, just thinking of her body, or her curves. Oh god, the man he was had better self-control than that.

"We are going to have to find a barren mountaintop somewhere before I kiss you again, Ellie. I don't want to control myself around you anymore."

"Hey, you aren't the one trying not to explode all the hotels while simultaneously wanting to jump on three very hot dragons." She turned a deeper shade of red.

Even the coloring on her cheeks was making it hard not to pull her into him again.

"True, and I will do my best to make this easier for you." He conceded, trying to keep his distance, even as he stepped closer to her. She tightened the towel, the flimsy barrier almost laughable considering the fire that was waiting to escape.

"You're still not making it easier." Damn. The low moan that was dripping from her voice was going to do him in.

"But you aren't moving away, are you?" Yeah, he was doing a shit job at making it easier, but it was nearly impossible to move away from her right then. Both of them were trapped.

"Drake." The word ached over him as he pressed his lips to the salty skin of her forehead.

Damn that moan.

"For what it's worth," he whispered in her ear, holding the towel around her as she continued to lean into him, the smell of steam and smoke that was surrounding her intoxicating him into an even deeper stupor. "I would be honored to let you ride on my back, or to ride you. In any way that you would choose."

"Let's heal that beautiful dragon of yours first," she teased with a wink, her voice still choked with need.

He knew it was impossible. He knew that no one could heal him, but right then he didn't want to fight her. He wanted to imagine carrying her up to the mountain cave where he had hidden his hoard so long ago, show her the precious stones, and be with her.

"I might actually be hoping that you can do it," he whispered, his voice a husky roar as she giggled, as he stole one deep kiss and practically threw himself out the bathroom door.

If he stayed in there one minute longer he might be the one responsible for the explosion this time.

4

ELLIOT

DRAKE LOOKED LIKE HE HAD BEEN FORCED TO SWALLOW frogs, and the wriggling things were trying to push their way back up.

I was sure I looked the same, my own amphibious nerves were on the rampage after Killian nearly walked in on Drake and I.

It was only seconds after our steamy little interlude that Killian had announced their return. My hair was still wet, Drake's face was still flushed, and thankfully Killian and Zoe were none the wiser. Well Killian was oblivious as far as I could tell, Zoe was giving me some serious side eye.

She either knew, or her guess wasn't that far off.

Not that it mattered either way, but I didn't need her to try to give me the sex talk again. Between her and Suvi I was efficiently traumatized.

I was well aware of how all of that worked, thank you very

much. I didn't need two old ladies trying to explain the finer details.

If I had to guess, however, I would think that the look was more thanks to the weird knotted blanket thing that Killian was holding out to Drake in a painful banner of faded beige. Seriously, what is with American hotels and the color beige?

Boring. Bland. And if I had to guess, the color of pure evil.

The beige evil was drowning the remaining joy of the last few minutes. Drake's head was hung low, his face twisted into a scowl that was boiling between anger and pain.

"You can't be serious?" Drake stepped away from his brother, his pained expression flitting to mine before he looked away and my stomach dropped. I knew that devastation well.

"Yes. I am. This will work, Drake. I used blankets to help keep you warm in the high altitude, the knots will help me to be able to easily hold them in my talons for the full flight," Killian finished holding out what was clearly a knotted blanket basket, self-impressed with his own ingenuity.

And I guess, in a way, it was ingenious. You know, if you wanted to be carried around like a stork baby. Which, you know, was exactly what Drake had said would happen, and exactly what he had feared. He was clearly caught between raging and breaking down, and I already had a glimpse of that last one. It broke my heart enough the first time, my phoenix was already prickling in its own frustration.

That's it, I was going into full-blown protector mode.

Phoenix bristling, I squared my shoulders, I was in this for the whole nine yards. I may only come to Killian's chest, but I was going to make myself as big and ominous as possible. Too bad I couldn't control the whole skin-fire thing yet.

I would bust into this thing looking like a mad fire demon if I could. That would set them straight.

I cleared my throat, just as I was struck with a distorted image of me running through the room naked and on fire, arms waving in the air and my elegant cough turned into an odd and completely unattractive gagging sound, which thankfully pulled everyone's focus and earned me a concerned look or two. Whatever.

I so had this. Fire or no.

"We don't need that Killian, I can carry him."

Killian blinked in confusion, holding the weird blanket fort up, as if he was deciding if I could fit inside of it too.

"I don't think your claws are big enough to hold this." I didn't miss that little bit of mocking in his voice, my phoenix didn't either, and she was pissed.

"Are you saying I'm small?" I totally squeaked in frustration, puffing my chest out as if it would make me bigger. It's something that worked if, you know; I was a bird, and didn't have boobs sticking out at Killian.

Which of course he noticed, his eyes widening as his voice caught.

"I'm saying that blankets and brothers are thick and heavy and I don't think you can handle it."

Zoe snorted from the other side of the room, Drake stepping

toward us with the clear intention of stepping in the middle. I was protecting him dammit! He needed to back off.

"I can handle it!" I yelled before Drake could get too close, not sure who or what I was shrieking about anymore. "I may not be a massive dragon but I can wrap my hands around anything you and Drake have for me."

And then I realized why Zoe laughed, and why Drake was getting ready to plow in between us. Even Killian was snickering, realizing what he had said, and how I had walked right into it.

"Oh my god!" I shrieked, taking a step back. "That's not what I mean. I mean, I can carry him. He can ride on my back."

You better believe that I thought that out pretty damn carefully.

Killian's smile pierced the corner of his mouth, making his dimple pop and pull at his facial hair. That look could have easily done me in, but Drake was standing nearly directly behind him, his own smile shining through the warm brown sugar of his eyes.

Damn. And I thought having two of them beside me was trying, this was pulling me close to eternal damnation, and they were standing on the other side of the room.

Pull it together, Ellie. I could get this under control.

"I wouldn't mind carrying him on my back and I am sure the fact that I turn into a burning rocket will help keep him warm when we are over oceans and stuff."

My phoenix ruffled indignantly at being called a burning rocket, but I ignored her.

I turned into a giant Phoenix, which was on fire. I don't know what could explain that better than calling myself a giant burning rocket.

We should clearly be more focused on the fact that we were going to get to fly over a freaking ocean, because as I was still geeking out about; Rydaim was in Spain.

This boiling rocket was going over a fucking ocean!

And I was going to take Drake with me, even if I had to *accidentally* burn the blanket basket right before takeoff.

"How do you know you can even carry anyone, Elliot?" Zoe asked, looking up from where she had been busying herself near the couch with what looked like a towering pile of bed sheets. "Are you sure you won't just burn him to a crisp?"

"I won't burn him to a crisp," I hissed between the clench in my teeth, she really wasn't helping me plead my case.

"But how do you know?" She was clearly prodding me now.

"Because he's my mate, Zoe. We are bonded and shit and we will go dive bomb pelicans and touch clouds and stuff, all while on fire. And not burning to death." Okay, so maybe that last part didn't sound as cool as I had hoped it would.

"Are you thinking about that movie again?" Yes. But I wasn't going to admit it. I loved Falcor and if I was going to have that moment she couldn't take it away from me.

Punk best friend she was, she chuckled all knowingly and went back to tearing and knotting bed sheets, I wasn't about to ask what that was for.

"I am going to carry you, Drake." I was firm, unfortunately he was clearly the only one who believed me.

"Thanks Elliot," Drake smiled appreciatively.

I gave him a quick nod in reply, but I was back to staring at Killian, our self-appointed leader of this operation, who was quickly reverting to full on scowl mode again. His shoulders drooped and the knotted blanket monstrosity fell to the side. Zoe gave me one side-glance, probably in warning, but I fully ignored her.

"What?" I said, throwing my hands in the air. "It would be easier to have him ride me than whatever that is." I guess those words wanted to slip out anyway, you know to join all those thick things I am wrapping my hands around.

Killian made a weird choking noise while Drake turned to a nice flush color, even Zoe gave me another side glance, but I plowed on, determined to force the phrasing into oblivion.

"It's either that or hijacking a private plane. Which would probably be easier..."

"Never mind the fact that you could possibly burn Drake to a crisp. Have you ever flown over an ocean before?" Killian interrupted, stepping toward me in that slow calculated way that always sent my stomach into an acrobatic flip.

He already knew the answer to that. I may have danced a bit when he revealed Rydaim's location, screeching about how I was going to get to fly over an ocean.

"No."

"What happens when you get exhausted and need to rest?"

Land. Duh.

Except I wasn't completely sure if I could land on water. Would I float like some kind of burning swan boat, ready to travel over the ocean of love? Or would I sizzle and disintegrate into ash and have to do the whole reborn thing that I was pretty sure was going to hurt like hell, not that I had done it. It would come up eventually, but maybe not on water. What happens if all that ash floated away and there wasn't enough of me left to do the whole reborn thing. I clearly didn't know enough about it to be able to predict any outcome.

Either way, I knew what he was trying to do and I was already furrowing my brow in determination.

"Make you carry both of us." I smirked and his scowl become a permanent fixture on his face.

Oh boy, he didn't like that.

"I'm not letting you ride..." he faltered, we all knew exactly what he was going to say. Even Zoe had stopped trying to make sheet art.

I raised my brow, ready to battle him just as a knock sounded on the door. I jumped, half expecting Dabria to be making a visit, but Zoe answered it without so much of a word, swinging the door wide to let Suvi inside.

With all that had happened the last few days I had almost forgotten that Suvi was following us to Denver.

Or even that she existed.

Without the circus everything was so topsy-turvy.

"If you would have taken the rooms I give you I wouldn't have to track you lot down half way across this god forsaken city," She mumbled, giving each of us a wicked glare before pulling out her pipe. Oh, hell no, stinking up her office was one thing, but I was going to sleep in these rooms.

Well, at least I wanted to, we were probably going to end up leaving before that.

"I don't want to clean your voodoo out of the walls, Suvi. Put the pipe away," Zoe said, having abandoned the sheets to lean against the back of one of the many chairs, looking as calm and collected as she always did.

I guess Zoe did hate the pipe as much as the rest of us.

Suvi gave her a look, clicked her tongue and complied, shoving the pouch of rancid leaves back in her pocket. She didn't seem too happy about it. Well, until she saw the giant ugly scorch mark in the table, the still burning embers stretching over almost half the surface now. The dragon had been burned away sometime while Drake and I were having a completely normal conversation in the shower.

Yeah, that sounded as believable as bear racing competitions.

"Is that it?" She asked, sticking the tip of the pipe in her mouth and gnawing on it as if it was lit.

Zoe gave her a nod, her eyes drifting to mine in hard little nubs of fear, right before both Killian and Drake made a move to do their whole protect and deflect thing like they had done at the airport.

Odd move considering that we were facing Suvi and not a blood-thirsty vampire.

My happy little cucumber persona was beginning to deteriorate into a neurotic pickle. I gave the boys as much of an answer-demanding glare as I could, but neither of them said anything.

Because everyone was back to staring at the table.

"Is it...?"

"The travelers mark," Suvi cut Zoe off, hovering her hand over it before turning on me. Instead of the wrinkled stare of rage, however, she looked amazed.

I don't know how that was more terrifying, but it was. I stepped back, right into the shoulders of both Drake and Killian who wound their arms around my back, Drake at my waist, Killian at my shoulders.

I braced for the hormonal impact, ready to fight off the need to jump on backs or bones or whatever I could find. Their touches were spreading out in a wave of radiating heat. My veins were on fire, the beating heat spreading out from Drake's fingers. My bones rattled with the heat from Killian's wide palm as it tried to pull me into him. My knees were knocking as everything began to swell and I was hit with the very clear image of them sandwiching me in a different way, arms and legs tangling.

Heat spread, but I took one shaking breath, determined to control it. Or at least hold on to it as long as possible. I wasn't facing a skin fire quite yet, and I was sure Suvi would drown me in blue tea before that happened.

That would make for a show as I broke my way into Rydaim.

Blue skin would make me inconspicuous as shit.

"What is a travelers mark?" Unsurprisingly, my voice

quivered, the simple words sounding way more lusty than you would think was possible.

Drake noticed and stepped away, letting his fingers linger on my waist as long as possible before they fell away, leaving my veins to pulse and throb in a different kind of longing.

Killian stayed. But one I could manage.

"Your soul calling for another." Simple answer, but while everyone else was looking just as confused as before, I was fairly certain I knew what she was talking about.

"Is that why I felt like I could reach through the table and grab him?" Suvi's eyes widened, so I plowed on. "Or why I saw him in the bathroom?"

"You saw him in the bathroom?" Okay, without context that one made no sense, no wonder she was looking at me in an eyebrow quirking question of my sanity.

It wasn't a good sign that I wasn't the only one questioning my sanity.

"She saw an image of him, in the dungeon in Rydaim." Killian was really not making it sound any better.

"When?" Suvi ripped the pipe out of her mouth, her angry little eyes digging into mine as she snarled. Nostril flaring, teeth flashing snarl. It sounded like a wild animal before an attack.

An attack that I really didn't want to be on the other side of.

"After I drank the thing Killian gave me and I passed out." Okay, so her look was getting worse, I really wanted to step back, but Killian was still holding me against him so tightly that even breathing was becoming difficult.

Luckily, that glare was no longer directed at me.

"And what did she drink?"

"Something that Callay gave me." This was really starting to sound like a whole 'I heard it from my cousins, uncle, second niece who works at a bar and heard it from a red-head' thing.

I didn't regret drinking it, but I wasn't a huge fan of the smug smile that was starting to spread back over Zoe's face. Drake looked about as ready to bail from this as I was, perhaps we could both take off and soar to Rydaim ourselves.

We could totally take them all ourselves.

I tried to step away from Killian, and out of the line of fire, but he was holding me in pace, his fingers pressing into my shoulder as if he needed the support.

"And where did Callay get it?" Zoe didn't want me to drink it in the first place and was obviously ready to jump in, but Suvi held up a hand, wiping her smug expression.

"I know exactly where Callay got it," Suvi's accusational smile had turned into a wicked gleam that I had only seen a few times before, most recently in Stacia's room. You know, that one that looked like a murder scene.

I'm actually surprised I hadn't had any bad dreams about that yet, of course, I also hadn't had much time to sleep and dream about blood filled rooms and freaky little girls with ominous proclamations.

"And how do you feel, child?" Suvi pulled me from my blood-filled memories with a jump and I jerked out of

Killian's arms. At least she wasn't looking at me as though she was ready to destroy anything anymore.

"Like I need to get the fuck to Rydaim and kick Ceres' face in." Brutal, but that wasn't new. I had felt like that from minutes after my dragons had plunged themselves into my lives.

"And after the spell?"

"Spell?" Was that what had happened to the table? I looked to the still smoldering table in question, but Suvi shook her head.

"No child, what you drank was a spell. I have an idea which one she has infected you with, but I would like to be sure before I tell you what to expect."

"She?"

"What do you feel now that the spell has filled you?" Her eyes narrowed into mine, her teeth clamping around the pipe as she ignored my question and took a step toward where I stood, my dragons each taking one large step closer to me, flanking me like bodyguards.

"I *need* to be there. We *need* to be together." Saying it aloud was only making that soul-pinching need a stronger pull. "I need to go to Rydaim."

Suvi sucked on her pipe, as though she was trying to inhale the memory of the feet-leaves she puts inside of them. Feet-leaves and an intense stare that was now burrowing into my soul. Maybe she could see into it, because damn it all I was feeling pretty stripped bare right then.

"Your soul is connected to that of your mates. This is the

sign of the mark that connects your souls." Her eyes were still digging into me, although she gave the table behind her a nod, not that I could look at the still smoldering table. I was pretty sure she had witch-locked my gaze to hers. If that was a thing, and it was because looking away from her right then seemed like a dangerous mistake.

"The Travelers Mark is most often seen in the black magic of the Fae that roamed the woods near Russia before the Dragons coaxed them into their service. It is old magic, and I am not sure how your soul prodded it into being. But with enough practice you could move through these marks to the connecting half. I haven't seen it done in more than a century."

"I could travel…"

"Through the table, through the vision of your mate. Yes."

"I felt like I could." The mumbles were so soft that I wasn't sure that even Killian could hear. Besides, they were all still looking at Suvi, their mouths sagging like some cartoon character after eating hot sauce.

They may be shocked, I was just happy I wasn't genuinely a head-case.

Win-Win.

"Thanks to the spell you have swallowed, the binds on your magic are starting to disintegrate. Your memory will follow behind. You will remember everything in your life, and have access to all your power no matter what binds I have placed on you. Without those binds, however, you will also be able to be tracked by those who seek you. The time for hiding is over, now you must fight, and if the bones are correct your life will certainly find a wall that even you cannot traverse. A certain end is waiting for you. But you must face it before it reaches too far out of your control. You need to get to Rydaim, all of you. It is time to end this."

She finished sternly, and I really wanted to give a celebratory grin. The old witch thought I should go to Rydaim, I should be thrilled. Probably would be too if everything she had said wasn't raging like ice and fire in my soul.

My win-win had just turned into a win-death, and not any death, Certain. Fucking. Death.

She had just said that, right?

Clearly, she had. Killian was now looking ready to steam roll me out of that room as though the Zombie apocalypse was heading our way. Maybe he was, he had never answered my question from dinner. I really had no way of knowing if Zombies existed or not.

"You say death is there, and then say we should go there anyway," Killian asked, pulling me tightly against him, I wasn't about to try to pull away this time, his warmth was perfectly comforting given the current situation. "We were going to go, but now I am second guessing that."

Suvi smiled, the grin looking more like the smile someone gives you before they murder you.

At least we weren't surrounded by blood this time.

"Changing your plan will not change what awaits you." Yes, Suvi, please get more cryptic and fucking frightening, because we all need that right now. "If you do not stay together and the binds remove themselves, she will be found and she will be unprotected. Your current path is true."

Zoe gave a sigh before nodding in understanding, although Drake and Killian were still huddled around me in their signature walls of muscle.

"You know what you need to do." Suvi gave us all one last nod before she left, tearing out of the hotel room so fast that I barely heard the click of the door. For all I knew she just moved through the massive pane of wood. I was still staring at where she was, and the burning table right behind.

The table I had almost moved through.

A Travelers Mark. I wanted to say that it was right, but it gnawed at me all wrong, like I was missing something.

"What do we need to do?" Drake asked, his hand reaching to wrap around mine.

"I know I need to not get killed." Mine was probably not the answer that he was looking for.

"And yet you wanted to join us on an expedition into hell." Zoe's voice was way too lighthearted for what she said.

"Well, when you put it that way…"

"Me." Killian cut me off, still scowling at Zoe who was now going back to her nonchalant fabric ripping. "You all want to join me, and after that I am not convinced that still isn't the best option."

"Well, if you leave me here I'll just explode into flame and move through a table to get to you, so that may not be the smartest option either." He knew I was right, he clearly knew I was right, or else he would be looking at me, instead he was stepping away, looking at the table.

"So," I prodded carefully back into the conversation. "We leave at dawn?"

"Yes, and Zoe can carry Drake."

"But I..." Killian turned on me, his emerald eyes glinting dangerously and cutting me off.

"Drake will not ride you, Ellie girl," he stepped closer to me, the low growl of his voice rippling over my spine and sending an orchestra of hormones twisting through my chest. "I will be the first to do that."

"Like hell..." His smile drowned my shriek and he stepped away, thankfully giving me space to breathe.

"Meet at dawn, on the roof, we will fly into the city in the bay and go through the back tunnels. You three will be dressed as slaves for the market." The tone of command was clear in his voice, accentuated only by the incessant ripping of fabric. "We will get in, get out, and destroy anyone who gets in our way."

I wasn't a fool, I knew exactly who he was talking about. Who he was ready to destroy.

Let's hope I didn't end up being the one in the way, because if this shield was about to break, anything was possible.

5

JARRON

THE COLD STONE PRESSED AGAINST JARRON'S BACKSIDE WITH the unrelenting force of a cattle prod. The ridges of stone cut into his back and thighs until large portions of his body were beginning to go numb, His bones ached, his skin pulled and cracked until it felt like it was going to peel from his bones in the hunt of a good moisturizer.

But above all, he was cold.

He had never been cold in his life, and now, his body was rattling with it.

The stone, the air, the slow drip of cave water that fell from the ceiling to form a pool near his feet, it was all frigid. It seeped into him like a weight that he couldn't shake, bleeding into his bones and rattling over his spine. The longer he sat, the worse it became, and after hours of leaning against the wall, shivering against the stone, he was beginning to wonder how much more he could take, and how mortals could *take* it at all.

He had this filthy dungeon chamber to thank for that little insight into their world.

Everything about this room was toxic to him. The shackles around his wrists and ankles dug into his flesh, infecting the bleeding rings of skin with their poison. The bars that stretched over the single high window spread magic into the air, even the stone that dug into him with expert level torture drained the spell over him, infecting him. The magic of his father's Fae was everywhere, locking his dragon inside his chest, keeping the beast and its powers trapped, and left him sitting here, bleeding and broken.

It was bad enough feeling like a mortal, it was even worse being trapped in the cold, feeling like a dying mortal. Dabria had favored the knives the Vampires had made from her scales, and blood was still seeping from the wounds that lined his sides and back. Scarlet fluid had dried against his skin, tightening uncomfortably and pulling at his arms and back, further twisting what he was sure were a few broken or dislocated bones.

He was going to die and he had no way to stop it.

He had been here so long that he could no longer feel even the faintest of purrs from his beautiful dragon. Well, except for a few hours ago when his skin had buzzed, his dragon had grumbled and Elliot's panicked voice had filled the tiny prison. Her voice had been everywhere, pulsing over the stone and drifting through the air. It had taken him a moment to locate the voice that was emanating from a tiny spec of light in the corner near the door. He had questioned if it had been her, until her promise had come, and he knew only one person who was foolhardy enough to say such things, and apparently powerful enough to project her voice halfway across the world.

He wanted to be amazed of her, probably would be too if he wasn't so terrified of what she said.

She had promised him safety, promised him rescue. His heart had clenched as she had promised him she was coming. The words were still a twisted echo in his heart, fear eating at what was left of his resolve. She shouldn't be here, none of them should be here with what he had learned. Both were very dangerous, stupid things that they shouldn't be doing.

Knowing them however, they were already on their way.

Imagining Elliot's Phoenix as it soared over the ocean, and whooshed into the mountain that surrounded him brought warmth to his icy exterior, his heart heating as the dragon that was trapped inside tried to fight past the binds to reach her. To protect her.

Hearing her voice had heated him in a whole different way, and the two converged in a wave of power and energy that should have been impossible due to the dratted iron and stone that was restricting him. Perhaps it was possible to push past these binds, it was old magic and if he could find a crack he was certainly going to expose it. Break it apart and walk right out of this prison as if it was nothing.

It was not possible, but feeling the warmth of Ellie's memory wash over his skin ignited the hope. And perhaps a little bit of a day dream.

He may not make it far, but the look on Parris's face as he stood from the binds and swallowed him whole would be worth it. It was unfortunate that he received so much joy from watching his fire destroy, or else he would have swallowed the vile man first. That, and the taste of ash and death that lingered from Vampire bones lodged in his teeth was not one he was interested in repeating.

He had been commanded to bite the heads off one of the beasts more than forty years ago, when the creature had been found conspiring against Parris. He still remembered the taste, the feel of ash and bones that stuck to his teeth. Jarron worked his jaw at the memory, the taste too strong even now.

Vile things.

He would repeat it again without question, however, for Ellie. He would not regret the taste either.

Any daydreams were wiped from his mind as the heavy door to the prison swing open, his muscles tensing and pulsing as a pair of tall leather boots stepped through the door, splashing the layer of blood and water that lined the floor with the toe of her shiny shoe.

"Wonderful," Dabria growled, her lip curling into a sneer as the residue trickled over her shoe, her cold eyes turning to him as if the fault was his.

Could have been, it was his blood after all. But the idea didn't disgust Jarron as much as it should. Her face was making the whole thing quite worth it. Restricting a smile, he laid his head back against the stone, his injured shoulder throbbing with an agony equal to a shift as he turned to the snarling female.

It really wasn't a good look for her.

"Why, hello Dabria. I didn't expect you for another day at least. Are you so eager to dispose of me?" He was careful to keep each word calm, each syllable smooth as he hid any sign of the agony that he was tangled in.

Not that he was fooling himself that she didn't know, even speaking of his impending death so casually was tensing through his chest and igniting the pain in his bones. Try as he might, he couldn't keep the pain from his eyes, and it was that that she saw, her own eyes sparking with the icy chill of her dragon as she stepped closer, carefully avoiding the blood-soaked puddles this time.

"Not quite yet, we are still waiting on your darling brother." The ice in her eyes grew and Jarron fought a shiver of fear that was winding down his spine, pushing into him.

There was so much hunger in her eyes that for a moment she didn't look like the icy dragon he had watched grow up, pushing her way into the throne room - in every sense of the word.

Right then, she looked so much like the Vampires did when they were looking to feed that he pushed himself against the wall, smelling the air for the rancid aroma that always accompanied the blood-suckers. As far as he knew, it wasn't possible for a Dragon to be bitten by a Vampire and turn into a blood slave or a member of the coven.

With all the discoveries of the last few days, however, he wasn't going to keep fooling himself of their truthfulness. Luckily, she smelled like little more than the mountain snow that had always accompanied her dragon. There was a hint of a vampire there, but he was sure it was there for other reasons, reasons that made his stomach twist and turn.

This time he let his face twist in disgust.

"What do you need of him? You obviously hope to end me, that should be enough for your pitiful revenge." The snarl of Jarron's disgust seeped out with his words, his eyes narrowing as Dabria took another step closer.

She was close enough now that she could easily injure him, if she was so inclined. He knew he should tread carefully, but his hatred of her was too high for him to care. Besides, if she got close enough he could land a punch, it would be worth it. He might fully disconnect his shoulder in the process, submit himself to more stabbing, but again, totally worth it.

"It is not pitiful. But it is revenge. I had hoped that killing you would help him see the light, help to understand his fault and come back to my arms. I will make him a King, and I will be the perfect Queen to match!" Her voice raised in octave and excitement with each word, with each step that she took toward him. So close now, he was sure he could land a punch if she just leaned down. "But then I saw him with that mortal whore, his hands all over her, her eyes undressing him."

Any thought of punching the dragon left, his fist tightening against his limp leg and shooting pain through his shoulder and arm as though he had been stabbed. Hatred blossomed over Dabria's face, her eyes gaining that malicious hatred as she looked past him, into the slimy wall of the prison, into a world beyond.

"What do you mean you saw them?" The growl was out now,

although it lacked the power he was used to with none of his dragon behind it.

"I mean, that I went to say hello, to tell Killian of your predicament. See if he wanted to help." Her voice matched the taunting scowl she was giving him, and his insides swirled, as if he knew what was coming. He had heard her, he knew she was okay, but the twisted hatred in the woman before him was making him doubt that.

"It's so nice having so many Dragons under my control. Thanks to a little bit of my magic that I left in your brother and his *mate*," the word spat off her tongue and Jarron jerked, his head turning painfully to her. "I found them quite easily at some disgusting restaurant in Denver. Burned the thing to the ground, hopefully burned the fucking whore a bit too."

"You burned..." The two words cut against his heart, slashing through the already tense and angry muscles that lined his back. His fist tensed again, the hard rock of his anger pushing into his thigh as she leaned toward him.

"I burned your brother's mate, he won't be able to stay away, and then you both will taste the same bitter end as your siblings." Her eyes dug into him, her face only a few inches from his now. "One covered in ash, one covered in blood."

Her taunt was clear, her supposed win screaming from her eyes. She was basking in her victory, it was unfortunate for her that she was also very, very wrong. Ellie couldn't get burned, and his end would be nothing like his siblings. He kept both thoughts locked in the back of his mind however, focusing his internal monologue on the ice in her eyes, and the appalling rotting core of her soul.

"I can only hope to meet an end such as theirs," Jarron said, his smile stretching as the faintest howl of his dragon rang in his ears, his blood heating as he swung his arm wide and smashed the hard rock of his fist into her jaw.

She howled at the impact, stumbling back through blood and water until her back slammed into the opposite wall, a stream of profanity shooting from her mouth. Jarron's shoulder was on fire, ripples of agony shooting through his neck and down his arm with such intensity that he wouldn't be surprised if the bones from finger to nose had begun to crack and splinter.

He refused to make a sound, however, nothing beside the grunt as he shifted his weight against the wall, holding his arm against him as he stared her down. Every howl of his pain ripped from his eyes, digging into the woman who was now staring at him with a violent intensity.

"You horrid, disgusting..."

"You will not win, Dabria," he cut her off, letting the last whisper of his dragon's growl impregnate his words, the threat more of a prediction, even if she didn't know that, at least he would die knowing that the end would come. The smile spread wider with the thought.

"Oh, I already have," she hissed, her hand pressing against the quickly darkening skin on her jaw. "Perhaps I need to remind you of that."

The cold air that had been destroying his falsely mortal body since he had been thrown in here turned to an icy chill that reflected in the ice of Dabria's eyes, reflected in the purple smoke that was drifting from her lips, seeping out of her with each word.

"Fire is nice," she hissed, the words he had heard thousands of time sinking into him dangerously now that they were directed at him. "But I prefer ice."

A ripple of blue spread from between her teeth, shooting out of her as though it was fire. Fire that did not burn. The temperature of the air dropped as the ribbon of ice smashed into the stone above his head, showering him with flakes of snow colder than sin, each speck burning his exposed skin in sparks of white. The flakes came faster, burning like acid as they froze the fabric of his shirt into iron, the liquid power of her dragon spreading over the fabric, just as it was spreading over the stone, spreading around him. Encasing him.

"Perhaps your end will be in ice, a different end for each of Ceres' unfortunate children." Her ice was spreading over his skin now, crippling his fragile body and popping his visions with sparks of black. He couldn't move, his teeth couldn't even chatter. Everything was too cold. Everything was too dark.

"I wonder what end Killian will meet. Perhaps we will torture him with his mortal. Tear her apart in front of him. Perhaps you can tell me something to speed up the process, to make her squeal like a pig."

"I will tell you nothing. She will destroy you," he whispered as the world froze around him.

6

ELLIOT

I HAD LOCKED MY DOOR.

Not that a lock would keep either of my guys at bay if something were to happen, but after what happened with Drake, I needed some kind of barricade.

Just a little bit of breathing room.

Not that I didn't mind what had happened with Drake, I would be happy to find myself in the same situation again. With Drake. With Killian. With Jarron. I doubt I would be able to control myself as well, however.

Hence the lock.

I needed the lock, because just lying on my bed, trying to keep my mind clear and my breathing regular was providing a difficult enough challenge.

My hormones, and my imagination, were quickly going into overload.

I swear I could feel his hands as they moved over the skin of my side, as they trailed over my back and up my spine to my neck. Laying in my sheets with my eyes closed, my hands knotted against the thin fabric of my cami, the memory of his breath was tickling over my neck, mixing with the still damp strands of my hair and pricking my skin into a heat. Gooseflesh rolled over my arms, my phoenix ruffling in an even deeper need.

A freaking cavalcade of man-jumping need.

"Will you settle down? We can't do anything yet." Both me and my phoenix needed the pep talk.

My pep-talk clearly wasn't helping, however, and the heated memory was going to become dangerous if I wasn't careful.

I needed to focus on something other than the glittering touch of Drake's magic hands and get myself to sleep. Dawn was coming way too fast and I was still hoping to convince the powers that be that allowing Drake to ride me was in everyone's best interest.

Ugh.

The images were loud and lusty and beautiful. And so much fucking trouble.

Literally.

Growling loudly, I rolled over and pulled the blanket over my head as if the beige and blue down comforter of the overly soft hotel bed would drown out any image of hands and lips and forbidden riding.

I however was doomed, my mind was full of the feeling of

Drake's soft touch, Killian's powerful kiss and way too many limbs.

Limbs were everywhere, tangled in blankets, running over legs and hands. My mind began to drift with the image of Killian's muscular back hovering over me, his hair falling around us, hiding his kiss. Hiding his...

"You're quite the saucy little minx, aren't you?"

I knew that voice. I fucking hated that voice. I wanted to rip apart the owner of that voice.

My eyes snapped open, but instead of the steamy dark of my hotel room, it was the ominous dark of the cave that Dabria was apparently obsessed with.

Dark stone stretched around me with that same frightening Kaleidoscope, the red glittering sun beaming from the end of the tunnel. It was familiar in all the ways that I didn't want it to be.

"Might be. Wanna see how hard I bite?" I taunted into the darkness, my trapped mind swinging me around wildly, looking for the gap in the unending tunnel she liked to trap me in.

I already knew there wouldn't be, but it didn't matter, I wouldn't be here long. I just needed to hide my thoughts while pissing her off enough that she kicked me out of her mind, or I kicked her out of mine.

Either way, I was going to teach her to stop popping into my mind.

"You can't bite girl," her voice was right behind me now, her icy breath a soul dampening chill against the fantasies she had pulled me from. "You couldn't even do more than hide and whimper as the roof to the restaurant came down."

Brows furrowing, I turned to the voice, if only to dispel the shiver of ice she was sending over my skin. I expected the mirror of the cave she trapped me in, I expected the ice of her breath to dissipate in the grey stone.

Instead the chill in the air grew, the bitch herself faced me. Her long dark braids were pulled back from her face, the ebony of her skin elegant against the darkness of the cave, making the bright blue and purple of her eyes pop.

She was beautiful, and it was only enraging me more.

"Well, I had Killian to protect me," I pushed a dreamy sigh out of my voice, her eyes flashing darkly and sending my stomach into an energetic swoop. "He won't let anything happen to me."

Yeah, I was laying it on a little bit thick, but as he was the one weapon I had against the ice queen, I was going to use it. The only problem was, was that this time it didn't seem to be working. Her eyes were growing darker, the ice in them sparking dangerously as she stepped closer to me, heels clacking against stone with a soul wrenching grind.

"Yes, because he's been so great at protecting those around him. His own brother..." She sighed, clicked her tongue at me with a look of bristling disappointment. She was mocking me in the hopes of getting a rise, and it was working, but not in the way she had hoped.

My heart turned to stone in my chest, every single muscle in my back tightening so quickly that I could feel my wings begin to uncoil from my spine, my phoenix desperate to rush out and destroy her. To save Jarron.

No! Stay down! I was sure the flames were licking over my skin, if I had skin in this place, and I really hoped I didn't because both my emotions and my Phoenix were on high alert, ready to bust out.

Pushing everything down and into that damn box was my new priority. And she was making it really fucking hard with her ugly smile spreading over her face, taunting me and pushing the need to hide everything about me away. I was boiling too much, and really wanting to send some of that boiling energy right into her face.

Damn it. Control.

"Jarron will not burn. We will not let him..." My voice was smothered by the snarl of my phoenix, the sound rumbling in my ears and over the stone. I knew my flame was beaming from my eyes, but Dabria didn't react, well not in the way I was hoping. Her smile was reaching 'creepy haunted doll' level now, she even had the glint of doom in her dead eyes. I guess the bond of Suvi's magic hadn't been broken quite yet.

"Why do you care?" Dabria continued, "Killian has chosen you as his mate. Your heart belongs to him... not to Jarron. You should be happy we are ending him, giving you a clear path to your own crown."

What the fuck? Every other time I had prodded her with the fact that I had won Killian's heart she had erupted in frustration. Now, she smiled, now she prodded. Now she was bringing it up as if it was something to celebrate. It was as if she knew about Jarron, about me, about everything.

Well, maybe not about me. I mean, she didn't see my fire-eyes of hate a minute ago, but she clearly knew something. I hated to think about what.

Or worse, what they had tortured out of Jarron.

And there goes the twisting fury of both my soul and my heart. There was something about her that made me want to rip her head from her shoulders, and that feeling was coming back again in spades. I tried to push it in the box with every other wicked thought that I was supposed to be keeping from her, but it just wasn't going.

Fine. She couldn't see the fire in my eyes, so I might as well let it shine. Even if just to melt some of her ice away.

"I care for what Killian cares for, and Killian cares for his brother." I carefully stepped around each word, watching her reaction, and wishing that everything about her wasn't quite so bone chilling.

We aren't leaving him with you. Because I'll rip your head off before that happens. The threat was real.

Her smile twitched, and I was sure that she heard me, I hoped it was the part about me ripping her head off. Mostly because I was sure boring mortals could do that if they were deranged enough. And also, because threatening her was still a lot of fun.

"Perhaps you should care a little more."

"A little more than what?" I was sure my disembodied head twitched an eyebrow.

"If the life of someone I cared about was in danger I would be caring a whole lot. I wouldn't be having fantasies of someone else's love in a hotel room half way across the world."

And there it was. Bitter angry Dabria lived on.

"Don't like it? Don't watch. You aren't getting him back."

"Maybe not in the way you think." Her dragon was rumbling now, the air dripping with ice as the walls of the cave began to crack and glow in a startling blue. "But you are still helping me. And I'll prove who his true match is. You don't deserve the lust he has given you. Those dreams don't belong to you."

Lightning ran through my veins, every single muscle tensing as she laughed, the sound low and deep and menacing. I really didn't want to think about how much she had seen of that. Hell, I really didn't like the idea of her in my head at all.

We hadn't really talked about the whole tracker she had put in my head, but clearly it was still there, leading me right to her, and her right to me.

Right as I roared my way into Rydaim.

She would know when I would get there. She would know when we would all get there. I needed her out of my head, and I needed her out now.

Game on.

"Haven't you already done enough damage, Dabria?" I was full on snarling now. if I couldn't piss her off enough to leave on her own, then I was going to push her out.

"Not yet," She smiled, stepping closer to me, close enough I could feel the chill of her skin. I didn't let her get any closer.

Focusing all my energy, I shoved her away, using invisible hands or mind power or whatever I had in this place to get her as far out of my head as possible.

I expected nothing, but she stumbled like a newborn and fell right back on her ass with a little thump. Braids flinging, legs kicking, she looked ridiculous, and I laughed far louder than I should have when facing a dangerous ice dragon. Which, awesome for me, made Dabria even more pissed than before.

Her icy eyes snapped up, boiling with a blue flame that was downright freaky. I was used to fire filled stares, but this, she looked like she was going to shoot icicles out of her eyes.

I stepped back, well, I thought I stepped back, and she jumped up ready to charge me, or eat me, or freeze me like some kind of cruel statue.

"You bitch," she snarled as she ran at me.

"No!" I yelled, pushing my hands forward and realized a second too late that that was exactly what I shouldn't be doing. The bristling heat that had been boiling under the surface exploded out of me. "Shit! No!"

I tried to stop the flame, to stop her, but the flames were everywhere, swallowing the cave in a bath of darkness, my eyes flashing open to Killian's worried face as he crouched before me, gently pressing the hair out of my face.

So much for the lock on the door, good thing I really fucking needed him.

I pulled myself out of the lingering sleep, forcing my breathing to calm even as my heart rattled in my chest like a jet engine.

"Are you okay, Ellie girl?" he whispered, his fingers still trailing around my ear, caressing the clammy skin. He was way too calm for the marathon my nerves were running. "You were yelling..."

"Dabria," I gasped, the single word shivering in my mouth. "She was in my dream."

Killian's eyes filled with flame, smoke spreading over his skin as his shoulders squared in an ominous wall. He didn't move, but the single pulse of muscle pulled him above me, his bulk towering over me protectively. The fire in his eyes was frightening, but none of the fear filled my soul. It only blended with mine, our fury colliding.

"What did she say?"

His hand warmed as it moved around my neck, clutching me protectively, as though I would slip away, back into her mind. I wrapped my fingers around his wide wrist, the skin scalding beneath my hand, but I didn't let go. Maybe I was afraid of slipping away too.

"It's not what she said It's what she saw." I admitted, my head aching from the lack of sleep. Or from the fact that some freaking ice dragon kept pushing her way into my head.

I'd like to push something into her head.

Like fire javelins.

Which she probably knew about now. Yeah, I totally should have ripped her head off when I had the chance.

"What did she see?" His fingers were little pricks of fire against my neck now.

"My fire. I shot fire at her, I was trying to get her out of my

head, to break whatever tracker she placed inside of me."
Watching Killian's expression shift with each word was like
watching the live action version of an emotion board. He
went from worried, to concerned, to scared, to pissed so fast
that I was sure I missed a few.

"She knows."

I could only nod, the fury in the low rumble of his voice
froze me, and not in the uncomfortable hormonal way.

"But I pushed her out. And I'm pretty sure I broke her
tracker bull shit."

"Knowing you, you shattered it. Which couldn't be more
perfect, because it's time to go." His hand left my neck as he
stood, as he threw open the heavy curtains that covered the
windows of my room and let in the streaming light of dawn.
"She's out of time anyway."

The dim blue sunlight streamed over the floor as he
strolled back to me, pressing one hot kiss against my
forehead before throwing off the covers and chucking a
hoodie and jeans at my head. I guess that's what I get for
not putting my clothes away, everything was accessible.
Including some overly lacey underwear that was now
laying on top of me.

"Wear those."

He smirked and I scowled.

Who knew that my pretty underwear obsession was going to
cause so many problems.

"It's time to go," he said, pulling his focus from my clothes to
where I sat, the strap from my cami drifting down my

shoulder. "It's time to make Dabria quiver in her knee-high boots."

"That I can do."

I couldn't move fast enough. Screw her and her demented mind control. I was ready to show her what that fire could really do.

7

ELLIOT

I WAS SUCH A WEIRD COMBINATION OF HOT AND COLD THAT IF I didn't know any better I would think I had turned into a 50-year-old woman experiencing hot flashes. Not that there was anything wrong with that, but being an immortal, I never expected I would experience it.

Of course, for all I knew this was nothing like what hot flashes were.

This weird tornado of hot and cold that was both deflating me into a snow demon, and twisting me into a fire pillar.

Everything inside of me was hot, so much hotter than when I would normally leave my phoenix form. Blood was boiling through my veins; my bones were trying to pull themselves apart with the heat.

I was sure, if you could peek inside I would be nothing but fire. Of course, you had to get past the frozen exterior to see any of that.

My skin was covered in goose flesh and my nipples were

poking out so far that they had turned into massive headlights. I could direct air traffic control if I needed to.

Of course, the whole nudity thing seemed to be all my fault.

Killian and Zoe had landed gracefully in the tiny village in Spain, Zoe letting Drake ride on her back, much to my frustrations. It was probably for the best though, because I was nowhere near inconspicuous enough for a night landing in a tiny village. When I landed I did so in a fiery heap of feathers and sparks, throwing myself into the stone building of the alley with such force that I was still expecting someone to come around the corner and scream at us about curfew and drunkenness or something.

Which would have been fine, except it seems the dragons had a special skill that I did not. That of keeping their clothes intact when they shifted.

I didn't even know that was possible! They stood without even a scuff, or scrape, or hint of ash on them.

Zoe was wearing what was possibly the most inconspicuous outfit ever. Hoodie, hat, and jeans. She was the matching hipster tourist pair to Drake, who while he may not have shifted was really testing my self-control with the form fitting jeans and sweater combo he had going on.

He looked rugged with his chestnut hair dancing over his forehead, his eyes burning into me. I could even forgive the fact that he was wearing socks with his sandals.

Leave it to Drake to be able to rock a sweater and sandals and somehow look even sexier.

Killian, of course, was wearing his suit, the grey pinstripe still perfectly pressed after a flight over the Atlantic. There wasn't even a drop of ash or scorch on him.

And then there was me, and I was wearing nothing. Because, you see, a birthday suit isn't a friggin' birthday suit at all!

Well, unless you counted ash. So, I guess I was wearing an ash suit.

And there was no such thing as a fucking ash suit.

Even when Killian had happened upon my naked ass in an alley I still had a shard of underwear. I mean, it didn't cover anything, but it was there. That had to count for something.

Flying over most of the United States, over an ocean, and then to a tiny little village on the edge of the Mediterranean Sea was proving too much for my poor little shifter to be able to contain even a scrap of the clothes Killian had thrown at me a few hours before. It was all long gone and I was totally nude.

The chilled breeze ran over my skin, flicking my long red hair around my face like ribbons. I was sure that I looked like Venus, but without the giant oyster shell, as I tried to hide boobs and crotch, my occupied hands allowing my hair to fan around me. Okay maybe there was more side boob and renegade nipples, and a bit too much hair in all the wrong places. Long hair and a beach breeze did not mix.

But it was beautiful in my head, even if Zoe was looking at me like I had lost it.

Killian wasn't even trying to hide his desire for me, I was pretty sure he was trying not to drool while he took off his suit jacket and very quickly wrapped it around me.

I don't think I could have shrugged into the thing fast enough.

Not that I was uncomfortable being naked around them anymore. But in an alley, covered in ash, while everyone stood in their clearly inflammable clothes was making me a tad bit embarrassed. Besides, Killian's jacket was warm and my skin was still freezing in the beach breezes. I was going to burrow in that sucker.

"Does this happen every time?" Zoe was very clearly trying to hide a laugh, which was pushing me closer to that red-faced embarrassment eruption.

"Do you mean, do I burn up all my clothes and emerge covered in ash in the middle of random places?" I questioned my voice was a full octave above what it would be normally. "Why yes, yes I do. And up until about ten seconds ago I thought that was normal."

"Well, it used to be." Zoe wasn't even trying to hide her snicker anymore. Which was awesome. Maybe I shouldn't try to hide my need to explode into a burst of flame?

I gave her a look, and she freaking snickered. The bad part about having your best friend off on a rescue mission was that she was going to push your buttons, when you are standing naked, in an alley, surrounded by the royal children of the dragon king who wants to kill you.

Wow. My life got weird.

"What is it? A royal thing?" I asked grumpily, it had just hit me that I was about to walk in to an underground Dragon city full of my enemies, flanked by the crown prince and his two dead siblings. Well, not dead. But no one inside knew that.

"No, it's all Killian's fault," Drake said in something that was half gasp-half grumble.

"It's what happens when a stubborn dragon hoards something that has a habit of burning up on reentry," Zoe said, prodding her brother who was quickly readopting his trademark scowl. "You all learn a new skill."

"Well, you should have expected me to be naked, then. And you," I gestured toward Killian, whose scowl was beginning to melt away. "You saw me in the alley, so you should have known..."

All air sucked from my chest, my heart rattling in my ears as Killian laughed.

"You bastard!" I gasped, affronted. "You knew!"

"Knew what?" He was chuckling too loud for me to take him seriously.

"You knew, I would burn my clothes."

I wasn't the only one to be upset now, Drake was looking nearly as furious.

"Man, you are a bastard, Kills," He said, his eyes little specks of flame that were dragging up my long legs, and lingering on the hem of Killian's jacket. "No wonder she was nervous. Thinking of all of us together. Naked."

Did he have to say it like that, like sex and honey was dripping from his voice?

God. Could it get any warmer? Any more prickly and needy?

The visions of those two twisting through me in an all too graphic display. My voice choked and I clenched my legs together; very, very aware of where Drake and Killian's eyes had now drifted.

Yeah, okay, so nudity was very clearly wanted by all of us.

"I ain't got nothing you haven't seen Ellie girl," Killian said with a wink, carefully sauntering toward me like some 1950s boss man.

Heat boiled, need and sass blending together with my still boiling temper and I don't know what happened, I couldn't stop myself...

"Unless it's so small you can tuck and hide it, then yes, yes you do have some *things* I haven't seen."

Zoe and Drake exploded in laughter, the sound echoing through the dark alley like a million bells and snorts and whatever else. It sounded like someone was herding hyena cattle through the ancient roadway.

I, however, met Killian's shocked face head on, folding my arms in his suit jacket in smug defiance.

Shots fired big boy. Come at me.

Too bad for me, Killian took one large step forward, placing his hand on the side of the building behind me and leaned in. He was so close that I was bathed by the smell of his dragon's flame, by the musk he always wore, by the deep green of his eyes.

Damn it. Maybe he could have come at me a bit slower?

Any smug retort I could have come up with vanished in the

moss of his eyes and he smiled, the side of his mouth pulling up in a tease.

I expected some big retort, some perfectly placed clap-back. Instead I got one word.

"Soon."

He smiled, leaned closer, until I could feel the warmth of his skin radiate over me, and then he pulled away. Leaving me to fall against the wall in a heaving mess of breathless desire.

Oh, my fucking hell.

Breathing was a thing of the past, which was fine, because I obviously didn't need air, I could just breathe him in for the rest of my life and be perfectly happy.

Soon. Who knew one word could be so fucking hot.

"Okay." Yeah, my comeback was that bad, and it thankfully shot me out of my dazzling mind-melting confusion.

Killian chuckled, and tossed me what looked like a pile of rags, turning away to give Zoe and Drake the same.

"You two can wait to change until we get to the cave," he said as Drake gracefully caught his rags. "You," he continued, turning back to me, "Need to give me my jacket back."

Damn it.

Okay retaliation received. I gave him a look that said as much.

You win this round, bud.

"No problem," I said, stubbornly wrapping my arms around

the soft warm, and perfectly aromatic material. "I mean I have these rags so I am clearly set."

What I thought to be rags were actually torn and stained sheets from the hotel. The corner of one was emblazoned with the double H that marked the hotel's logo.

I guess the mystery of Zoe's sheet art was solved. Not that that helped to know what I was supposed to do with it.

"Yes, you are," Killian said, his hand still held out to me. "Jacket, Elliot."

"Are we going to a toga party that I wasn't aware of?" I teased trying desperately to bring both oxygen and sanity to my depraved mind.

Killian froze, eyebrows pulling together in clear confusion.

Meanwhile, Drake snickered from where he was quickly busying himself with the white and brown fabric that Killian had handed him. Folding it in weird squares or something.

It all looked like knots to me, and mine even more so.

"I'm not sure dragons know what those parties are," Zoe said from beside me taking stock of Killian's confused yet incredibly curious expression.

"Then why am I being handed sheets if not for some sort of frat drunkenness?" I held up the sheet-rags, the things were knotted and torn until it resembles nothing. I wasn't sure if it was a hat, a dress, or a giant dragon diaper.

Although the thought of a giant dragon diaper was humorous, I had no interest in witnessing the other side of that.

Sick.

"I thought we were going to save Jarron?" I asked, letting the useless fabric fall to the side.

"We are," Killian said, still holding his hand out for his jacket. "You will be dressed as a slave to be sold in the market. Zoe is dead, Drake is supposed to have been eaten alive by Jarron, and you don't exist. Which means that I am now stuck with the pleasure of sneaking three people into a city that I live in, that is under siege, where my brother is captured, when only one of us can fly."

"Well, at least I can fly us out," I said with a grin, "That would be a nice 'fuck you' to them all after our inevitable success."

"Yes, if we want all of the Vampires, and Dragons, and Fae chasing after the trail of a Phoenix. Dragons don't leave trails of glittering feathers and fire behind them. Dragons don't glimmer in the night sky as though they are meteorites falling from heaven." I didn't miss the fact that his voice had lowered, that same gravelly voice rumbling over my skin as he moved back into my air space. Damn it. I would not let him suck me in again. I could fight this. "They don't sing songs that pull at your soul and swell your heart until you think you can explode."

"Do you have any plans of letting me breathe, tonight?" I asked, leaning against the alleyway in an attempt to find oxygen, or stability.

"Not until you give me my jacket," Killian said his voice a low murmur as he leaned in close his hot breath running over my cold skin. I was barely able to restrain the shiver, although moving was proving to be an impossibility. I was frozen underneath him. "As sexy as you look in my jacket, and as much as I enjoyed seeing you standing there, naked," he dragged the word out and all of the blood rushed to my belly. My knees locked, my stomach pulled into a tight little knot and the warmth in the base of my gut ignited. My Phoenix bristling and pushing against me, begging me to rip the jacket off and fling myself into his arms.

I was so not going to let that happen.

Not yet.

Yet.

Oh god. There I go blushing again.

"I need you to take the jacket off, "Killian continued. "I need you to put on those rags, and submit to my every command."

Twisting need, burning want. Oh lord, how was that so hot?

But more importantly, how was I still standing?

Thank God Drake had cleared his throat, his own blush ripping over his cheeks like a steam. He wasn't going to rush over and stop whatever madness was about to happen, but I didn't want to think what would happen if he did.

The building behind me would be toast.

"Nope. Jacket is staying. I don't think I can... submit." Yep. Totally squeaked, but not in nerves. I was genuinely having trouble keeping myself against the wall.

"That can come later. The jacket is coming now."

I swallowed.

"I think I'll keep the jacket on, thank you very much,"

The jacket was becoming part of me with how tightly I was holding it against me.

"Elliot," Killian whispered, "you can't wear my jacket into Rydaim. If you want to go in on unseen, you need to wear these."

He pointed towards the fabric in my hand.

"Oh."

"Let me help," Killian's hand trailed over the shoulder of the jacket, his thumb peeking around the fabric as he began to pull it off my shoulder, his hand warm against my collarbone.

"Seeing as an explosion is imminent, I am pretty sure I can figure it out." Yes, my voice was in a full-on stutter now.

I shrugged out of the jacket as fast as I could, throwing it at Killian's head and wrapping it around his ridiculously perfectly sexy hair and half-smile before he could catch it.

Which was good, because I didn't need his jewel-bright green eyes glistening at me as I stood there in my ash suit.

Jewel-bright green eyes.

Good lord, I was clearly losing it.

The faster I got into this toga party outfit, the better.

Sucks to be me, though, because unfortunately untangling these sheets was a chore unto itself and required far more brain power than I had available right then. It was all knots and tears with no clear place to put arms or heads.

Utter disaster was striking.

By the time Killian had uncovered his face, I was still standing there, staring at the fabric, in a full-on reveal of my very pointy breasts and my very blushing bottom.

"Damn it!" I growled, tangling up the fabric more. Because that would obviously help.

Clearly, I had resorted to using toddler logic.

"Slowdown, honey, you're going to tangle it more." Drake's hand was hot against mine, his fingers soft as he slowed my frantic attempts to untangle the mass of fabric, freezing me in place.

Last night, he had stood in the exact same place, him just as clothed, me just as naked. And both of us a blubber, hormone-infused mess.

Now, he didn't even seem to see it. He stared right into my eyes with that gentle smile tickling at the corner of his mouth, glistening in the honey brown of his eyes.

If I hadn't already frozen in place at his touch I think that look would've melted me to the ground. A big pile of icicle-fire, if that was a thing. Which it had to be with how I was boiling and freezing at the same time.

"Let me help you." Drake took the fabric, carefully working each piece around each other as he undid the mess that I had created until he had revealed a hole big enough for me to step through.

He held it out for me, patiently waiting for me to step into it, his eyes melting into mine.

Warm, desirably Drake stare.

I stepped in slowly, my toes pointed as I pranced into the circle of fabric and Drake lifted it around me.

"This seems familiar," I joked as he lifted it over my hips, over my chest.

"We never did get that date," he whispered as he pulled me closer, the fabric like a lasso over my bottom now. I jerked forward, closer to him.

Closer to his warm eyes, and that little dimple that was peeking out from underneath his facial hair.

"I haven't really had the best track record with dates," I was determined to keep my voice stable, even as he continued to roll the fabric over me, untangling it to something that hopefully resembled clothing.

Or, at the very least a tiny barrier between me and the heat that was radiating off him. He was the summer sun, his warmth pressing into the air, wrapping around me like a warm blanket just out of the dryer, pulling me in to him. Pulling me closer.

It was just me and him and my very inconvenient inability to take a full breath without everything shaking and shivering in need.

God dammit these dragons were really trying my patience.

"I think I'm willing to risk it," his voice whispered over my skin as he smoothed the fabric over my hips and my abdomen, his fingers brushed against my skin in a rumble of electric sparks.

"Damn you all," I gasped, not a drop of the irritation I was trying to push out making an appearance. "Can't a girl throw herself into the Dragon's pit without falling into a hormone overload? Give me some space."

I knew pushing Drake away was going to be an impossibility. If I so much as touched him, my very hungry Phoenix was going to pull him right into me.

So instead I practically threw myself down the alley, trying to arrange the tangles of fabric that Drake had placed over my shoulders.

Yes, it was still a toga. Well, a toga in the apocalypse. There were too many rips for it to be much of anything else. I was going to be slippin' nips all over the place in this mess.

"I would have to agree with Elliot," Zoe snapped, throwing the knotted toga fabric over her shoulder with a flare.

Seeing as she didn't burn her clothes like us commoners, she didn't have to put it on quite yet. Jerk.

"As much as I would love to participate in an orgy, and I don't, we really need to get out of here." She was already halfway out of the alley.

"Wow. Gross." My stomach was flipping and it wasn't all in disgust.

"Agreed," Drake said, giving me one last longing filled look before he stepped toward Zoe, and what I assumed was the path to Rydaim.

8

ELLIOT

THE MORE WE SCALED UP THIS MOUNTAIN, THE MORE I realized exactly why Dragons live in caves, and not people.

Well, state-of-the-art caves according to all the Dragons I was surrounded by, although I wasn't convinced that we weren't just heading to some big massive opening with a few carvings and piles of jewels. I was going to be really disappointed if one of them didn't hoard jewels. As it was, the only hoard I knew was Killian's and while his suits were insanely intoxicating, they seemed a little bit off for me as far as cave dwelling dragon was concerned.

Which brings us back to the cave. And why Dragons live in caves and peoples do not.

Dragons can fly into those fuckers.

As a faux-people I was currently plagued with a mind numbing near vertical trek up the side of a mother fucking mountain.

My bare feet were cutting into jagged stone and rock, numb

little fingers clawing at ridges of a freaking mountain. I was going to start falling apart, lose an arm or some shit.

I might be getting delusional.

Maybe the lack of oxygen was getting to me. Although it was more likely because I was directly behind Killian. Thanks to the incline of the mountain and the way I was practically crawling up the loose rocks like a mountain goat, I was given a great view of certain pinstripes stretching over certain legs, and backs, and an overly muscular ass.

Shit.

I grabbed at some rocks in an attempt to follow behind, and about five gave way, sending a mini avalanche below me, and me skidding down toward the ledge I had just traversed, and would probably lead to certain death. Well, for a mortal. But I was supposed to be mortal-ish right now, so it would create a problem if I burst into flame.

Double shit.

"Are you sure you can't just summon your dragon and carry us in?" I asked for what was probably the thousandth time, trying to disguise my slightly heaving breath as I continued to pull myself up the stone. "I mean, you carry us in your claws or something, right?"

You would think with an entire lifetime of climbing silks, working out, and generally being a muscular badass this wouldn't be too hard. I had done enough hikes that it wasn't a big deal. Mix that with my Phoenix-Fae superpower blood and this really should've been a walk in the park.

Yeah, right. Dragon's and their freaking caves.

"First, you don't summon a dragon. And second, I am not carrying you in my claws, Elliot." Killian growled ahead of me, heaving himself up another large outcropping of boulder and pulling the fabric of his suit tight. I looked down, just as more rock began to slip.

"You are supposed to be a slave, Elliot."

"Yeah, but do they normally climb up the side of the mountain?" I asked as I scurried over the rocks, barely catching them as they slid again, thankfully this time Zoe was there to hold me in place.

"We are supposed to be going that way," she whispered, I rolled my eyes at her.

"The slaves are already inside." Killian's voice was hard, the sound dragged away on the back of the brisk wind that wound around us.

I had pulled my hair into a messy side braid, that was helping the whole Venus problem I had had earlier, the rags I was wearing with the other.

Well, at least it was helping as much as they could. I had predicted nip-slips. And I had received nip-slips.

Thank god Killian and Drake were hyper focused on guiding us up the mountains. Although I had received a good number of snickers and crude hand gestures from Zoe. She had seen me naked more than anyone else. And not all of it due to changing rooms.

You get the silks wound too tight in an s-wrap and you'd be shirtless in no time.

"The slaves that are traded come from other purchases or

children that were born while in captivity. All the Fae that remain in the world are inside of Rydaim which is why we have to sneak you in."

Ugh, every word in what he said was a stoning for my soul. A whole people, trapped. Enslaved. Phoenix screaming, my skin felt as though it was on fire and I was instantly ready to bust on in there ready to burn some vamps.

I didn't even know these Fae. But I was part of them. And I wasn't okay with any of it.

"Well, almost all," I said under my breath, watching my hands as I pulled myself up more of the rock, waiting for smoke or fire or whatever wanted to make an appearance in my heated state.

It was only slightly shaking hands and overly cold fingers, however.

"Up the mountain is the best way for us to get inside," Zoe said with a gasp, she wasn't trying to restrain her heaving breath. At least I wasn't the only one who was having trouble. I mean the mountain pretty much went straight up and down.

Normally people would use ropes and harnesses and stuff for this kind of thing.

But not us. I mean, we could all fly if we fell. Well, everyone but Drake. Seeing as the guy was now hanging from one hand and swinging his legs above his head, I didn't think we had a problem.

Between the circus and the mating-thing, and just all around starting to fall in love with the guy, I had forgotten that he was, in fact, a world-renowned rock climber.

Watching him swing and lift himself up with what appeared to be no effort was probably what he felt like watching me on the silks.

I was picking my jaw up off the floor, or the rocks. Thank goodness I didn't leave any drool behind.

"It's the same entrance I used to get out," Killian said, oblivious to my ogling as he pulled himself onto a tiny ledge and reached down to help me up.

I grabbed his wide palm eagerly, he could pull me up this damn mountain if he wanted to.

He looked awfully goofy standing on top of the mountain in a perfectly pressed suit, hoisting up a gorgeous hipster fire eater, and a toga clad frat girl in the apocalypse.

Good thing Drake didn't need help, but he was also scaling a mountain in socks and sandals. So, you know.

Let's hope we didn't make the evening news.

"Are you ready for this?" Killian pulled me against him as he lifted me, and I promptly stepped to the side.

"I'm ready to kill some Vampires, save my guy, and get out." I said, arranging my toga to something that I could pretend was more modest. "I am not ready for anymore hormonal explosions."

Killian laughed at that, the sound rich, welcome and happy against the chill of the wind. He was the only one that was laughing, however. Drake and Zoe stood, frozen in place, just behind Killian, both of them looking at the same thing.

A narrow opening in the stone.

I am pretty sure my heart turned to lead. Caves had always looked like little monstrous openings in the earth to me, frightening crevices that were ready to pull you in and devour you. This one appeared to be the epitome of that, the caves that all other caves were based on.

White rocks from the mountain pressed from the top and bottom like frightening teeth, the jagged edges ready to rip and tear and devour you before pulling you into the dark abyss just behind.

You know, like a certain dragon king I am putting myself within arm's reach of.

I swallowed. Because I needed more visual evidence that we were walking into a nightmare.

But I needed to be here. We needed to be together. Nightmare or not that thought was a battering ram I couldn't ignore.

"This is like the worst kind of homecoming," Drake said I stepped up to him, Killian walking right past us and into the frightening mouth-cave as though we were going to conquer the thing.

Kill the beast!

"Well, I am wearing a toga, so I guess it kind of fits." There was no laugh for that, just a glare, a sigh, and Drake's hand wrapping around mine as we walked forward, preparing ourselves to be swallowed by the mountain.

"I'll protect you, honey," He whispered, all warmth gone from his eyes. There was only fire and determination now.

"And I'll protect you." I wasn't about to tell him to let me be a bad-ass on my own. Not right now. But I sure wasn't going to let him think he was alone in this.

"We are going to get eaten by this mountain and slit this nasty King open from the inside out!"

I was defiant, yet confident.

And judging by the look on Drake's face, really, really naive.

"Please be careful, Elliot."

His words were pained as he pulled me toward what I thought had been a small dark opening but with each step it expanded into a gaping hole the size of a semi-truck, cut into the side the mountain.

Damn it. I was sure Killian's dragon could soar into this easily. Just like every other massive, dangerous dragon that was on the inside.

Holy fuck.

I knew I needed to be here, but I was really starting to question that decision.

Drake had told me before that Rydaim was a fortress, but this massive opening didn't make it seem very fortress-like. Walking through the thing, I felt like an ant on the way to some extravagant, and utterly horrifying party.

I wondered if this is what Cinderella felt like if she had, you know, crashed the royal ball wearing nothing but a couple of strips of muslin. Oh! And, if the ball happened to be at the home of the person who wanted to kill her the most.

If anything, it would make the fairytale more interesting.

Forget the whimpering girl waiting for the prince to carry her away.

Instead, Cinderella comes barging in in her rags ready to kill them all with her fucking glass slippers.

"The Cinderella Massacre." I said aloud, forgetting too late that all of the conversation had been in my head.

"What?" Drake asked, his fingers tightening around mine as he continued to escort me into the cave, the darkness swallowing the air around us.

"Nothing," I whispered, aware of where we were and what we were about to do.

I certainly wasn't going to go gouging anyone's eyes out with my shoes. Even if I had some.

Which I was kind of wishing I did right about now.

The chilled wind that surrounded the mountain was even worse in the cave. Here, it was an icy whipping wind that brushed over my skin like the devil himself was trying to seduce me.

It really didn't help that with each step into the cave everything grew darker, everything grew colder, until I was following a blob of a shape that might be Killian, and clinging to a hand that I hoped still belonged to Drake.

The mountain monster had devoured the light as quickly as he had devoured us and I shivered, I was really ready for this cold to end. I had never been this cold in my life and I was over it already.

"Are you okay?" Drake asked with a squeeze of the hand,

thankfully his voice sounded like him. One less mountain demon to worry about.

"Yeah, I mean if you count walking into an eternal darkness of damnation. I'm fine." I sounded way more hysterical than I thought I would.

"Darkness?" I could just imagine his eyebrow lifting, that cute little dimple popping with his curiosity.

I'd seen the look enough, even if the dark shape that was hovering in front of me looked nothing like that and he was becoming more and more like a twisted monster in my mind.

"Can't you see?"

I shook my head, realizing too late that he couldn't see that. Well, I couldn't see that. He could, because he chuckled and wrapped his arm around me, pulling me into him and smothering me with his usual scent of pine and rain.

"No, I can't, but seeing as we are going into a cave ruled by a man who wants to kill us both let's limit the opportunity for explosion." I smiled, hoping he could see it, and unweaved myself from his hold in a duck and weave that I had done many times before.

However, I hadn't done it in a cave, with an uneven floor, that was so dark I couldn't even see my nose. I realized my folly about two-seconds after I begun tumbling head first toward my doom.

I braced for impact, expecting jagged stone to cut and bruise more than crash pads in the gym.

Thankfully Zoe caught me before face met stone, although

with the smell of wet and moss that was filling my nose it was probably too close for comfort.

"Damn it!" I shrieked, cringing as my voice echoed violently, turning my profanity into a low monstrous growl. Damn cave, way to live up to your name. "Is there like a light or something that we can use, like, I dunno. Dragon fire! "

Zoe chuckled, placing me on my feet and shifting the tattered toga over my shoulders. Awesome. I wonder what fell out now.

"Sure, but you gotta ask the man upfront for that."

"Killian! Is there any way we could craft a torch or something? Or maybe I can catch something on fire?" I asked, putting my sweet voice on and turning towards where I assumed the front was.

Considering his answering chuckle came from behind me, my guess was obviously the worst it could be.

"You are supposed to be a magic-bound Fae ready for the slave trade," he began, "No magic."

"Okay, fine, but you are clearly a dragon. And aren't you a prince or something?" Yes, I was purposefully prodding him now, "Can't you forge a torch and light it with your totally awesome dragon flame?"

Killian's shoes tapped loudly in the dark as he approached me, at least I assumed it was him by the two specks of green that were now digging into me.

"I could. But we are getting closer to the heart of Rydaim. We need to be careful, and you Ellie girl need to be quiet." He spoke in a low growl as he reached me, the dragon fire in his eyes giving a frightening shadow to his features. He looked like a haunted floating head, and I stepped away.

Well, more like shuffled, tripped and fell back into Drake with a shriek.

So much for being quiet, or stealthy.

I was starting to doubt that this was going to work effectively. The uneven floor was cutting into my soles, and there were pitfalls everywhere.

Thankfully Zoe took pity on me, one line of dim blue flame shooting from her and running over the stone directly above, shimmering over us in the faintest of lights. It didn't let me see much, and it clearly wouldn't last long, but at least I could take one breath and see enough to take stock of the cave, and the situation.

Not that I could do much of either with the way Killian was looking at me. The scowl had pulled his eyebrows so low that they were very nearly fusing together.

"I say we need to be quiet and inconspicuous and you go shrieking and lighting fires." Killian straightened his jacket and stepped away in an attempt to calm his dragon, not that it was doing any good. The beast was growling so loud I was sure it sounded like thunder in the village down below.

"Take a breath," Zoe grumbled flipping her hair as she sent another faint streak of blue up to the ceiling. "We are still far enough away that unless someone has found this tunnel we should be safe."

"And you said it was abandoned?" Drake was looking at the flame with as much question as Killian, edging his way closer to me as if he was going to tow me out of here at a moment's notice.

"Yes, there was no one here. I doubt anyone knows this exists." Killian turned from his siblings to look at me, his eyes dark with his flame, but there wasn't a scowl in sight. His face almost looked sad. "It's not too late to go back."

"I'm not going back, Killian," I whispered, shivering as another of the icy cave breezes ran over my nearly bare skin. "We are here. We need to finish this."

"I can't believe you talked me into this," Killian said, tucking some of the hair that had come loose from my haphazard braid behind my ear.

The touch was hot and I shivered, something that he would normally smile at freezing his face in worry.

"You heard Suvi. It has to be this way Killian. We have to be together. All of us." I said as if that somehow solved everything. It only made Killian scowl deepen.

I was beginning to think the thing was going to be permanently glued to his face. He clicked his tongue, straightened his jacket and went back to leading the charge through the cave as Zoe's fire dimmed, and the conjurer of the flame froze in place, a look of horror on her face.

"Do you smell that?"

Normally, I would question her sanity, but I knew Zoe, and I knew her affinity for smelling things. Especially, supernatural scary things that cling to leotards and cave rock.

Drake turned around slowly, his eyes growing wide, and the

last of Zoe's fire extinguished with a hiss and plunged us into darkness.

Well, plunged me into the quietest, fucking scariest darkness ever. I could hear them breathe, I could hear my heart rattle in my chest and the low growl of Killian's dragon begin to reverberate in his. All the sounds were made worse by the liquid darkness. I didn't think I could get more scared.

"It's a vampire," Zoe hissed.

Well, damn it, I guess I could get more scared.

"Drake and I will lead them away," Zoe barked as shuffling feet and fabric and hissed swears began to echo on all sides of me. "Killian take Ellie to your home and we will meet you there. It's the same one, right?"

"Yes," Killian growled, right behind me now, his hands firm around my waist. I guessed his game a moment before it happened.

"Don't you dare," I hissed, trying to dodge his attempt to lift me over his shoulder and instead stumbled against stone and lunged myself right into Drake. With the way he gasped, he had clearly not been expecting it. "We can't split up. We need to stay together."

"And we would," Zoe said, lifting me away from Drake, whose hand was soft against my hip, and leaning me against Killian who instantly wrapped his arms around me, lifting and holding me against him. "But right now, we need to be safe. We will be back together soon."

"Or we could stay together now," I grumbled as Killian threw me over his shoulder, my bum sticking in the air as I slammed into his back with a soft 'oof'.

"I need to protect you," Killian growled, holding my legs against his chest as though they were precious property.

"*We* need to protect you," Drake corrected from right in front of me, his hand soft on my cheek as he coaxed me to turn, coaxed my lips to press against his, to open and let him in.

He kissed me deeply from where I lay helplessly thrown over Killian's back, the older brother's large hands running over the exposed skin on the back of my thighs. Killian's touch warmed through my muscles until I was a pile of goo, Drake's kiss setting my veins on fire. And I moaned, loudly, and completely lost to it. I melted into Killian as his touch trailed over my skin, my hand clinging onto Drake's neck and tangling in his hair.

Everything was on fire, everything was too hot, and with a shriek from Zoe I opened my eyes, Drake pulling away as I grabbed for him, and my hands glowed brightly in the dark. It wasn't smoke, or the shimmering flames of gold that Jarron and I had conjured before. Instead it was a light similar to what I had seen in Suvi's office.

The bright white orb sat on my palm, reflecting light onto every inch of the dark cave, and worse, right onto Drake and Zoe's concerned faces. They had seen it before, and they knew exactly what it was.

Well, they thought we did. There was something different about this one. This wasn't the pure orb of white light, there was a green ribbon of smoke that was sparking through this one, almost like lightning. It pushed against the edges of the orb, like it was alive, like it was desperate to get out.

"Put it out," Drake gasped, taking a step closer as though ready to touch me, but thankfully thinking better of it.

"What is it?" Killian asked as the light began to fade, the orb shrinking back into my palm like the setting sun in the desert. Because that looked normal.

"Nothing," I said, knowing that no matter how I answered that it would not help our current vampire stalking situation. Thankfully, Zoe seemed to understand that.

"Go," Zoe gasped, her eyes still wide as she stared at my hands. As she prodded Killian forward.

I looked up from the whispers of smoke as they dissolved, jostling around on Killian's back as he ran, as I stared through the cave, towards Zoe who was now spitting lines of fire into the dark, and Drake who refused to look away until the pitch black of the cave swallowed us both.

I could still hear the flame, I could hear each pant of Killian's worry, feel his muscles press against my stomach as he continued to run. But it was the sound of Zoe and Drake's screams that I was waiting for.

It was the screams I hoped would never come.

9

KILLIAN

"You can put me down now!"

"Shh!" Killian was insistent, the snap sounding like a whip in the dark cave they continued to weave through. But even with the snap of his voice, Ellie had been much louder, her screech a long drawn out echo that would bring the vampires, or whoever was following them, right back on their trail. Zoe and Drake had barely been able to draw them off, and having the beasts find his siblings was bad enough.

He had to protect Ellie.

"Silence Ellie girl," Killian said with a low growl as he shifted his weight, and her right along with it. Carrying her over his shoulder had been the best option in their race to escape whoever was tailing them, but with how much Elliot was shifting her weight it was very quickly becoming more of a hindrance.

He had almost been knocked sideways into a wall once, and missed a turn another time. Although that time he had been distracted by the stained fabric that was barely concealing her. Well, not so much the fabric as her.

"Not until you put me down," Ellie grumbled, thankfully quieter this time as she attempted to shift again and sent him off balance.

"Knock it off," he growled, the sound more from his dragon than from him, and quickly jostled her back into position. Damn her and her stubbornness, now was not the time for her to get all up in arms and demand to run back and fight. Even in this situation, her foolhardiness was going to get them in trouble. Having her here was dangerous enough, having her stubbornness here was another thing altogether.

Killian picked up the pace, turning another corner as they grew closer to Rydaim. Closer to his home.

He had expected this leg of the journey to go flawlessly, get Ellie to his home, have Callay watch her while he retrieved Jarron and then a race back out. Now nothing was as cut and dry. With Zoe and Drake lost somewhere in this maze of caves he had no idea what their next move would be. Of course, any first move only came after they were to reach his home. If she insisted on running herself or slowing him down by complaining and sending him off balance and into walls, he had no idea if they would make it that far.

"We are almost there," Killian said, working hard to keep his voice level. "Then I will put you down."

"Or you will put me down now and let me run like the capable person I am."

So much for being quiet, even his dragon was grumbling at her foolishness. Killian turned the opposite direction of where they were headed, determined to break the trail in case anyone heard that outburst, and pushed his dragon deeper inside of him. While it was amazing to have such control of his creature, his emotions were way too volatile right now to make that safe. Shifting into his dragon right now would spell disaster.

"Does this have something to do with that feminism stuff?" Killian asked as he set them back onto the right path, they weren't far from the point in the cave that would break into Rydaim now. Just about a quarter mile more.

"Because I am in full support that…"

"No, it has everything to do with the fact that I have legs!" she was irate, but irate in that way that always made her face turn red and her freckles pop. Killian smiled, he loved the fire in her, both temper and supernatural.

"Put me down," she continued, emphasizing each word with a kick of her legs.

"Not yet," Killian said, lifting his arm higher up her thighs to get a better grip on her, and playfully swatted her behind with his free hand.

She yelped a bit, and jerked in his arms.

"Stop fighting me Ellie girl," he whispered, his voice husky and low as he worked to keep his need for her at bay. "You don't want to know what will happen if you push me too far."

She froze against him, her hands knotting against his suit jacket as she pushed herself up, the motion slow, controlled, and thankfully not sending him into a wall.

"Does this have anything to do with what you said before?" The shake in her voice was like a flame against his already powerful need. "About submitting."

"It's too early to tell."

"You're lying," she was whispering now, her voice dragging over his skin as he stepped into another tunnel, this one leading right to the wide alley behind his house.

"Am I?" Killian teased, rubbing his thumb over the warm flesh of her thigh. The soft skin peeked out from underneath the torn and stained bed sheet, taunting him.

"Do I want to know?" Elliot asked, pushing herself up to stand against him as he slowed to a walk, his hands tight around her bottom as he held her high.

Her hands were strong against him as she supported herself there. He was sure she didn't even need him to hold her legs against him. Hell, the girl could possibly hover right there if he let go, judging by the amount of flame that was in her eyes.

"That's up to you," he said, giving her another swat, and this time letting his hand linger on the roundness of her for a moment longer.

He wouldn't do anything more, he didn't dare, feeling her skin grow warm as she battled and squirmed underneath him was enough.

"What the hell, Killian?" She hissed, keeping her voice low as he stepped into the alley and gently lowered her, letting her body press against his the entire way down. He was sure the useless fabric that she had deemed a toga was sliding all the way up in the process, revealing every inch of her. He didn't look, he didn't care, he was too trapped in the glittering golds and reds in her eyes, the fire burning brightly in her, her hair lifting to soar around her as so many of the Fae in Rydaim did when their magic was close to the surface.

He had never seen this in her. It was frightening, this power that was in her. More so, it was amazingly beautiful. Watching her was taking his breath away, sucking his raw dominance back against his chest.

"Beautiful Fae," he whispered, tucking a strand of hair behind her ear, not that it stayed still, the thing lifted into the air as though it was riding in the slowest moving breeze ever known.

"What?" Ellie asked, following his hand and nearly shrieking at what she saw. Well, she would have shrieked it Killian hadn't covered her mouth, which proved to be difficult seeing as the girl was trying to jump away from her own hair as if it was trying to eat her.

"What in the world is that?"

Killian couldn't help but smile, letting her twist around in the alley, trying to move away from her own hair as a dog tries to chase its own tail. Which was fine, until her movements became so erratic that she was going to catch the attention of the few dragons that were streaming past the end of one of the side pathways on their way to the main square.

They were close to his home, but they were also close to whatever his father was planning. Executions always take place in the square and if they were already on their way down then time was not on his side.

He had let his need for her get away from him. They were nearly too late as it was.

"Will you settle down?" Killian asked with a hiss, pulling her into him until she stood, her breasts pressed against his ribs.

"What is happening, Killian? Is this some Dragon nonsense?" Her eyes were wide, her panic clear, which made sense. Seeing your own hair fly around your head had to be disorienting.

Killian smiled and smoothed the hair over her head, thankful when this time it decided to stay flat.

"It's not nonsense, it's magic," a tiny voice cut through the dark, it's sweet joy instantly recognizable. Killian relaxed, much of the pressure that had been rampaging through his muscles calming.

Elliot however, tensed and spun in his arms, flinging her arms forward as if she was going to attack whoever had joined them. Okay, not as if, she was ready to lunge at the tiny Fae.

"Do not hurt me, Elliot," Callay said, stepping into the light even as she put her hands up. "Yours is a fire I cannot survive."

Callay's eyes were wide, her fear even deeper than when she would step between Killian and his rage. Although, if she truly could survive his fire, it was making sense as to why she had thrown herself before him all those times. Killian couldn't help the chuckle, tricksy little Fae. She may be a little bit of a liar, but it didn't make her any less brave. Killian knew the destruction his temper could cause.

"Callay," Killian said, Elliot's tension releasing, her smoking hands thankfully dropping to her sides. "I would like you to meet Elliot."

Callay's silver eyes flashed, her smile spreading wide as she took a step forward, although she did not extend a hand. She stood just out of reach, staring at Ellie as though appraising a fine wine.

"Nice to meet you," Callay said with a smile and a gentle nod of her head. "You ready to kick some trash?"

"Finally! Someone who knows how to get stuff done." Elliot said, trying to wiggle out of Killian's arms. He wasn't having it, which only earned him a deeper scowl from his spunky mate. "What did we say about smothering, Killian?"

"Please don't encourage her." Killian grumbled, ignoring Ellie and increasing his grip. "And I know how to get stuff done!"

"If you are including carrying me..." Ellie began, the fire in her voice reaching a height that Killian knew not to play with.

"I am including how to get you here in one piece, and not devoured by cave stalkers." He hissed, trying to keep his voice low and them out of notice from the increasing flow of dragons.

Elliot was making that difficult, she was reacting to his temper like a flame to gasoline.

She gave him a look and finally wiggled herself away from his grip, the ripped shift she was wearing twisting on her torso and partially exposing her breast.

"I kept you alive, Ellie girl," Killian said, dropping his voice low in the hope of blocking Callay from the conversation.

Killian towered over her as he reached up to replace the ripped sliver of fabric over her breast, careful to keep his fingers from her skin, even though he could feel the warmth of her firebird wrap over his hand, pulling him in.

"I would really rather not explode."

"I think everyone would rather not have that," Callay snapped, pulling their focus. "If you guys are done with the pillow talk, can we go. I know why you are here, and I'm already afraid you are too late."

"Too late? What do you mean?" Killian's voice was hard as he turned to Callay, the girl's lips pressed into a tight line as she nodded once.

Anger and frustration ripped through the prince and he took a step forward, the tiny Fae twisting her hands one over the other. Her fear only rattled him more, his dragon dripping fire against his tongue as he stepped closer, forcing the Fae to look at him.

"Everyone is already gathering in the square."

"Is there more?" Killian snapped, but the Fae nodded her head. "Strangely, I ascertained that much."

Killian growled in frustration, stepping back to Elliot. He needed to be near her, but not smothering her. The girl had enough fire in her eyes that he was sure he would hear about it. He needed to know she was okay, to be there if she needed. Or if things went bad.

Danger was everywhere, add the risk of failure to that and

Killian was on edge. They had come here to save Jarron, and the sooner he could go do that and get her out of here the better.

Zoe and Drake were on their own. If he had to leave Jarron he would, even if Elliot would never forgive him.

He would do everything to keep her alive.

It was what he was about to do that was scaring him the most.

"No, there is not *more*. Your Highness." Her voice shook and this time she took a step back, her eyes wide as she looked from Killian to Ellie and back again.

"Then we aren't too late," Killian said, running his hand through his hair as he turned away from the two women, toward the end of alley, and the brightly lit street that was quickly becoming clogged with people.

He needed to find Jarron before he reached the square, any chance of interception would be lost if he got there, and the stealthy removal he had planned would be blown to bits.

Ellie couldn't be there for that. She couldn't be anywhere near there for that.

"Callay, how secure is the house?" Killian turned away from the dragons that continued to stream past the alley to face them, the Fae was back to smiling while Ellie couldn't have looked more concerned. Well, knowing her, she could.

"As secure as it always is," the tiny Fae sparked, bouncing on her toes. "I haven't let any of Parris' men, or the bastard himself inside. And trust me, they have tried."

She was clearly proud of herself, there would be time for

accolades later. Right now, he was expecting to have to put out a fire.

"Wonderful," Killian began, turning to Ellie and gathering her hands in his. "I would like you to take Ellie there and wait for my signal. I need to get Jarron."

"Yes, of cour--" Callay began before being steamrolled by a girl whose eyes were devoured in her red-gold flame.

"Like hell if you will!" Ellie snarled. Thankfully quiet, even with the fire he had been expecting. "I didn't come all this way for you to hide me away in your house..."

Her voice was lifting too high, and although Killian didn't dare check, he was sure that some of the passersby were sure to notice. Heart pounding, he quickly scooped her up by her arms, and took a step deeper into the shadows of the alley, pressing her against the hard stone of somebody's house.

She stood there, her face twisted in boiling rage, heat radiating from her skin and pressing into him as he leaned against her.

Damn it all, it was nearly impossible to stay angry at her.

"No, you came because me leaving you alone wasn't safe." She cranked an eyebrow at that, turning her nose towards Callay before turning back to him, her eyes narrowed in defiance. "You must stay at the house. It is too dangerous to come with me for this."

She opened her mouth, clearly ready to rage, but he stopped her with one soft fingertip against her lower lip. The soft, wet, skin nearly froze him in place.

"Beautiful Elliot," He began, his voice soft. "I will not smother you, but you do not know this enemy as I do. You are here, and that in itself is making me want to rage. I need to keep you safe, and to do that you need to go with Callay."

"Fine. But you have to promise me that I will get to explode something before the day is over," she said breathlessly as she leaned back against the wall, her head and shoulders pressing into the stone. He was sure she had moved away in an effort to get air, he certainly needed some. But the position she had chosen was too much, her lack of clothing was doing nothing to hide her figure.

"No promises," he gasped, his voice choked. "But I have a feeling you will accomplish it anyway."

He tried to laugh, but the sound choked in his throat, dead and broken. Her hand pressed against his chest, the tiny thing laying over his frantically beating heart, he was sure she could feel the thunder of the organ.

"Then at least promise you will come back to me." She was calm, longing, her hands needy as they pulled at his suit.

As they pulled his heart in two. In all the times he had left her before he had never felt anything like this. This longing, this need. He could already feel his muscles rip apart in want of her.

Not to mention that his dragon had turned into a furious demon inside of his chest.

Leaving her was suddenly feeling like an impossible task, but he had no choice.

"Take care of her Callay," He whispered, not looking away

from Ellie, from the beautiful fire in her eyes, from the hope that peeked out of her smile.

Lifting her up to him, he pressed his lips to hers. His lips, his tongue traced over her mouth, tasting the fire on her breath as she kissed him back. Her tongue joined the dance, dragging over his lip, and he about lost it.

Thank God she pulled away when she did. "Promise me, Killian. Promise you'll come back."

If only she hadn't asked that. He couldn't lie to her, he would never lie to her, but he couldn't leave her in this hell without hope, either.

"I couldn't leave you," He whispered, setting her back down to the ground, letting his hands linger against her shoulders, her neck, her cheek, as if he was trying to memorize everything. He knew he was. As much as he didn't want to admit it, he was.

One last kiss, this time against her forehead, and he was gone, pushing himself into the dark, and toward where he hoped his brother would still be imprisoned. Before he regretted everything.

He had no way of knowing if he was too late. He had no way to make a plan. He had to run, and find them, and hope for the best.

"I've never seen him quite so gentle before," Callay said behind him, her voice fading away as he turned the corner, back to the dungeon before it was too late.

10

DRAKE

Drake's feet hurt with every step as he followed Zoe through the underground tunnels.

Somewhere in their escape they had turned the right combination of tunnels to lead to a place that he knew, a place that he had spent so much time in he could navigate them blind.

These tunnels were familiar. He had snaked his way through this place hundreds of times before, first as a boy, and then as an adult when he and Zoe where building up the resistance. He knew this maze, and he knew that the vampire that was tracking them would lose them far before they reached their destination.

They needed to get to Killian's house, but that was not where Zoe was leading them.

He knew her, and he had a faint idea as to why. Not that he could ask right then.

They had to lose whoever was tracking them before he

could go peppering his sister with questions. No matter how well hidden their destination was, anyone can find it if you follow the right people. And their vampiric tracker was certainly following the right people, whether he knew it or not.

They had to keep running. Which was hard as years living as a mortal had nearly turned him into one. His sandals were his normal pair he wore when hiking, and the socks had been a logical choice to keep his feet warm when soaring over the Atlantic. The two together made running impossible, and running for over twenty minutes damn near agony.

He didn't have time to think about it, however. He let his feet ache, his heart throb, and his muscles whine as he followed Zoe in one direction, and that tight little cord that bound him to Ellie pulled him in another. His dragon was practically screaming in fear at having been separated from her.

Perhaps there was truth in what Elliot had been saying, but he couldn't question it now.

Forward. He had to continue forward.

Drake wasn't one to argue with his creature, but as the cave grew colder and the air was drenched in that familiar damp weight that he had grown up in, he couldn't make himself follow her. He had not returned to Rydaim for over a decade. Even as close as he was, his heart was having a conniption being back here. There were too many memories, too many traumas that he had never wished to revisit.

And yet, here he was, running through the caves he had

been captured in, surrounded by the smell of blood, sweat, and that heavy weight of stale cave air.

"Well, I said it couldn't get worse," he grumbled to himself, Zoe chuckling darkly beside him as she turned around a wide corner, pulling them in the opposite direction of the wide cavern that Drake was sure would be their final destination.

"What you aren't bleeding are you?" She was very clearly frustrated with him, even though she was laughing.

"Nah, a little blood when being chased by a vampire is nothing," Drake teased. "We came here so we could stay together, only to be separated anyway."

"Don't remind me." That one was clearly a growl, each word snarled from behind clamped teeth as she turned and led them down another tunnel. "At least we aren't with Killian. I can't imagine his rage right now."

"Ellie can handle it." He was certain, although it didn't quench his need to run back and protect her.

They currently had their own problems anyway, and as long as they had dragged the vampire away from the others, he was protecting her. Thankfully the smell of death that had followed them from the moment they had arrived here was growing fainter. Now, if he could stop his feet from cramping, the faint smell of iron that was now drifting from him made it clear he was bleeding.

These shoes were not made for running and a strap or a seam or something was now triggering a bright red stain to blossom over his socks. The rubber ducky design was ruined.

"Get on my back, will you," Zoe demanded from beside him, her mind was obviously in the same place his was. "We are almost there and I would prefer you not attract every blood sucker in a fifty-mile radius."

"They will still be bleeding, Zo." Yeah, he couldn't disguise the fact that he was huffing and puffing now, and Zoe shot him a look that even in the dark was clearly disappointment.

"Obviously blood is the least of our problems. Get on my back you weakling."

"Zoe I..."

"Get on my fucking back, Drake!" He clearly didn't have any choice, and even if he did, the fact that she was now lifting him into position like he was still a toddler made that clear. "I can carry you all day if I need to."

"It doesn't solve the blood problem, Zoe." he was more sour than he had intended.

"Yeah? Well don't scream or I will rip your fucking head off." Ah, there was the Zoe he remembered, he had no chance to bask in the familiarity, or welcome her back before the warning suddenly made sense and a line of dark red fire ripped through the darkness of the cave in two quick spurts, each one cauterizing the bleeding gashes on a different foot.

Hot damn. Screaming was the least of his problems right then. His dragon was nearly ready to burst from his bones at what it perceived as an attack. The only thing that could burn a dragon was dragon flame, and Zoe was clearly putting that to the test. Her flame may not have the poisonous after effects of Killian and Jarron's fire, but it still hurt like a mother fucking fire demon was trying to devour him.

Every bone was cracking apart, a white-hot heat rippling through them as the flesh curled, burned and thankfully began to heal, not that it helped much, he could still feel the flame inside of him, and he could still smell the roasting char of his own flesh.

That was really doing nothing to help the traumatic flashbacks that running through this cave was plaguing him with.

A snarled whimper ripped from his chest, the sound loud enough that he knew trouble was on its way.

"What the fuck did I say about screaming?" Zoe snarled as she turned another corner, giving his feet enough time to heal before she dropped him again.

He barely restrained the howl as the still pink and healing calluses and burns smacked against rough leather shoes and jagged stone.

"It was a whimper, Zo."

"That doesn't make it better. Keep up and I won't do anything drastic." The smile that she fixed him with was sure not reaching her eyes. For being such a benevolent big sister, it was sure easy to forget that she had a hard as iron side that would lash out and burn you.

Being back in these caves had brought it out in her, just as his fear was becoming a quivering burden. He had never been the bad ass that his siblings were.

He wouldn't be able to wear socks comfortably for a week.

And he loved socks, no matter how much of a stupid human delicacy they were.

Each step throbbed, his muscles screamed, and his chest burned for lack of non cave-infested air. But he kept forward, keeping his agony locked away as they turned the last few corners and were finally facing the faint glow of The Forgotten's massive underground hideaway.

He had been a child when he had fallen into the space accidentally, The Forgotten nursing him back to health before he could run back to his family, his tiny head full of a million questions. How could a people who were so nice to him be treated so poorly? Why would people say they were so bad?

He didn't understand, and he didn't stay away either. So, a century later when Zoe had tentatively broached the subject of saving them, of overthrowing their father, he knew right where to begin.

Even through the pain and trauma of being here, in Rydaim, this place brought a feeling of home. This was the homecoming he wanted.

Instead, they ran into a ruin.

The place had never been a shadow of the regal city that Rydaim was. It had always been the filthy underbelly of a world that people would much rather pretend did not exist. When Drake had first discovered it, the biggest building, if you could call it that, was the main hall that served as church, gathering space, and refugee center. It was barely half the size of the grand throne room and made of boxes, discarded wood, and stones that they had pulled from the sides of the cave and the underground river that moved through the center of the cavern.

Over the years more houses, more tents, more lean-tos had been added to the large cavern until it was a bustling space.

Drake wasn't sure what had happened to the survivors after the coup. He had no way of knowing. But with the way the buildings and tents were scattered, and the large hall was slowly collapsing in a smoldering ruin, he would have to guess that none of this damage was old.

This was new, just as the blood, and carnage of those who didn't survive whatever massacre happened here was. Drake's heart twisted as they moved further into the ruin, Zoe moving just as slow as they looked from one tangled body to another, the pressure in his chest becoming unbearable at the bloodied feet of a child sticking out from underneath some still burning fabric.

He wanted to take those feet between his hands, find a way to heal them, to take all the pain and blood away and make everything better.

But he couldn't move even a step closer.

The knife that was placed against his throat wouldn't let him.

"Not one more step dragon boy or I'll pour your filthy blood all over this mess." The sharp hiss of a woman dragged over his skin, twisting against his spine. He half expected it to be Dabria with the strength of the threat, but he did not recognize this voice despite it being that of a woman. Which was no help.

He had a fifty-fifty chance of being correct with that.

Ice flooded through Drake and he complied, not that he couldn't take whoever it was behind him. They didn't smell like a vampire, but they didn't smell of dragon either. Attacking an unknown assailant was never wise, lucky for him he also had backup.

Zoe spun around at the voice, her eyes on fire as she faced whoever the hell was behind him. The blade pressed harder and Drake cringed as the sharp point pressed into his neck. He had held out hope that it wouldn't be sharp, but that was for naught, at least it hadn't broken skin.

"You too, sister," The girl snapped, her hand wrapping around Drake's collarbone and pulling him into her. Surprisingly, the girl was nearly as tall as he was. Her arms were as filthy as The Forgotten, but she was much too large for that kind. "One step and the little one gets it."

Again, another prick of the knife against his neck. Drake inhaled with a hiss, purposefully making it a bit more dramatic than necessary and earning himself a look from Zoe. She clearly didn't seem too concerned about whoever was behind him, fitting seeing as she was not the one with a sharp knife pushing into her neck.

"We aren't moving. Calm child," Zoe said, her eyes calm as she raised her hands, palms open as if to show she didn't have any weapons. It was a foolish motion for any dragon. Why would you carry a weapon if you could breathe fire at will? If for the reason alone, this woman was very clearly not a Dragon. "We aren't here to hurt you."

"Ha! You've come to finish the job of your damn pale skins. They sent others too, I can end you just the same." The woman let out one cold laugh, jostling Drake more and this time the knife did cut into his skin, sending a tiny dribble of warmth over his neck.

His dragon growled loudly inside his chest. The tiny nick may not hurt more than a cut while shaving, and he had done that many times in his life, it certainly was aggravating his dragon. The creature was rising up in his chest. Damn it. The last thing he needed was to lose control of the beast now.

"Tell your beast to cool it," the girl snapped, still keeping herself behind Drake. "I can remove his head before either of you can shift."

"Well, he can't shift," Zoe said, sounding as bored as a housewife talking about vacuums. "So, I mean…"

She shrugged and Drake was pretty sure he was going to punch her once he got out of this. What in the hell was she doing?

"Of course, he can," the girl said, shaking the knife against him in clear agitation. "He's a dragon. I'll take off his head!"

She pressed the knife harder, and Drake inhaled with a growl jostling against the woman. He had had about enough of this.

"But can you remove mine?" Zoe said, a smile peeking on the corner of her lips as she took a step forward. "I doubt you could even reach me before I would turn you to a crisp."

"I'm not alone here," the girl snapped, although the shake in her voice was giving her away. "And don't worry, you will be gone long before you can shift."

"Can you two please stop the pissing contest," Drake was

barely able to get the words out thanks to the knife as his throat, each word scraped the knife deeper, sending more bits of red over his neck. "We aren't here to finish you off. We are here to help."

The girl laughed at that, the sound deep and rumbling. "I'll believe that when I see it. No one helps The Forgotten. Well, except the golden prince, but he is probably bleeding out over the main square by now."

There wasn't a laugh left in the girl's voice. Which was fine, because the taunting playfulness in Zoe had sucked it all away, her eyes burning with the fire of her Dragon as her anger prickled dangerously.

"We can't be too late." She gasped, the pain in her as loud as the thunder in Drake's heart.

It was why they had come.

"We don't have time for this," Drake growled his voice more Dragon than human as he reached up, placed his hand over that woman's and with a clear voice let his dragon rumble the instruction.

"Drop the knife, let me go and take two steps back, you have no fight with us."

Barely a second passed before the knife clattered against the ground, Zoe snatched it up as the girl stepped back, stuttering in noncoherent fear over what was happening.

Only then did he turn around to see the victim of his silver tongue. The woman appeared to be in her early twenties, although there was no way to truly know within the supernatural realm. Judging by the state of her long messy hair, the rags she wore as clothes, and the dirt that covered her, she was clearly Fae.

Although how she was here, or who she served he could not guess.

The girl's forearms were uncut.

She looked at him in fear, her wide green eyes dragging between the brother and sister as Drake's danger alarms kicked into overdrive.

"How did you do that?" She asked, her voice visibly shaking now.

"Who is your master?" Drake asked, ignoring her question as he stepped closer, letting his silver tongue run free.

The girl shook her head, fear clear in her eyes as she tried to fight the pull of his dragon.

"Sasin owned me, but I slit his throat the night he tried to take me in his bed." She said, the words strong and proud, even though her eyes were afraid. "No one owns me."

The last words came out all on their own, unbidden by Drake's dragon. They were tough, proud, and the wide smile that spread over the girl's face perfectly matched it. Drake couldn't hide the smile from twisting over his own face. At least the tenacious spirit of this place hadn't left.

"And you don't know who we are?" Zoe asked, the heat that was radiating off her skin enough to heat the cave overnight.

The girl shook her head, scoffed, and popped her hip.

"Should I?"

"Well, we have been dead for over a decade, so probably not." Zoe laughed, flipping the knife through the air.

The girl's face twisted in curiosity, the facade of strength that she was trying so hard to present slipping away. She couldn't even keep her hip popped. She stood, back straight, hair flowing gently in a nonexistent breeze staring at the two of them as though she had been punched.

"I'm sorry?" Her voice choked, "you're dead?"

"Not technically," Drake provided, straightening his sweater and trying to wipe away the blood that had dripped onto it. "Why did you think we had come to finish you off?"

The girl's focus twisted from Zoe, to him, although the look she gave him made it clear she was still trying to decide if they were dead or not.

"Because Parris and his rats will stop at nothing to collect all the Fae. And you are clearly part of that collection squad. But let him know, our blood is not for sale. And I'll stop him when he comes back."

She eyed the knife that Zoe was still flipping through the air, her brows pieced together as she stepped closer, tugging at the ripped and torn t-shirt and jeans she wore.

"I'm sure you will," Zoe mused, brandishing the knife to get her to move back. "What's your name, kid. I want to know who is going to save us all."

Zoe's prod sent the girl fuming, her eyes flashing dangerously.

"Fallon." The word snarled from her. "I'm not a kid, and you aren't here to help us. No dragon will help us, not anymore. Not with that pale skin behind them."

Drake's stomach twisted, his focus drifting to the war zone. Of course, it was Parris.

"We aren't with him," Drake said. "We are dragons."

The proclamation sounded more like a threat and Zoe scoffed, the sound trapped between laugh and cough. That was helping. Zoe was playing this all too dangerously. Fallon may not seem powerful, but anyone who threatens to rip heads from dragons should not be taken lightly.

He had been around Ellie enough to make that rule golden.

"You say that like it makes any difference." Fallon was popping her hip again.

"It does." Zoe flipped the knife twice and catching it easily before winking at the girl in a look that was clearly supposed to put the girl at ease.

Instead, she only looked more frustrated at Zoe, still eyeing the knife as though she was ready to lunge for it.

He wished she wouldn't. There was no way that was going to end well.

"Looks like a Dragon, walks like a Dragon, and certainly speaks like a Dragon. You aren't welcome here." Fallon clicked her tongue, eyeing the knife like a lover before turning the gaze on Drake. The needy look in her eyes made his stomach flip. "How did you do that? Make me come over here? Is it a vampire thing?"

"He has a silver tongue," Zoe provided, making Drake jump.

They were never honest about that least of all with supposed enemies.

He hated using it in the first place and always avoided it at all costs. Admitting it was a whole other gut-wrenching situation all together.

He bit said silver tongue and settled for a scowl.

"Nonsense." Fallon said with another click of her tongue, folding her arms over her chest. "Only one person had that gift and he's..."

"Dead?" Zoe provided with a bit of a laugh, now admiring the handmade knife.

"Although he isn't dead by a few years, just a few days. That is of course if you believe the rumors."

The girl narrowed her eyes at them as if a sharper gaze would help her identify the two people that she clearly hadn't seen before.

"You guys are full of shit," she said before she moved to run.

Unfortunately for her, Drake expected it. Foolish girl. She claims to have killed her dragon master, but then runs from the princess and her silver-tongued brother.

Perhaps she really didn't recognize them.

"Stop," Drake said, the single world laced with the power of his dragon and sending her to a screeching halt.

"Damn it!" The word was a yell, and Drake let his smile stretch, both he and Zoe taking wide steps toward where she stood, now frozen among the broken planks and shattered stone of the once proud meeting hall.

"Damn it is right," Zoe laughed, coming up behind Fallon and casually putting her elbow on the girl's shoulder, leaning on her as she swung the knife before them, the hand carved stone glinting and shining in the flickering fires of the slowly dying city. "Why don't you take us to whoever else is down here, or I can have my brother ask you nicely to do so."

"Br... Brother?" The poor girl was officially in a tizzy. "The princess?"

"Now she gets it!"

Normally, Drake would agree that the title fit his exceptionally beautiful sister. Perfect hair, legs for days, and a fire that could destroy anything with nothing more than a little bit of steam. Right then, she looked so menacing, that there wasn't a scrap of princess in her. Well, unless you count the princess who avenges the crown from an evil tyrant mercilessly killing anyone who stands in her way.

Which, ironically, was exactly what they were here to do.

Drake, however, couldn't bask in the wicked wonder that was his sister. Not right then. "Zo, what about Jarron. She said..."

Zoe's face pulled together as she looked from the now quivering Fae to her brother. Drake, did not join the poor girl in the pre pants-wetting party, however. He had been on the receiving end of that look enough.

"We have to trust that Kills can take care of it. Elliot said she needed to be here, so let's put our faith in whatever wonky magic that girl is going to pull out."

"Kills?" Fallon interrupted, her voice shaking even more,

Drake half expected her to collapse right then. "Do you mean the prince? Killian? Your... your brother?"

"Yes." Zoe said, still swinging the knife, although the girl was no longer looking at it. Her eyes were digging into Drake,

"That's who the execution is for." Any threat, any laugh, any taunt had left the girl's voice, there was only a painful truth that dug into both of them, accentuated by the dark green of her eyes as they began to shine.

The sound of Drake's sharp inhale was drowned by the sound of the knife as it hit against the floor.

"What are you talking about?" Zoe asked, swinging the girl around to face her. "I thought you said that Jarron..."

"Is set to burn Killian out for high treason, in the square today."

"How do you know this?" Zoe continued, her hands wrapped around the girl's shoulders as she brought her closer, shaking her.

"It's why Parris is cleaning out The Forgotten." Fallon continued, her voice broken as Zoe continued to shake her, the hostile movement calming with each word the girl spoke, although it wasn't in calm, it was in pure genuine panic that soaked into the air and nearly drowned Drake. "He says its protection, everyone knows it's food. Only bodies are returning."

"A thousand vampires high on Fae blood, and the last of Ceres line on display in the square." There was nothing good about this, and Drake instantly regretted admitting it.

"Shit. It's a trap."

"Well, what the fuck did you expect Zo? Grab her, she knows too much now, we have to go. We need to get there."

He knew he had pushed his dragon into his voice, he knew they would have no choice but to follow him.

He would pay for that later, but right then he didn't care.

If it was a trap for Killian, it could easily be a trap for Ellie too.

11

ELLIOT

"This is it," Callay whispered, her hand a freakin' vice around my wrist as she dragged me through one dark alley after another, and towards a door that was out of place in the midst of the smelly alleys of Rydaim.

A bright white painted rectangle of wood and glass was embedded amidst the dark stone. A light, or magic, or another freakin' dimension glowing from the other side and making it look even more like a magic portal against the hundreds of other doors we had passed. So far, I was not impressed with everything I was seeing. This city didn't seem so much like a beautiful Dragon paradise as a festering tangle of tunnels.

Jarron had explained the city like a high-tech cave paradise. I think a dank tunnel and a pile of jewels would be a better fit.

Callay dragged me through the white door before I could really start to freak out about what was on the other side and I squinted as my poor little eyeballs were assaulted by a light so bright I might as well have been dragged into the surface of the sun.

"Sorry," Callay whispered, flicking off a bright light with a click. "I enchanted it to keep the Vampires away, I forget how bright it is after the alley."

"It's no problem," I whispered, furiously blinking my eyes in an attempt to banish the retina burn and the instant headache that was now rattling in my head.

I had enough tiny spots of light in my vision I could connect the dots and make a dead president.

Now was not the time to have dead presidents in your vision, however. I needed to see, because I needed to be able to attack. Although Callay appeared to be the other half to my kick-ass self, I didn't know her enough to really trust her. Especially not here, in underground Dragon dungeon of doom.

I had no idea what awaited me there, and I really hoped I wasn't being thrust into the not so trustworthy arms of a scorned lover. I had already had enough of that with Dabria.

I guess that's what I get for accidentally bonding with an amazingly hot sex god. At least with Callay I could take her, I may only be a bit taller than her, but as long as she didn't shift into a tiger or some shit, I was set.

Well, unless she keeps trying to burn my brains out with a vampire light.

"Better?" she asked, as I continued to blink my eyes in retina burn banishment and little bits of the world around me came into focus.

A counter, tile floors, a sink. A few more blinks and I could clearly recognize the room as a kitchen. Well, a kitchen if I had died and gone to heaven. I don't think I had ever seen anything so big, so white, or so clean before.

And I thought the vampire-repellent light was blinding.

"Yeah," I gasped, still letting my vision settle as my bare feet squeaked on the overly large tiles. I didn't want to think about what gunk my ashy feet were leaving behind. I felt out of place considering the kitchen heaven we had arrived in. "Except I think you brought me to the wrong place. There is no way Killian lives here. It's so... white."

Even as I said it, I was struck with images of beige hotel rooms and perfectly trimmed beards and expensive steaks in high-end restaurants.

"Oh. Scratch that."

Callay grinned broadly before she giggled and pulled me the rest of the way out of the kitchen, through an equally as immaculate hallway and up stairs that I was sure were lined with gold. Like actual gold, and not the leaf kind you see in opera halls and stuff. We are talking plated gold that glittered over everything and covered the beige carpet in sparks.

I will never question Killian's taste in hotels again. It was all starting to make sense.

"Between Killian and Jarron it takes some work keeping this place the way they like it," she said, finally dropping my hand and leading me towards a golden door at the top of the stairs. "They have very particular dragons."

Foolishly, I had assumed that it was all them. The

cleaning, the amazingly perfect kitchen. The reminder of Callay's true role in their world was a painful upset against my spine. I'm not even sure how I could forget, given that Killian had dressed me in a toga so as to look like them.

A slave.

Well, a slave about to be sold.

Which in no fucking possible way made it any better.

Except that Callay looked nothing like that, her clothes were clean, her hair was immaculate and fell in soft silver waves down her back, laying over a crisp jean jacket. Her style sense made her look like a perfect little bohemian beauty. Sneakers, scarves, perfectly ripped jeans. It looked good on her.

We were about the same size, the same build. Even our hair was about the same length, the same gentle curls winding down our backs. I would have asked to borrow some clothes if I wasn't sure I would burn them to bits at some point in the next few hours. We still had to get out of here, and I was for sure going to fly my ass out of this cave if given the opportunity.

Or if I made one.

If Dabria was around, I was definitely going to make one. Show her what my fire could really do.

It was going to be epic. Like jaw dropping, put that bitch in her place level epic.

"I will say, I've put my touch on a few things," Callay said with a smile as she continued up the stairs, pulling me past a landing that was painted in white and green and up a second set of stairs, this one lined in dark wood.

I could already see the difference in the boys with just that. The walls glittered as much as Jarron's eyes, as much as his skin when his dragon was close to him. I think I might have been getting an idea as to what Jarron's hoard is.

Ugh. Thinking that brought the stabby pulling feeling back to my heart. My phoenix was having a hard time staying put, and I was having a hard time convincing her to stay put.

"Put your say in?" I asked, staring at the beige carpet as I tried not to think of the gold in Jarron's eyes.

"Yeah, like this painting," Callay said, coming to a stop and pointing out a weird oil painting of kittens and a vase. "It's like five hundred years old. I'm sure it cost Killian a lot but I asked for it because it's goofy, and because it drives him nuts. I mean, look at that cat's face. Medieval cats are ridiculous."

She laughed like it was the funniest thing in the word, but I was stuck staring and picking my jaw up off the floor.

Ridiculous was not the word I would use to describe what I was looking at.

"And don't worry about telling him, he knows." She continued as she reached the landing and turned around to stare at me. "He hates that kitten about as much as he hates his dad."

"Kinda looks like him too," I mused, knowing full well that I had never seen Ceres.

But the thing definitely looked like what I assumed Ceres to look like.

Its ears were in the wrong place, its eyes were too close together, and if she hadn't told me it was a cat, I probably wouldn't have recognized it as such. It looked more like a dog, especially with the oversized bone looking thing that he had in his mouth. I squished my eyes together to see it better, and my stomach instantly twisted.

"Is that...?" I couldn't believe what I was seeing,

"Yeah, he's carrying a dismembered *member* around like it's a chew toy," she said, reduced pretty much to hysterics now. "A cat and his big old flaccid peni."

I swallowed my laugh and stepped away from the painting, not really wanting to see more. But now that I had seen it, I couldn't look away. An ugly cat carrying around an equally as ugly piece of genitalia.

Seeing it there was making me all sorts of uncomfortable. I think my rampant virginity was showing. Not that I didn't think about it, or want it, or understand it.

But seeing it in a cat mouth.

Holy shit. I was going to back this crazy train right up.

"I think I hate it." *Think* was probably not the right word, but for the sake of not being rude it fit. I was pretty sure Callay could see through the lie anyway with how she was smiling.

"Good," she said, throwing her arm around my neck. "Then you two will have quite a lot to bitch over. Penile stealing cats deserve lots of bitching."

She grinned, and I stared at her. I mean, I had grown up knowing I was weird, and being treated like I was the bizarre step-child Suvi had found on the side of the road. I think Callay might be pushing me off that pedestal.

"I'm not quite what you expected, am I?" She said with a wink and a smile, stepping away from me to lean against the wood paneled hallway. "Did you expect all the yes ma'am's and no ma'am's? A bowing and groveling slave?"

I could only stare at her, I mean, what the fuck do you say to that? So I stood there, jaw working, while her smile spread.

"I knew I was going to like you. I gave up a lot for this whole thing, but meeting you?" Her smile grew she nodded once and pushed one of the dark wood panels, letting the thing swing in revealing a door I hadn't seen before. "This might all be worth it. I mean, assuming the show is worth it."

"The show?" I asked, following her in, my mind immediately going to some circus performance or tour production, I tried to twist my mind around it, well, until I followed her through the door and heart, stomach, and even my back bone fell to the ground with a clatter that I was pretty sure she could hear.

It was Killian's bedroom.

I mean, it screamed him so loudly that it couldn't be anything else.

Everything was painted with his dark surly personality. Black and green accents covered the walls, the furniture, even the bed spread on the massive four poster in the middle of the room followed the same color scheme. The plush down blanket covered what was clearly a very soft, and very springy mattress. I didn't even try to stop the image of us rolling around in those sheets together.

The bed, his bed was making my skin heat. Well, I guess it was less the bed and more the desire of what I would want to do in the bed. I gulped and locked my legs together, carefully following Callay into the room. Thankfully, she was pretending to be politely oblivious to the hyperventilating that was occurring behind her.

God, it even smelled like him in here. Mint, musk, and smoke. I almost asked if there was another room we could go to, considering that Jarron lived here as well it was too much to risk her taking me there. I had just seen Killian, I could control this pull and desire.

My heart, however, was still trying to rip itself apart in want and need of Jarron. I didn't know if I could emotionally handle seeing his room, although I would imagine it held lots of gold.

Gold and white and far too many bathroom products.

Now that I was in Rydaim the pull I had been fighting since seeing the map, since seeing him in the bathroom was turning into a ridiculous anchor that was pulling me towards him, towards the fountain that I had seen on the map, towards the large black box of the dungeon.

He was steps away. Knowing that wasn't helping my need to go all gung-ho and rescue him. I was sure it wouldn't take much to convince Callay to help.

At the very least she must know where the fountain is. Although, if the state of those alleys were any indication, I have a very limited desire to see it. Sewage fountains were really not my thing.

"I would show you the collection." Callay said as she shut

the door behind me, giving a very large and very ominous door to my left a nod. "But I'm not allowed in the main room. I wouldn't risk upsetting Killian and his dragon. They would flip. I have no intention of losing any limbs."

The wide steel door was set into the wall to my left, the massive security system beside it had way too many bells and whistles for me to understand what was going on there. It was clearly going to require a retinal scan and a blood sample though.

"What? That?" I teased, nodding toward the monstrosity of hideous technology. "I am pretty sure I can break through that. Well, in a zombie apocalypse anyway."

"That would be the only time I would risk it," Callay said with a smile, stepping toward one of the black and green drapes that hung over the windows and throwing them open. Light and dark shimmered over the fabric like an oil slick, just like Killian's dragon, as if I needed more of a reminder as to where the motif had come from. "The vault covers more than half of this floor. I'm ninety percent sure he has a second kitchen and bathroom stocked back there."

"Good lord, how many suits does he have?"

"A lot," was all she said, securing the shades and stepping away from the window.

Bright yellow light filtered into the room, streaming over the dark hardwood floors in streaks of silvery fairy lights.

"I enchanted these so no can see in. So if you want to see Rydaim..."

"You mean there is more to the city than stinky alleys?"

Oh, please let it be true. After everything they had said I had been looking forward to seeing some grand underground city. Well, that and I really didn't want to see Jarron tied to a sewage fountain.

I didn't want Jarron to be tied to anything, but a sewage fountain made all of that infinitely worse.

Sick.

"Much more." Callay stepped away from the window, letting the light stream in and my eyes focus on the city that lay just beyond. The roofs of at least five buildings lined either side of what was clearly a street, but they weren't roofs like I had ever seen before. The shingles, the slats, everything was all carved from stone with enough intricate detail that at first glance it looked like the tile shingles that I had seen in Greece and Spain when we had toured through this part of the country last year.

My phoenix screeched loudly as I stepped closer to the window, the sound echoing over the wood and stone of Killian's bedroom and I jumped.

I had no idea if Suvi's shield was going to hold this far away from her, or if it had already broken. Now would be the most inopportune time for that to happen, add to that my tendencies to bust my way through that shit, and I wasn't holding my breath that I was going to make it through this unnoticed, or unheard.

Luckily, Callay didn't so much as blink at the noise, so I must be okay. Which was good seeing as I currently couldn't focus past the amazing world that was revealing itself with each step I took toward the window.

It was so much more than grimy alleys and foul odors.

Rydaim was made of gold and glittering jewels. They weren't piles, but they were everywhere, and it was beautiful.

I guess all those online supernatural encyclopedias had gotten something right.

Took them long enough.

Everything was stone, and glass and every single precious gem known to man. They glittered and sparkled and gleamed against the mirrors that hung from the roof of the cave in shapes and designs that looked more like pieces of artwork than reflective lamps that snuck the sunlight in to the underground masterpiece.

The houses looked like the Gothic architecture of the 1500s that I had seen throughout Europe for most of my life. I had always been in awe of the gargoyles, the flying buttresses, and balconies and every single intricate carving that made me long for Shakespeare and romance.

Now, I was in the middle of it.

Except everything was encrusted with gold and jewels, each house, each business, more intricate than the last as each family attempted to outdo each other. With the way the carved cobbles of the road reflected the light from the ceiling, I was sure that competition extended around the homes as far as their owners could push them.

It was beautiful. It may have been the glittering girl in me, but I had clearly been swept off my feet by a city. I could totally live here.

Well, I could, until I looked up to the stone sky of Rydaim.

A wide red, black, and yellow sun was set into the ceiling, it's round surface gleaming dangerously as it looked down on everyone like some all-seeing eye in a fantasy novel. That alone was creepy as hell, and then I saw the shapes and images that were set into the sun, the gleaming stained-glass bleeding over everything.

People. Dragons. Dragons devouring people, and way too much blood for anyone to feel comfortable. And yet, dozens of people, dozens of dragons wandered through the streets below as though it was a comforting blanket and not some frighteningly prophetic hope for the future.

The frightening creep factor had been turned up to eleven.

"It's the throne room," Callay whispered from beside me, clearly following my horrified gaze to the roof.

"Well, no wonder it's horrifying, the man behind the curtain is just as bad." I shot the window my best glare, part of me wishing that I would sprout some super power that would shatter the thing from here.

Nothing happened however, not even a crack.

Fucking Phoenix-Fae powers. They never worked when I wanted them too. My phoenix bristled inside of me, pushing heavily against my chest as she heated my bones.

Okay, okay, point taken.

"We could fly up there and destroy that thing, easy." I was clearly talking to my phoenix, but luckily Callay didn't seem to notice.

"You know, I've always wanted someone to break through the ugly thing," she said with a smile, her eyes gleaming with a bit of wickedness as she stared at the thing. I really hoped that look wasn't normal, because she was suddenly looking downright frightening, hair flowing around her as mine had in the alley.

It didn't look nearly as freaky on her as it did on me thanks to the glistening silver of her hair. The gentle movements made her look like some ethereal smoke was swirling around her. I probably just looked like I was on fire.

She looked like magic was ready to explode out of her.

It was kind of terrifying.

"Maybe I'll throw the bastard King out of it. Let him fall to the ground like a rag doll." I was probably looking just as crazy now, the imagery of that was wonderful.

"You mean until he unfurls his wings and flies back up to eat you with one gulp." She raised an eyebrow at me and my well laid plans imploded to confetti.

Okay, maybe not well-laid, but it would certainly be funny.

"Well, I'll have to rip those suckers right off before I do then." I was smug, and possibly over confident in my abilities.

"Haha. Okay, if you say so little Fae." Her voice was all laughter, but it might have been lead for all the good it did me.

The city was forgotten as I turned to look at her, her silver eyes shining as her hair continued to fan around her face.

"Do you know what I am?"

"I know what you are going to do." Her hair was alive and

her voice was deep, something that got worse as screams and shouts echoed through the window toward us.

I had been so focused on the carvings and the glittering roads that I hadn't noticed the massive circular fountain in the middle of the square at the end of Killian's street.

The thing was as horrifying as the massive glass sun and thanks to the bright red fluid that flowed in the place of water, even more traumatizing.

Hopefully, the color was just the reflection of the stained-glass monstrosity directly above it. We were almost too far away for me to tell, and the throngs of people that were now choking against the stone structure were adding to that.

It was their screams that had pulled my focus, and the screams and jeers exploded as I stared, as the hundreds if not thousands of people broke apart, making way as at least seven people barged their way through the throngs.

Fists and food pounded the air, covering the group that approached the fountain until I could only see their heads, the blondes and blacks and reds all blending with the crowd that if it wasn't for their movement I would miss them completely. Except that I recognized those dark black and blue braids, and I recognized the floppy blonde.

My heart knew what was going to happen a minute before it did.

"No," Callay and I said together as the advancing party broke through to the fountain. A tall greying man dressed head to toe in black led them all, followed directly by a blonde-haired, pale-skinned demon who was dressed just as darkly.

Those two needed no introductions.

Ceres and Parris.

And yes, he was just as ugly as the medieval cat.

"Ugh. Can I kill them now?" I snarled, my phoenix raging and screaming inside of me as the men waved and smiled to the crowds like Santa Claus to children.

This gift was not wanted.

Seeing Jarron made me want to throw myself out of the window. Flame was already trying to take over my body, I could feel it rumble underneath my skin, ready to roar to life, to explode into being and soar down to save him.

"Not yet." I said to myself, pleading with my soul as a foul looking guard dragged Jarron onto the edge of the fountain and threw him down. His head smashed against the cement with a thud that I could hear from there.

His face was already swollen and bruised, I didn't want to know what had happened. I didn't want to see what was coming.

I didn't understand how he could be there, how Killian had failed. He was so strong, so capable. So doomed.

The black and blue braids emerged right behind Jarron, a smug looking Dabria prancing onto the fountain and stepping between Ceres and Parris like some demented pet.

She wasn't the last ones to join them.

Another guard dragged a battered and bloodied body onto the fountain, the bulk, the hair, the ripped and tattered suit immediately recognizable.

"No," I gasped, Callay's soft scream joining my outrage as

Ceres began to yell about death and salvation, his torrential voice only mumbles through the glass, mumbles through the out of control rage that I no longer wanted to control.

Killian had been captured. They were all in trouble, and if any of these fools thought I was going to sit back and watch this happen they were beyond mistaken.

Foolishly, I tried to control my breathing, tried to formulate a plan when Dabria looked up from the neck of the man she was nuzzling. Her purple eyes flared clearly across the square, over the road, and dug right into mine. Seeing me.

No, Callay said she had enchanted the window. She wasn't seeing me. She was hearing me.

Well, I would give her something to hear.

I hope you are ready to burn, bitch. You have taken not one, but two of my mates. I am going to melt you to the ground.

Her pride melted to shock, and then to fear as she tugged on the sleeve of the vampire. Not that it would do her any good. I would melt him to the ground too.

This was going to be messy. But also guaranteed amazing.

My Phoenix was screaming, my blood was boiling and I already knew there was no way I was going to be able to control this.

If I was going to save them, I might as well make it memorable.

"Oh shit," Callay practically screamed from beside me as my skin turned to flame. "Xi was right."

12

JARRON

Jarron had never assumed he would be on this side of an execution.

He had been on the other side his entire life. He had placed the enchanted shackles on the wrists of thousands who were doomed to die. He had bound Dragons who had defied the kings' orders, restrained Fae who refused to bend. Thousands of people he had led to the fountain, thousands of people he had doomed with his fire. He wondered how many of the ones he had burned before banishment were still alive, how many of them had died from the slow burn of his golden fire. And worse, how many of them had truly deserved what they had received.

How many were actually guilty of the charges that led to their death, to their burns, to their banishment.

He already knew the answer to that one.

None of them.

None of them had been truly guilty.

Just as he was not truly guilty, just as Drake had not been. As Killian wasn't.

At least he wouldn't have to burn, and damn, another of his brothers.

Not that watching his torture was any better.

Killian's screams rang through the darkened alley outside the back entrance to the dungeon that Jarron had been kept in for the last few days. The once powerful heir writhed in a pool of his own blood, the red fluid mixing with water and what Jarron was sure was urine as he writhed on stone carved cobbles, the bright blue blade piercing his side again and again.

Each time it pierced his flesh, Jarron cringed and attempted to look away. He didn't want to see this, hearing it was bad enough. Short of having his eyes forced open, however, he had no other choice. Every time he looked away, the guard that held his chain knocked his fist against Jarron's jaw, forcing him to look back.

To watch the blade pierce his brother's side.

Watch the vampires kick and slash, and the last of his fiery attempts at rescue fizzle away into a wisp of smoke.

Dabria stepped forward, placing the heavy shackles identical to his own around his brothers wrists. With the snap of metal they restrained his dragon, his fire, and his ability to heal. Not that Killian would be able to do any of that with how deep the blade plunged into his side.

"Father, you must listen to me," Killian began, his voice gargled through the blood that was pooling in his mouth and drizzling down his chin.

Jarron tried to shake his head, to warn him not to say anything, to warn him that the old man was no longer their father, but instead a shell. He wasn't even able to give more than a slight nod before Dabria shrieked and kicked the side of his head, the heavy sole of her shoe pounding against skin and bone in a crack of pain that sent him tumbling to the ground in a tangle of limbs, torn clothes, and shackles.

He faithfully kept the scream of pain inside, even though his vision was flowering with red at the impact. He would not scream, even if they chose to rip his spine or his wings from his body.

He would not scream.

Jarron lay on the cold stone of the alley, his vision in line with his brothers, the elder's eyes fully green in the absence of his dragon. A lone tear dripped over the bridge of his nose, falling into the pool of his own blood as they stared at each other.

Pain. Anger. Failure.

Jarron may not have been able to deliver a warning to his older brother, but the message had clearly been met anyway.

The blade, Dabria's bitter laughter that dripped over the stone. They were fucked.

Doubley so, as knowing Killian he was stubborn enough to come to Rydaim on his own, which meant that there was no backup coming.

Which meant that unless the two of them were going to pull out some kind of miracle, they were going to die.

He was fully accepting of that. At least he thought he was. The tears that were now falling free from both of them said otherwise. He didn't want to leave her.

In some twisted reality he was honored to have his name join the thousands who had risen up against the man over the years, to count himself amongst the souls who had been murdered because one man had an insecure ego.

And now that man didn't even exist.

"Do you have anything else you wish to say to me, son?" Ceres asked, the last word bleeding with mockery as he stepped forward, his dark cloak drifting behind him.

Killian snapped his eyes shut, clearly trying to call his dragon to bring his fire forward, but nothing happened but a bit of smoke and a pained grunt as one of the guards forced him to sit. Thankfully Jarron was left alone, left to bleed against the cold and somehow soothing stone.

It had been a glorious rescue attempt, Jarron would give him that. Killian had run in, fire streaming, hair waving, screaming like a demon hell bent on burning each vampire to the ground so as to face Ceres in a battle to the death.

It might have worked if vampires could burn, or if Dabria wasn't perfectly controlling their father. But his foolhardy brother had known neither of those at the time.

He hadn't had a chance even before he started.

"Do you have any other bones you would like us to break?" Parris mocked as he stepped into a fresh pair of trousers one of the other vampires had brought him, his last pair burned away by the dark fire of Killian's arrival. "I am sure we could find a few more places to stab."

Parris wasn't even trying to make a show of talking to Ceres anymore, he smiled widely at Dabria, the two of them sharing a laugh as the woman walked from me to Killian, her long braids swinging down the back of her leather jacket.

She had always dressed too much like Parris. Now it was even more obvious.

"I don't know Peri," she crooned, the nickname ridiculous for him, especially coming from her. Killian cringed as she roughly grabbed his hair and pulled it to the side. "He looks pretty defeated to me. All bloody and crying and pathetic."

Her voice twisted into a hideous childlike mockery as she roughly pulled his head around, tugging his long hair with violent abandon.

Jarron cringed as she threw him back to the ground, his face compacting hard with the rough cobbles of the alley and sending a hollow thunk against the stone. He had been at the receiving end of her ruthlessness enough the past few days that he could nearly feel the pain ripple over his skull.

"Let my father decide what to do with me," Killian said, stubbornly keeping his voice as deep and powerful as he could, pushing himself up like a slug in an effort to see them. To look at the man who for some reason he still held out hope in.

Jarron had clearly not been as effective at conveying that bit of information to his brother.

"Your father has already decided," Parris said from beside Jarron, the Vampire's slimy pride rumbling over the cave and up Jarron's spine as he pushed himself to sitting, his shackles grinding loudly against the stone.

"I would like to hear it from him." Killian's stubborn hope was only going to bring him more pain. Jarron tried to warn his brother, to plead with him to stop, but the subtle head nod only got himself another rough smack on the side of the head, sending the red and black spots into a deeper fury.

He should really heed his own advice.

This time the scream of pain almost escaped. Not that it would have mattered anymore, the man who cared about such things was gone, something that Killian finally seemed to have caught on to. The king didn't even react that time, not to Killian's plea, not to Parris's rough treatment of his 'golden son'. Even his trademark laugh was missing.

"I think Dabria forgot to turn him on," Jarron forced out through the pain that was flowering over his head, blocking out his vision in pops of color that he was beginning to believe was blood. They only grew as another fist, or perhaps another boot made contact with his skull and more blood red flowers blossomed over his eyes.

"You bastards have played your last piece then?" Killian's voice was a growl in Jarron's head, the black and red world blocking everything out and making everything seem more dangerous.

"Oh no," the tap of Parris's shoes echoed through the stones that Jarron lay on, his vision slowly coming back as the blood in his eyes faded away, although it did little more than let him see Parris's ash coated shoes, and Killian's blood-stained knees.

His dragon was probably pissed. Jarron knew for a fact that was one of his favorite suits.

"You are our last piece and you are going to help us finish the job, both of you."

"We will never help you," Killian growled, his stubbornness burning into Jarron and making his head ache. Now was not the time to threaten the pompous vampire. "We will make you pay for what you have done. All of us."

"Oh, how cute," Dabria crooned. "They think they have a chance."

Ice and flame ran over Jarron's spine as he carefully shifted his weight, moving his head to see his brother, kneeling before Parris, covered in blood like some kind of martyr. A beautiful, clever, not a stubborn asshole kind of martyr. He could have kissed the idiot. He hadn't come alone.

Even if he had only allowed Zoe to come along on this rescue mission, they were very clearly saved.

His dragon was trapped in his chest, but he could feel the creature rear up. Its claws scraped against his rib cage at the hope that they could get out of here and race to her, to protect Ellie against the beast that was steps away from finding her. From the monster that created her.

Jarron could only hope that Killian wasn't dumb enough to have brought Elliot with him. He knew the girl would try, that she was tired of being surrounded by her protective dragons. But, with what he knew, coming to Rydaim would be a death sentence for her.

With Zoe, they at least had a chance.

The hope was probably too clearly painted on his face as his guard grabbed his shackles and forced him back to his feet.

"What a glorious day for a reunion," Jarron said with a laugh, trying to catch Killian's eye, but the man was solely focused on Parris. "All we need is a little bit of silver fire to make it the best it can be."

That got his attention, the vampire turned with a smile, the reference to both Drake and Zoe filled him with even more hope. It also earned him another fist to the side of the head.

God damn it. He really couldn't wait until these two stopped using him as their punching bag.

At least now there was the faintest bit of hope that that would happen.

"Tsk. Tsk. You should know better," Dabria said, her voice right before him, the ice of her fire bleeding through the air around him, shivering in his bones. He had barely survived her icy attack from yesterday, he knew he couldn't survive another. His vision was all black now, his head hanging pathetically on his shoulders.

"So, should you," Jarron mumbled, the words barely escaping through the pain, and so broken that it earned him another laugh. "You will pay."

They laughed again, before scraping and grunts filled the air and the party began to move, guards and vampires pulling them from one alley to another and toward the already filled streets. Toward the crowded fountain.

The alley had been dark, cold, and silent in comparison. Walking into the street was like walking into a battering ram of light and noise, everything hitting against his pained bones and exploding in his skull with enough pain that Jarron expected his vision to blacken again.

Bright light beamed from the mirrors in the ceiling, the screams and jeers and taunts of the crowd erupting as they broke through the dark and into the mob. It was a mob, hands were everywhere, pulling tugging, ripping the hair from his head and the clothes from his body.

He bit back the screams at each touch, the pain flowering over him and joining with all the others as each step took him closer to the fountain.

Ceres' shell led the way through the crowd, the grey streaks in his hair picking up more of the light than usual, making him look like some kind of devilish saint. Although that could have been because it was reflecting off of the deathly cool skin of the Vampire who was on his heels. This was all more Parris's show than Ceres, although no one knew that.

Well, not yet.

The two of them smiled, waved, laughed, and jeered with the rest of the crowd. Their movements as one. Two frightening twins, meandering through the throngs like rock stars. Seeing his father now, Jarron felt a fool for not realizing earlier that the man was no longer in control of his own mind. Ceres was too foolhardy, perhaps too flighty for the king that had raised him.

Ceres had always loved a crowd, always loved a good execution. But this cantering flamboyant man was too much.

He was nothing more than a cruel representation of the

woman who lusted after him. A mirror of what she saw in him, and not necessarily what really was.

Or perhaps even what Jarron had seen in him.

Jarron cringed as a tomato hit his back, the cold, wet blob seeping through his filthy shirt. It was the first of many. After that one, more food and more rocks were hurled his way, peppering against his head and back in a violent rainstorm. Killian's growls and shouts from behind echoed the same onslaught, the blindly following Dragon rising up in attack.

He had expected this, but it didn't mean he had to take it. He lifted his shackled hands above his head as he chanced a look back at Killian, desperate to know what was going on.

He had hinted at the chance of there being back-up. With the Vampires strutting and Dabria busying herself with strutting through the spotlight, now was the time to get the information he couldn't in the alley.

The two brothers' eyes met, and Killian's head jerked to the north, away from the fountain that they were being led to, and toward the large estate that the two brothers had shared for nearly a century.

Wonderful. She was close. He could only imagine the riot that would occur when Zoe would make her appearance; the once dead princess rising up to save her brothers. The thought filled him with enough joy that a smiled stretched over his face as he was dragged onto the edge of the fountain, the large base the usual stage for Ceres' evil acts.

Cement and stone scraped against his knees as he was

pushed back down to the ground, Killian forced down right by his side.

"How close..." Jarron began, desperate to know what was going on. He didn't get more than the two words out before the guards on either side of them kicked them into place, forcing their faces to the ground as their heels smashed against their necks.

At least they were only kissing the cement and not Parris's ashy shoes.

Damn vampires.

"My people!" Ceres yelled over the crowd, earning himself a deafening roar. "My dragons!" Another roar, the sound growing with the whoops and cheers that ripped apart the pressure in Jarron's head.

"We have found the last of those who seek to destroy our kind! We have found the ones who do not wish to live as the superior beings we are!"

The main square of Rydaim filled with more shouts, but this time they were confused, pained. Questions echoed through the yells, Ceres palming the air as he asked for silence.

"You can imagine my surprise when I discovered my own sons to be part of those who seek to overthrow me, who seek to destroy the world that we have created." he paused, boos and jeers echoing over the stone as the foot that held him down was released and a strong hand pulled them both to sitting.

The pain in Jarron's head split with each movement, the world swimming in and out of focus as pops of red and black filled his vision. At this point he was sure he had a crack in his skull.

What was Zoe waiting for?

"We all know what the punishment for such behavior is," Ceres continued, "And while it is a shame to lose all my children, and to lose the executioner who has given us so much service. I see no other way. What say you? Shall they live or shall they die?"

The question was meant as a vote, as the last chance for either of them to survive, but it was all a farce. It was always a farce.

There was no plea for their life, there was only the screams of eager dragons, waiting to watch their blood fill the fountain, to rush forward and drink from the thing in the hopes of taking the dragons power into them.

It was a disgusting tradition, and sitting on this side of it, it was so much worse.

The crowd rumbled to a low murmur as Ceres stepped behind the brothers, placing a hand between them in preparation for the line of fire that would take their life.

This was it. This was the end.

Desperation ruled the prince as he looked to his brother, desperate for some answer, for some last-minute miracle. If he had brought them they should surely be making an appearance by now. Theatrics may be fun, but now was not the time for it. They were seconds away from death.

Ceres' hand was a brand against Jarron's neck, the burn of his flame so hot that he knew it would cauterize his flesh as it moved right through him. Burning his head from his body.

Jarron was barely able to bite back the scream, Killian was not so lucky. His pain echoed over the crowd and they broke into laughter, seeing the once crowned prince bend to pain like a foolish mortal.

"Of course," Ceres said, his hands lifting from the brothers. Killian's scream still lingering as Ceres laughed, and the eager malice that dripped in the air twisted into fear. "I can always spare a life if one of my sons chooses to prove his allegiance by killing the other."

Jarron could barely move. Even breathing hurt. Kneeling there, on the edge of the fountain every muscle twisted, increasing his agony at what Ceres was saying, at what he was to be forced to do.

Jarron chanced a look at his brother, hopeful for some impasse for some promise of a quick and painless death so that he may survive and defeat the bastard. Killian was not looking at him, Jarron was not even sure he heard. His focus was only on the peaks of the roof of his home, his pupils shaking in hope.

Jarron had already let his hope slip away.

He could only hope for a quick death now, the brief moments of hope that he had experienced already hurt enough.

"For these, my sons, I will pardon an heir if he devours his brother before this crowd. I will let them fight for their lives, and allow one to remain if he shows his devotion in the blood of the other. A battle to the--"

Screams broke through Ceres' speech, silencing the false king as an explosion rocked through Rydaim. Rock cracked and collapsed all around them, the ceiling splitting as the rumble of the cave began to split it apart. Jarron jerked at the explosion, his eyes flashing to his brother who now looked at the roof with a villainous joy.

What the hell!

Killian should know better than to bring a bomb into an underground cave. What was the idiot thinking? His damn brother, if they survived this he was going to be in a whole new world of pain.

The cracks in the cave spread as another eruption followed the first. Rock sprayed over much of the crowd as the top of Killian's house exploded.

The shrieks increased with the fireball that followed, with the glittering flames of red and gold that were now streaking over the crowd and spreading from a ball of flame that was singing with a tone more frightening that Jarron had ever heard.

It was beautiful, and even in their fear, much of the crowd fell silent. Of course, it would have been even more beautiful if it was not here, if she was anywhere but here.

Killian clearly wasn't smart enough to leave her behind.

"You idiot!" Jarron screamed over the crowd as the fire bird landed right before them, the flames falling away to reveal the beautiful and completely naked woman underneath. His dragon could have broken the magical binds that tied him right then if his mortal side wasn't so furious.

He wasn't the only one, Elliot looked ready to end them all with one snap of her fingers.

Which she did, but instead of Parris and Dabria vanishing in a flash of blood and smoke, he was pretty sure she stopped time.

13

ELLIOT

Holy fuck!

I had turned into a freaking bomb.

My rage ripped out of me as I stared at the boys kneeling before the fountain, Ceres standing behind them, his hands on their necks in a way that was clearly painful. Well, at least for Killian. He screamed at the touch, his face contorted in pain as he shook and fell back down to the ground. That scream was all it took for whatever super-bomb power I had inside of me to explode.

Everything shook as flames of the purest white raged over my skin, licking and fanning into the air as though I had been covered in Kerosene. Explosive Kerosene that exploded with the loudest damn bang I had ever heard! Even I jumped, Callay screamed some foreign profanity behind me and rushed from the room as the stone house around me ripped apart. I watched it happen in slow motion, watched the wooden walls of Killian's room splinter and break, watched the glass shatter, watched the rock behind it crack.

I was sure the entire thing was terrifying. Even if I could run from whatever I was becoming, I wouldn't. Well, unless it was to take me there, to that fountain and the two men that I was about to save.

"Leave the hard stuff to the girls," I smirked and let the white flame grow, my phoenix bursting from me in a blast larger than I had ever seen.

The flames of my soul wrapped around me, my bones twisting into the massive bird as the last of the stone and wood around me exploded into shards and rubble, leaving me open to the sky, free to swoop down to my mates, and to Dabria who was still staring at me in slack-jawed horror.

Ready to burn, bitch? I taunted as I took off into the air, streaming right toward the fountain in a ball of red and yellow flames, burning feathers trailing behind.

A scream ripped from my throat as I bee-lined right for them. All the rage, and panic, and fear that my Phoenix had felt over the last few days released in one scream of warning that sent everyone scattering like ants, desperate to escape the bomb that was racing right for them.

Everyone on the fountain stared as I landed, as my Phoenix fell away and I uncoiled to stand on the edge of the fountain. Covered in ash, and completely naked.

Again.

I was beginning to feel as though I could conjure some clothes if I could figure out how, the magic that was bursting through my veins was strong enough to do so. I could feel the power buzz over the screams of the Dragons behind me, feel it run over my skin as I stared at the dead-eyed vampire who had yet to look away, and felt the strength reach an apex.

Magic buzzed through my eyes, pressing against my skin and slowing my heart as I felt time slow, and everyone around me pulled to a stop as though they had been put on pause. The sound faded to nothing, the air pressed against my skin in that heavy weight that for the first time felt familiar.

Felt safe.

Of all the times for this to happen, this was the best.

Ceres stood, staring dead eyed into the crowd. That dumb blond Vampire was still staring at me like he was a waxworks, and Dabria was looking like someone had smacked her. Which was awesome.

Her dumb face alone made this all the better. Talk about wiping the smug look off the bitch's face. Take that Dabria.

Killian and Jarron were huddled into each other, which presented the first big problem. I may have stopped time, but who knew how long that would last. Seeing as I had never carried anything as a Phoenix before, I wasn't sure if I could pick them up and fly them out of here. No matter how strong I was, I couldn't pick both of them up at the same time and carry them out of here like some sort of epic firefighter either.

Now, that's a calendar I am sure a few men would love to see.

"Damn you and your big ugly muscles," I cursed as I stepped

between them, giving them my best glare, that they would neither see nor remember. "Screw memory potions, I need a shrinking potion."

The air wasn't quite so much of the sticky glue it had been the last few times and I was able to move without feeling like I was trapped underwater. Yes, it was a tick in the 'this is better' box, but I was still facing two of the biggest men I had ever seen and facing the prospect of having to carry them out of here.

Where were Zoe and Drake when you needed them. Not that it would help, they would be frozen too.

"Oh, this is bullshit," I grumbled, bending down to inspect the shackles. If I could burn them off that would at least give us a bit of an upper hand.

"Why don't you flash them out of here, Elliana. I know you can do better. I have seen better of you."

I shrieked and jumped so high that I was sure it looked like I was about to take flight. Judging by the slight chuckle that followed the announcement, I wasn't the only one to think so. The voice was a smooth taunt that ran through the air like butter. Repulsive, moldy butter that should have been thrown out a few years ago.

Straightening from my attempted take-off, I was careful to keep my shoulders tight as I turned, ready to face a stunned crowd and an angry mob, but everyone was still frozen. The air was still the low pressure of a time freeze, my heart was still thundering in a heavy slow pace that shouldn't be able to sustain life.

And I guess, in a way, it didn't. Because the man who faced

me, who saw me, and who was now smiling at me with all the greed and hunger of a predator, was clearly not alive.

"What?" The blonde vampire sneered. "Aren't you going to come give me a kiss hello?"

I stood, completely naked, before a vampire I hadn't seen before a few minutes ago. I knew of him, I did not know him. And yet, there was something familiar about him, something that was slithering against my spine and pushing me forward, my Phoenix screaming in a fear of retaliation I had never felt before.

She was scared. She pressed against me in a flurry of feathers and claws that was coating my tongue in both ash and flame. She was screaming at me to run away, scared of something that she clearly recognized, even if I did not.

The only other time I had felt this was in the room after Stacia had coated it with the fake blood. The blood meant to repel Vampires. To repel him.

Of course, the one time the time-freeze came when I needed it, it would malfunction and leave me stuck with a guy that if Stacia's ominous pre-death warning had any truth behind it, knew exactly who I was, what I was. Hell, a guy who might have even created me. Creepy.

Add to that the fact that he worked for Ceres and I was in big trouble. He probably wanted my blood as bad as the old silver-haired king, too.

Because, you know, Vampire.

This was just fucking awesome.

I scowled deeper, the need for face punching getting

stronger.

"Parris," I said, trying to put as much certainty in my voice as I could, even though I wasn't completely sure on who he was. If my phoenix knew him, and he clearly knew me, I was going to play along as long as it kept him in the dark, and me one step ahead.

"Hello child," he crooned, countering my step back with an even larger one forward. "You don't recognize me, do you?"

Well damn. So that clearly didn't last as long as I had hoped.

Better still play the all-knowing bad-ass, the more I could fool this guy that I totally remembered him and everything about myself before time snapped back in to place the better. I needed to come up with a plan to get Killian and Jarron, and now me, out of this mess. This pale loser was really not helping that.

"Why would you think I don't recognize you? You still look like the same irritant you have always been." Because, you know, vampires don't age. This was totally going to work. "I'm more surprised to see you here."

I waved my hands around, indicating the time-freeze, because I realized I didn't know the name for any of these things. And I highly doubted that 'time-freeze thingy' was what I had called it when I knew everything about myself.

And apparently knew him.

"So am I, to be honest," he smiled, leaning down to the water that flowed through the fountain.

Ripples moved behind his fingers, the tiny waves stretching over the red-tinged surface like a broken rubber band, moving out and in as though they had been snapped into place on repeat. As though any motion or movement here could not quite stick.

Huh. I didn't know it could do that.

"Well, don't let me stop you from breaking out your own welcome committee." He smirked, still running his fingers through the elastic water. Okay, so I was snarky in my past memory-life too, I could totally handle this.

"Welcome," I let every ounce of irritated sarcasm drip from my voice as I waved my hands in the air in false celebration.

I wasn't even looking at him, though, I was staring at the water as it snapped back to his fingers again. I resisted the urge to reach down and touch it, my mind desiring to know if it felt like glue or dough, or if it was similar to whatever weird weight lined the air. Even if I wanted to get closer to the nasty vampire, I didn't really want to risk washing away the ash, that was thankfully thick enough to cover everything. Instead, I took one big step back, closer to Killian and Jarron and gave the monster shackles that were around their wrists a piercing glare.

I knew I could burn those off if I focused hard enough. It really depended on how awesome my hybrid magic was, because those things were frightening.

"What do you want?" I asked, the sarcasm still coming on strong as I stepped behind the guys, hoping to block my attempt at controlling my fire from the vampire.

"You are here, so that is enough for me," Parris said, his voice dripping with a vile hunger as he stood from the fountain.

His eyes were just as hungry, just as frightening, as he

looked at me, taking one large step closer. I held my ground, even as the air rippled with a chill that I was sure was coming from him.

"You always told me about how beautiful it was. It seems I have stumbled across the correct blood combination, even without your help."

He smiled, and my stomach flipped in what was clearly disgust. Stacia had told me he had created me, and obviously his little experiments had not stopped when I had been swept away from whatever creepy kid factory he had.

"What poor little soul have you been manipulating?" I taunted, trying to keep my voice strong as I focused on my hands, on the heat that was always so close to the surface. Thanks to the rocking and rolling of my panicked Phoenix, however, my body was ice cold. Even my blood had a chill as Parris took another step toward me, his eyes dragging over my body as his tongue darted out to lick his lips in that same gut-twisting hunger.

Gross.

I didn't know if he was looking at me with the interest of biting or mating with me, but as far as I was concerned both were off the table. I needed to get my fire back in line and then I could burn that foul look from his face as easy as I had burned Stacia's wrist.

"No manipulation. Just a good old-fashioned cocktail of the blood of a few choice souls. Fae. Vampire. Dragon. A bit of werewolf. And here I am, with you. As I always should have been." He smiled, his eyes lingering on my chest.

Thank god I was covered in enough ash that it was equal to

a leotard or I might resort myself to hiding behind the two bulky princes that Parris's continual movements had placed between us.

"And how many did you kill to make that?" I let my eyebrow lift, countering his step so as to keep the Dragons between us, and at the very least, hidden from his hungry eyes.

Killian's shocked face was perfectly between us, his long hair dropping over his shoulder and tickling against my navel. A drop of blood that was working over his temple was slingshotting up and down, just like the water in the pond had. Back and forth, as though we were stuck between two seconds, and not frozen in one.

"All of them," He smiled, his wicked face stretching into a grin. "I would love to add you to my concoction, Elliana. Just one bite, let me lick you as you once loved me to do."

Double gross.

I shivered as though a ghost had moved through me, every nerve ending pricking into the fire that had been gone for the last few minutes, "I would never let that gross mouth get anywhere near me."

The words were a snarl, and his face fell, the greed and hunger settling into a grim fascination that sent another wave of panic over me.

"You don't remember me."

It wasn't a question, and I wasn't foolish enough to play dumb anymore. I was actually amazed that I had been able to pull it off this long. But at least now fire was rumbling over my skin, the once cold fear of my phoenix turning into an angry rampage.

"Nope, and I don't know who Elliana is either," I said with a smug grin, even though it was pretty damn clear that 'Elliana' was me, at least it wasn't something weird like 'Mellaninya'. Elliana was close to Ellie, I would take it.

"What an odd choice for this rebirth, considering all that we have gone through, together. I wonder if you thought it would help, not remembering us."

"Why would I want to remember *us*. I snarled, truly hoping there was no *us* to remember.

Heat was rippling over my skin now. I was ready, now the only question was if I was going to burn him, or burn the shackles first.

I had seen how fast vampires moved before, and it was enough to scare me off fighting the blasted things for good. You know, if I had a choice, and I didn't.

Winner, winner.

He was going to be first, and that smug look on his face was going to be the first thing to go, just melt it off like crayons in the sun.

Still gross. But also, very awesome.

It was going to be grossly awesome.

"But that's okay, I don't need to know you in order to melt your skin from you bones," I yelled like a banshee, the threat clear as it shimmered in the air and threatened to break the time barrier of whatever I had created.

The twisted little vampire didn't seem to notice, he smiled brightly, and stepped around Killian's frozen body, closer to me, close enough I could see the dead grey in his eyes.

"Would you really kill your creator?" He whispered. "I don't think you have it in you to destroy your family. Your true family."

I was pretty sure I had been stapled to the ground, hog tied to a rod, and doused with ice water. I couldn't move, and I sure as hell couldn't turn away from the twisted, pale man who was taking step after step to be closer to be.

"Family?"

Ugh. I hated the word in my mouth, I doubly hated it in regards to him.

"I am your father, child." The words dripped with hunger, the tone, the need, twisting my stomach so severely that I was expecting the contents to turn themselves inside out.

Father's don't look at their children like that. They don't talk about licking... like hell if I was going to finish that thought.

Triple gross.

Just really, fucking, gross.

I didn't even know how that worked with vampires, but I was pretty fucking sure he couldn't be my father.

"You're lying."

"Perhaps. But I believe you already know the answer to that," he smiled wider, the length of his fangs pulling over his lips, hitting against the abnormally bright of the cave. "You have already seen the signs, and I am sure your phoenix is practically screaming right now. She wants me. She wants to feel me against her. Let her have her way, come closer. I have seen that look in your eyes before Elliana. I know what you need."

Oh, like hell if I was going to give him the benefit of a win after that. Not that I could stop it, the twisted little menace was already chuckling to himself. He knew he was right, just as I did.

And it grossed me the fuck out.

"What?" I snarled, "the look that says stay away if you would like to keep your head attached to your body?"

He snickered, that sound was even worse than the melty acid in his voice, and I cringed. At least he was coming closer, it would make it easier for all the meltiness to happen.

"No, the look of defeat. The look of a lost little soul who is dying for direction. Are you ready to come home? I have been waiting for you, daughter."

Yeah, I totally made a 'I just swallowed a lemon because you are the most repulsive thing I have ever seen' face, and yes, he totally deserved it. I was really not ready to add Vampire to my list of paranormal oddities and even the possibility that he was right was making me more agitated.

Damn it. My phoenix bristled, the creature pressing against my rib cage with enough force that it hurt. First, my fire had nearly left, and now it was so strong that I was worried it would turn me into another freaking bomb. And, as much fun as it would be to see Parris's arms and legs scatter to the four corners of this cave. Killian and Jarron were way too close for me to give that new internal weapon another go.

"Sure, I mean, it's not like these Dragons are giving me anything I need." My heart felt as though it was being torn out of my chest when I said that. Parris' face twisted up in clear disbelief, but I didn't care, he was close enough now. The fire in my chest was hot enough that all the rage and frustration and anger brewed to the surface.

"Do you even know what you need, Elliana?" That twisted smile of his was going to haunt my dreams.

"I do. And it isn't you." My hands were rippling with flame as I lunged at him, my palms moving to immediately cover his pale face from forehead to chin. I spread my hands as wide as I could, trying to cover as much skin as possible.

His scream was immediate. The scent of burning flesh filled the air as he stumbled away, pushing me back in his attempt to reach the fountain and the water that would hopefully slow the burn.

Steam covered his face, the long grey tendrils drifting from him as he plunged at the water, never quite reaching it. The fluid slingshotted away from him, leaving him to burn.

And leaving me to try to burn the shackles from my dragons.

Which turned out to be so much harder than I thought.

The massive enchanted rings of doom barely even sizzled under my Vampire melting palms. If anything, the cool metal was almost a repellent to my Phoenix. She screamed and retreated, taking all that wonderful heat with her and leaving me feeling dumb, boring, and particularly not full of shifter magic.

Okay, so touching them was out of the question. I should have seen that coming, but I still had the whole fire javelin thing, although I could control that better when in my phoenix form...

"You little whore," Parris snarled, the anger in his voice making me jump. I was barely able to scuttle away before he reached me, his skin fully marbled now, his eyes terrifyingly bloodshot.

Or, rather than eyes, pools of absolutely terrifying red in a pool of dripping flesh.

His skin pulled and bubbled as he smiled, his thin lips tearing apart the skin like paper. I cringed, expecting blood, expecting the whole thing to warp into a horrifying red-tinged mess. But there was no blood, just the bubbling burns and blood shot eyes that were beyond horrifying.

"Holy fuck!" I shrieked, jumping to my feet.

That was all it took to pull my phoenix out of the hole the shackles had put her in. Her flame was making a grand return, ready to burn vampires and shackles and anything else I needed to destroy.

"Come here, Elliana," the demonic vampire roared, chasing me from my dragons and leaving him to stand beside them. "I will teach you to obey me again if I must."

His smile warped as he waited, his teeth glinting as he held his hand out to me.

"Yeah, I don't think I am going to ever *obey* you." The words twisted the bile in my stomach into an uproar.

"Fine, we can do it your way," he sneered, his head lowering toward Jarron's exposed neck. The threat was as strong as the glint in those ugly pointed teeth.

"Like hell if I'm gonna let you do that!" I yelled, pushing my hands out and willing all of my flame and fire and anger into bubbling rage, ready to twist through the air toward him. But nothing happened, not even a burst of smoke twisted from my hands.

Damn shackle enchantment must still be lingering.

"Fuck."

Parris laughed, turning from me to move Killian's hair to the side, revealing his already beaten and bloodied face and neck. Both of their necks ready for a bite.

It was then my phoenix erupted, her scream as loud and angry as mine was. Time twisted back into reality, flooding the once quiet world with the screams of fear. The few dragons that had their heads on straight were already rushing the fountain.

Not that they would ever make it. I was angry, and I was ready to turn into a bat out of hell, or rather a phoenix out of brimstone.

The title seemed fitting as I erupted into flame, my phoenix emerging long enough that I sent a line of glittering red flame from my beak, right to the Vampire and the now awake and bewildered Dabria.

It was almost like something out of a dream.

Dabria looked the same in life as she had in the frozen world, like she had been bitch-slapped.

Take that!

My phoenix pulled back into me in another burst of yellow flame, my bare feet hitting against the stone beside my boys as a shower of feathers rained over us, fluttering to the ground like little stars.

Burning stars.

Each one calling to me.

The Travelers Mark.

It was the same feeling, the same pull.

Let's hope I didn't fall head first into the fountain this time.

"Hold me!" I instructed to the two dragons behind me, my two mates leaning in with their shackled hands to grab my ankles, Parris now screaming as I turned to look at him.

He was scared, he was angry, he was desperate for me to stop.

That alone told me that this was going to work. I reached out and grabbed one of the still falling feathers, a zap of energy moving through me with the touch. Light and fire ignited in my veins, the energy of the feather and who knew what else sucking into me, and me into it.

And hopefully right to Drake, another part of my soul.

With a pop, the world began to swim, feathers and flame swirling around me. With the weight of a fifty-ton truck on my chest the world twisted into sound, to flame, and then to nothing.

I guess I could move through things, just not coffee tables.

"Holy mother of balls!" I exclaimed as the world opened back up, Killian and Jarron still kneeling behind me, and a large expanse of cave I didn't recognize stretching open before. "I can do freakin' magic."

14

DRAKE

CHEERS ECHOED THROUGH THE ALLEYS AS DRAKE RAN towards Killian's house, right toward the center of Rydaim. He knew he needed to get to Killian before he charged after Jarron. He needed to reach Ellie before she was left unprotected, but his dragon was pulling him in the opposite direction. His dragon didn't like being here in the first place, and the closer he moved toward the center of the city, toward where his brother had burned his dragon and cursed him to die, the more the creature was erupting in his chest.

Nothing about this place was safe, and he needed to get himself out, Ellie too. His creature could do that, his dragon was desperate to do that. He could feel the dragon rise up, ready to burst from him in a shower of sparks and fly out of this godforsaken cave.

He didn't need to remind the beast that this was the worst possible place for that to happen, even if he could fly. And he couldn't.

The creature growled indignantly as he continued to run

through the winding back alleys, the roads that led to the square flashing in and out of sight as they sprinted past them. There was only one row of houses that separated them from a hoard, they should be careful, but they needed to get there. Drake could only hope the sound of their race would be disguised by the crowds as they shifted from cheers to jeers.

"Do you think they are already there?" Zoe's question was strained by breath and fear as she caught up with him.

Thankfully she didn't seem too upset about his silver tongue having pushed her out of the cave of The Forgotten and toward Killian's house, not that he had meant to control Zoe, or Fallon. He would have to be careful, his dragon was far too close to the surface, and it was sure to happen again.

The possibility made him uncomfortable. He was not a fan of his gift, and accidentally using it always made it worse.

"The only way to know is from above," he said with a nod to the high roof of the cave, the thing looking as ominous as it had ten years ago.

His father and that frightening eye. He had always hated it.

"Do you want to shift or...?" He gave her a look, one which she quickly returned, the rising shouts from the crowd accentuating the panic in her eyes.

"Just keep running, if he's not there. If we've missed him," she paused, her voice shuttering in her own brand of fear. "We should be able to see from the top floor of Killian's house. Then we will know what's going on."

Her eyes flashed as she picked up the pace, sprinting past him.

The cheers picked up again, a roar of sound that rippled through the row of buildings that separated them from the main square of Rydaim.

"We are running out of time." Drake spoke more to his dragon than to his sister. The creature was still causing a ruckus inside his chest, and he was starting to think that he may need him.

He swallowed, hopefully he needed him more to breathe fire than to bend wills.

"I'm going ahead. Keep track of the caboose." Zoe smirked as she called back to him, sprinting her way past Drake and Fallon, who was trailing more than a few steps behind them.

"Come on, Zo. Don't do this to me," Drake yelled, but Zoe plowed on, giving him one more smirk as the crowd erupted again, this time louder than before.

The sound was so loud it shivered against the stone and even Zoe jumped, before picking up her pace even more. He half expected her to shift in an attempt to get there faster. If the alleys had been built to accommodate a dragon she probably would have.

The stone walkways were built for serving Fae, however, her dragon would rip this place apart.

Zoe disappeared into the dark, toward the sloping roofs of the larger houses at the end, the one in the middle like a homing beacon.

Killian's home. They were almost there. Please don't let them be too late.

Now was not the time for a leisure stroll, it was irritating enough that Fallon was interested in doing just that.

Slowing down enough to grab her arm, he began to tow her after him. Fallon hissed and tried to pull away, but Drake was having none of that.

"You need to move faster," he said, carefully restraining his dragon that time.

"I'm going as fast as I can," Fallon was full on whining now, and Drake nearly forced his power into his voice, he could hear his dragon growl, he was ready. "I don't even know why you dragged me along on this in the first place. He's your brother. He's your problem."

"He's your problem, too," Drake snarled, tugging her along a bit rougher than he normally would. "He only came here to save his brother, who has been working to save your kind for the last few years."

She tweaked an eyebrow in disbelief and pulled herself to a stop, and Drake right along with her. There was no time for this, and Drake's patience was getting pushed more than it would normally.

"You mean the golden prince?" Fallon scoffed as Drake continued to prod her on, at least she took a few steps that time. His glamour had clearly worn off.

"He's been working to save..."

"Well, he didn't save me. He lost an auction and sent me to some horn dog." She folded her arms over her chest, her fingers sparking slightly, although the sparks appeared broken, like the electrical circuit had been cut. Made sense, seeing as The Forgotten were not supposed to have any magic, all of that had been cut out of them.

She was conspicuously missing the scars from that procedure, but her magic had been affected anyway.

"You mean the one you killed?" Her smile widened at his question.

"You mean the one I dismembered before I slit his throat." Fallon's smile was reaching insane levels now, the grey in her eyes shimmering dangerously.

Drake fought the need to step back. He was very glad the knife had been left back in the destroyed city of The Forgotten. Not that it made her any less dangerous.

"None of that matters. Forget what Jarron has done. You know who Zoe and I are, you know what we have done," he fought the need to grab her hands and plead, the cheers were reaching an apex now and they needed to move.

He would leave her behind if he could, but Zoe was right - she had seen them. They didn't need that information getting out.

"I know."

"Then trust us." He tried to prod her forward, continuing to keep his dragon locked away, and his eyes free of both fire and persuasion.

It took an awful lot of his Dragon's strength to persuade with one look, not that he hadn't done it before, but the more of his strength he could save the better.

Wasting it on this girl seemed like a horrendous waste of time anyway.

Thankfully, she pressed her lips together and gave him a nod. Drake dragged her forward without another word, the jeers of the crowd pushing him toward Zoe, who had completely disappeared in the darkness of the alley.

Cheers pushed them forward, the girl running alongside him when the alley turned, pushing them past a tiny side alley that burst with light and screams.

The sounds of the crowd had changed, they were drifting to screams that rumbled with the shake of the earth. The rock below them rattled in an earthquake, the filthy windows on the few houses that faced the alley cracking with a snap as their frames shifted. Drake jumped, Fallon pulling to a stop as he did. Her eyes were wide as she stared at the cracked window, at the perfectly aligned break in the stone that stretched over the wall of the house and into the street, the long, jagged break running right between them.

Drake barely saw that, his focus was already shifting toward the house at the end of the alley, the one that had been their target, and the one whose entire top floor was now glowing with a peculiar shade of red and gold.

He had seen the color before, more than a dozen times, he had dreamt of the color, he would know it anywhere. But seeing it here, reflecting through the windows of Killian's house like a beacon, was only screaming danger.

"Oh god," he whispered, his heart pounding against his chest.

"What is that?" Fallon gasped, her bare feet slapping against the stone as she made a bid for retreat.

There was no running away anymore. Not for her, not for anyone

"It's a Phoenix."

"The Phoenix? But she's... That's not possible." Fallon was clearly approaching hysterics, odd for someone who had held a knife to his throat only minutes before. She was going to have to get her shit together pretty damn quick.

He didn't have time for this.

His dragon was screaming now, his own growl roaring through his chest as he started running, dragging her behind him.

They made it only a few steps before the cracks began to pull apart, the rumbling of the cave turning to a dangerous vibration that he could feel rattling every single one of his bones. He froze, turning up toward the brilliance of Elliot's light when the top of Killian's house exploded in a shower of stone in a blast that rivaled that of a bomb.

They weren't that far away now, and the shower of rocks and stones that rained over them reduced Fallon to tears, her screams nearly as loud as the bomb. Well, until she saw the brilliant bird that rose above the smoke of the explosion, rose above the flame and rubble that fell beneath her.

"Elliot."

Drake stood, watching his mate spread her wings, the glorious burning feathers of a Phoenix pressing into the air before she darted toward the fountain, towards the thousands of Dragons that were waiting for an execution there.

Well, she said she would pull out some kind of miracle. This was not what he had had in mind. This could very easily end in her death.

He needed to get there, and he clearly needed to get there five minutes before now.

"Stay with me, run, now." Drake pressed the full strength of his dragon into his voice, forcing Fallon to follow him. He really didn't have time for her bullshit. He needed to get to his mate.

He would have to figure out what to do on the way. Right now, he just needed to get there.

"What the fuck!" The girl snapped as she caught up to him, the panic and anger mingling in her voice like some kind of deranged tango. "Can you maybe stop doing that? It's freaky!"

Drake ignored her, ignored the gnawing regret in his stomach and plowed on. He could see the servants' entrance to Killian's house now. The white glass had shattered, the stone frame was broken and falling apart. Bits of stone and flame were scattered around it, they fell from the sky, they flickered from the inside as though they had been blown out from a bomb and not by the cracking of the mountain.

With all the destruction, and the fire that was sure to be consuming the fancy wood that his brother preferred, he was amazed the house was standing. Which was great considering that his sister was clearly in there.

He was ready to plow his way in after her when a spark of silver shimmered from inside the house. Dread plunged through him at the flickering lights, the unnatural glow swimming toward them as though it was stalking them.

As though the light, or whoever was attached to it, was ready to attack.

It was too white for a Dragon, too bright for a Fae. The possibility of it being a Vampire froze him, his Dragon instantly rearing in preparation for a fight. He knew he couldn't but he knew he would find a way.

The spark of light bobbed and weaved like a flickering star until it burst its way out of the door in the form of a small silver-haired Fae.

Callay.

He hadn't seen her in the ten years since the coup, since she had fought against her own kind, this was not going to be a reunion he was interested in having.

She was smiling, dust and soot covering her face and the clothes that were nicer than what he would expect of slaves. Interesting considering the last time he saw her she had been wearing the usual grey drab that the enslaved Fae wore. Her smile faded as she stepped through the broken glass of the door frame and saw Drake standing there with Fallon, his would-be assassin.

"What the fucking hell are you doing here?" She hissed, the words clearly not meant for the girl. She was looking right at him, her silver eyes turning into little orbs of sparking fury. "I sent you to Denver. Why the fuck aren't you in Denver? Elliot is one thing! Why the hell aren't you in Denver?"

Her rant grew louder with each word, with each step that

she took closer to him. Drake couldn't move; however, he might as well have been stapled to the still rattling stone with all the shock that was going through him.

"What in the hell are you talking about?" Drake's voice was hard, the growl of his dragon trying to rise up against the tiny Fae. Drake pushed it down. Her clothes weren't the only thing that had changed.

He had never known Callay to speak so openly, or so foul. There wasn't a drop of the *slave* he knew in the Fae before him.

"This sure as fucking hell wasn't part of the fucking plan!" Callay snarled, her lip twisting as she looked at something far past him, as though she wasn't even talking to him. "Damn it! That little demon tricked me!"

Callay may have never acted like she was equal with a Dragon, but she also never acted like she was losing her mind.

She was talking nonsense and he was certain he had never heard a woman swear quite so much, and he was bonded to Elliot, who would easily put most climbers and a few sailors to shame.

"Are you okay? Are you hurt?" Drake asked, his calm assistance drowned out by the screams from the square as they bolted back into being.

The glass and stone that littered the ground rattled and jumped as the screams increased, the sounds pounded toward them like an army on the march.

Drake's stomach wound itself into a knot as fear drenched

the air, the magic he had felt from Elliot's Phoenix swallowed by the shock, by the thunder of rampaging feet.

"What the hell is going on?" Fallon shrieked, the phrase stuck on repeat as the three of them turned toward the street, toward the sound of panic and anger that was very quickly heading their way. "If there is any chance of us getting out of here, or me running out of here on my own accord, I really think we should get on that right about now."

"Oh shit," Callay hissed, taking a step away from the door and trying to pull Drake behind her, her fingers digging into his sweater and grabbing the fabric in a need of escape. "We have to go, I have to get you out of here. She said to get you out of here."

"She?" The twist of Drake's stomach was turning into a hundred-pound dead weight.

Zoe.

She was in the house, and if she told Callay to get him out, that could only mean one thing.

"Where is she?" Drake was raging now, the sound of an angry mob growing endlessly closer. Callay was right, they needed to get the fuck out of there. But he wasn't going anywhere without Zoe. "Where is my sister?"

Callay froze in place, jaw dropping in a frustrated horror. "Zoe is here, too?"

Okay, so maybe she wasn't talking about Zoe.

"What the actual fuck have you guys done?" Callay's hair had gone into full on tornado now, the quickly flying strands only accentuating the angry panic that was lining her face. "We are so fucking fucked."

This was getting ridiculous. Drake had never seen the girl so unhinged, and the level of panic that was bleeding from her was adding to the wall of violence that was heading their way in a most unpleasant manor.

"Fuck!"

"Control yourself, Callay. We came to save Jarron and you." Drake had entered a full snarl now.

His Dragon was burning against his skin, and clearly showing in his eyes with how the panic drained from Callay's face. She stepped back, right into Zoe who had burst through the back door like a bolt of lightning.

The two of them hit the ground in a tangle of arms, legs, and thanks to Zoe - bright red fire. The powerful dragon jumped to her feet the moment she realized what was going on, hauling Callay behind her, who was now boasting a bright red burn on her arm. Callay was back to cursing and swatting at the skin, as if that would help.

No one else paid her any mind, even Drake's accidental prisoner was looking at the powerful dragon with a dropped jaw.

"We need to get back to the tunnels," Zoe said, her voice firm.

"To the village?" The girl said, the eagerness unmistakable.

"No, out." Zoe had already started moving and it took Drake a bit to catch up.

"What do you mean, out?" It was clearly Drake's turn to

become hysterical. "We can't leave them. Elliot is back there. I am not leaving her."

"That girl wasn't kidding when she said she was going to pull out a magic trick," Zoe said, the corner of her mouth twitching into an entertained grin. "She flew down to the fountain, jumped around in a freeze of time and vanished with Killian and Drake in a puff of smoke."

"Vanished?" Callay squeaked, stealing the question right from Drake's tongue.

Zoe nodded, "Damn Phoenix is causing more problems than she knows." Zoe picked up her pace, plunging them back into the tunnel they had entered the city from, the tiny opening barely large enough for even Callay to walk through upright. "She burned Parris, same as Stacia."

Zoe's voice had lowered, the rock twisting in his stomach as his dragon screamed in his ears, as if the creature knew what was coming.

"He ordered the vampires into the tunnels. He's ordered the tunnels sealed. We need to stay ahead of him or we are all going to be made into blood cocktails."

"Fuck."

15

ELLIOT

IT WAS A CAVE.

I mean, we had come from a cave, but this was a different cave. It smelled different, it looked different, and I was pretty sure it was nowhere near the underground fortress we had been in literally ten seconds ago.

Drake wasn't here.

Something in the back of my mind had told me to touch the feather, to grab it, that it would take me where I needed to go.

To Drake, not to a large underground cavern that may or may not be on the other side of the world.

This was the type of cave I had expected dragons to live in. Cold, damp, and miserable. I could even hear the wind howling from somewhere in the dark, the roaring train rippling over the dew-covered walls.

"We are in a fucking cave!" I shrieked, slamming my bare

foot in to the ground as if I needed reassurance that we were here.

Newsflash, this was all very, very real.

I was going to have to start accepting that all of these things were real, possible, and not some sort of sign of psychosis. Otherwise, I would be signing myself into an insane asylum real quick.

"This is a fucking cave!" I yelled again the sound of my verbal explosions followed by a low deep chuckle.

I spun around, hands up in preparation for attack, I was pretty sure I could send a pretty damn good stream of fire right then. But it was only Jarron and Killian.

The two dragons knelt on the ground, their hands restrained in shackles, looking as beaten and bruised as they had at the fountain.

"Oh my god," I whispered, dropping down in front of them.

My naked breasts bounced as I fell but neither male looked, and I didn't even flinch. "Are you okay?"

I wasn't sure which one to go to first. Killian looked far worse, the blood that was still pouring down his face was fresh and smelled of water and salt. Sitting there with my hands fluttering like mad butterflies, I could see the flesh around his eyes begin to swell, the injury from underneath pushing out, swelling from whatever had hit him.

Looking at Jarron was like looking into Killian's future. Most of the blood that had dripped from a large gash over his eye, and over his scalp had dried. The swelling around a massive bruise on his jaw wasn't nearly as rounded and a massive black-blue bruise was flowering over the skin. He had looked much worse when I had seen him in the vision in Denver. I wanted to be grateful that he was healing, that they were both okay, but my heart was breaking just seeing the two of them.

Not knowing what else to do, I threw my arms around both of them, pulling them into me and crushing every single bruise and broken bone they had.

"You're okay," I whispered to nobody in particular, although I pressed my lips to the tender skin of Jarron's cheek, and then to Killian's jaw. Both men groaned against my over excited greeting.

"Yes," Jarron moaned, turning to pepper me in a kiss of his own, "but if you aren't a little more gentle I am going to end up in pieces."

I backed away gently, trying to calm my worry so as not to continue to crush them, and to check that the ash was still providing adequate cover. We were good on both counts.

"I saved you," I said again, looking from Jarron to Killian,

Jarron grinned, and I nearly melted with the light in his smile. He was so handsome, even through the blood, even through the pain. He was still positive, still joyful. Still love.

Jarron may be smiling, but Killian looked about ready to explode, not that he could with those things around his wrists, I realized.

"Yes, darling," Jarron whispered, his eyes darker than I had ever seen them as he scooted closer holding the heavy shackles up to me. "Now would you mind taking these things off so I can give you a proper thank you."

"Or a proper scolding," Killian added, his voice dark and frustrated as he also held his shackles out to me.

There went my warm happy bubble of success.

"I just saved your ass and you are going to sit there scowling at me?" I spat, shooting an eyebrow in his direction, my hands beginning to heat as I turned to Jarron. "You can wait now. Or forever. I think I deserve more than that."

"You mean like a lecture on how not to expose yourself to the king who has hunted you for over a decade or so?" Killian was angry, his voice rumbled and rippled over the cave and I jerked.

"I saved you, Killian. Zoe and Drake were gone. You were going to die, and yet here you sit. Alive. I did that. And that king did nothing but stand there looking like a puppet who has lost his ass-hand. I even faced a vampire for you. You're welcome." I snarled the last words and scooted closer to Jarron, careful not to touch the metal around him and upset my already boiling fire. I needed that so as to destroy these ugly ass designer bangles that the boys had been suckered into.

"You faced a vampire?" Jarron asked, his voice shaking as he looked from me to Killian, but the stubborn pig-headed dragon of the eldest brother hadn't left yet.

He was still growling and glaring at the air around him.

"Yeah, that Parris guy wasn't affected by my time loop thing," I said, the new name seeming closer to the truth, or at least explained the weird bouncing liquid thing that I had witnessed. "And he's a piece of work. Seems Stacia was right. He seems to think I'm his daughter. Which I am so not sold on considering he also looks like he wants to eat me." Or lick my blood, but I wasn't going to add that one. "Besides, can Vampires even have children? I think I'm going to go with creepy as hell creator."

"I don't think you are his daughter by blood," Jarron said, his shackles shaking along with his voice as he looked between us, scooting closer with the faintest sparkling of gold in his eyes. "It's more than what Stacia said. He did create you, yes, but from what he said he has been creating children with different powers and abilities for years. And now he wants to take it one step closer."

"What are you talking about?" Killian snarled, his shackles grinding against the stone as he leaned in to them.

"Parris wanted Ceres to find Ellie. He wants her back. He wants to control everything. And now Dabria is controlling Ceres."

"I stunned Ceres' ass-hand?" I asked, the faint chuckle breaking out of my throat. "No wonder he was standing there like a useless lump. I broke Dabria."

Jarron gave me a look of question, but I was too busy chuckling to answer, the weird mental image I was getting only reducing me to more childish giggles.

"So, what I saw in the alley?" Killian asked, his voice nearly a roar over my fit. "They have full control."

Jarron gave a nod, his lips pressed together in a tight white line that was nearly as frightening as the darkness of his eyes. Any remaining laugh was sucked away.

"It's Parris," I whispered, the last few pieces falling into place. "It's Parris that wants to kill me?"

"Not kill you, rule you. He wants you for himself."

"He wants my blood and whatever it does for him," I clarified as if that somehow made it better.

Creepier maybe. Not better.

Jarron nodded, but Killian was quickly working himself up into a full-on rage.

"And you went off and flew into his life in a ball of fire." Killian's rage erupted, this voice echoing through the dark cave.

The supposed scolding, however, was bouncing right off of my back. I had had about enough of mister high and mighty.

"I fucking saved you Killian!"

"You should have let us die. We were ready to die for you."

"Did it ever cross your thick skull that there are people ready to die for you too," I raged, "Or even better that we don't all have to go off dying for each other like some crazy Kool-Aid drinking cult! Sometimes it's nice just to be alive, and walk down beaches and shit. That maybe we can kick some ass, shoot some fire, and live happily ever after in the end."

"I am supposed to protect you!" Nothing in his voice said protecting. Nothing in the way he sat with his hands in shackles said protecting. In fact, his stubborn bull headedness was so strong that I expected ribbons of black smoke to start shooting from them like some kind of cyborg.

"No!" I shrieked, my emotions boiling over and threatening tears. I pushed the hot ugly things away and let my phoenix and my fire boil even more. "You are supposed to support me. Love me. Whatever. But this whole act is getting us in more shit."

I waved my hands around furiously, sending sparks of what looked like molten lava flying from my fingertips. Jarron yelped and shimmied away, but Killian stayed still, letting the boiling embers fall against what remained of his suit jacket and filled the room with the smell of burning wool.

Which was gross.

"It's time to get off your high horse, Killian. I'm fucking strong too, and you are going to have to let me save you from time to time. I'm not dinging your ego, I'm treating you like you matter."

Oh, I was raging. Both of us were, Killian with his cyborg eyes and me with lava dripping hands that were now spreading smoke all the way up to my elbows.

At least I was running hot enough that my already smoking hands were pretty much ready to shoot a perfect line of scary metal destructive fire right toward Jarron's hands. Now, if only I could control my temper enough to not cause havoc. Metal destructive fire was one thing, I was suddenly very nervous what my fire would do to him. I had melted a Vampire's face off. I shivered. That image was going to haunt me for a while.

"Now, if you'll excuse me, I need to free your brother from these ugly things," I growled, anger and fire still dripping from me as I gestured to the shackles. "Let me know when you are ready to act like an adult and I can remove yours too."

I gave him a look, half expecting him to rebut and rage

about how I was being a petulant child. And maybe I was, but I had really had enough of his ego getting in the way. Thankfully, he said nothing and leaned away, his impassive face blanching as though he had been slapped.

Wish I had, because he deserved it. And if he tried to pull something like that again, I was probably going to have to actually do it. But not the face melting kind.

Yeah, I really needed to banish that image. It was nightmare inducing.

"Don't move," I pled to Jarron, the guy giving me one pained nod before balling his fists in an effort to hide his finger behind the thick metal shackles and turned away, like it was nothing more than a band aid that I was ripping off his skin.

Please let it be as simple as that.

I really wish I could close my eyes too, but that wouldn't turn out too well. Instead, I kept them open, hovering my palms before me and doing my best to aim for the rings of silver. It was hard to aim palm fire, not that I had ever done it before, and I really didn't want to mess it up.

I was pretty sure Jarron wanted to keep his hands. Hell, I wanted him to keep his hands.

I exhaled, it was now or never.

"Scream if I burn you," I said, letting the fire stream from me as the shaky breath left.

The cave exploded with light, the flame of my phoenix reflecting off the walls and making the previously dank space shimmer with color.

Jarron gasped at the light, the inhale turning to a shriek as the flame broke through the metal and he scuttled away from the ribbon of fire, and the melting shackles beneath. The old grungy iron bubbling into a pile of golden, bubbling iron.

"I'm free," Jarron whispered, shuffling over the rough rock floor to sit beside me, his hand soft on my back.

It was clear he wanted me to stop, his hand was soft, his voice calm in my ear, but I watched the metal bubble and heat, melding back into the stone never to hurt anyone again.

"There," I said as the last ring turned to goo against the stone, closing my fists and plunging us back into relative darkness. "You're free."

Jarron's eyes beamed as I turned to him, the gold slowly enveloping him as his dragon returned to the surface, now free from the powerful shackles.

"Are you safe?" Jarron gathered me in his arms, his hands soft against my back, my very naked and ash strewn back. I hadn't cared about that until that moment, but leaning against him, my breasts pressed against his chest, his hands over my back, all of those damn emotions came hurtling back. I clung to his shirt and when he pulled away, I brought the tattered piece of fabric with me, pulling it over his head and quickly throwing it on over me. Inside out.

It was nearly as ripped and stained as the toga, but I really didn't care. It would do the job, and I would be a little bit less apt to do something crazy.

Of course, me stealing his shirt did leave Jarron shirtless and that had always proved to be troublesome. But that was before his body had been ripped apart and mutilated.

"Oh my god, Jarron," I gasped, any explanation of why I had disrobed him forgotten as I leaned forward, my fingers hovering above the dozens of still bleeding cuts that crisscrossed over his chest. Gashes covered his sides, drizzles of dark blood seeped from the wounds as they attempted to stitch themselves back together. What looked like bite marks were covering nearly every inch of him in haunting white crescents.

I was scared to touch them, as if touching them would make them real. Just seeing them made it possible that it was a delusion. A bleeding, seeping, obviously excessively painful delusion.

"What the fuck happened?" I choked out, tracing the skin around the tender flesh.

Oh god, they were all so very, very real.

"Parris happened," Jarron scowled, pulling my hand from his side and holding it between his own. "Killian is right, Elliot. You are very lucky that he didn't kill you right then. If he didn't want you so bad he probably would have."

"Well, don't worry he won't be wanting anything from me for a while. I pretty much burned his face off."

"What?" Killian yelled from behind me, the grind of this shackles against the stone pulling me around to face him.

"He was going to bite you, so I melted his face." I held up my hands as if that settled it, but neither man had been there for Stacia's breakdown. They didn't know. "It seems my Phoenix fire has super vampire skin melting abilities..."

Both brother's looked flabbergasted, jaws and eyes too wide for what someone would consider normal shock levels. I, however, shrugged.

"I'm going to keep adding to my arsenal."

Simple enough. I was, however, determined to give them cooler names. I really wasn't up for adding 'melty hands' to my list of super-cool things I could do.

Weird.

"I know you don't want to let me go kick ass," I continued when neither brother said anything, "but you are going to have to actually let me do stuff. I'm pretty wiry and I'm not a huge fan of men swooping in to save the day."

I shot Killian a look, and while his answering glare probably could have melted his shackles all on his own, he still nodded which I was clearly going to use as a blood-signed contract.

"Thank you, Elliot," he said, his shoulders pulling together as he glared.

I rolled my eyes, close enough.

It took less effort to melt Killian's shackles from his wrists. Although I didn't melt them to bits when Jarron suggested saving them for a certain mind reading dragon that we still had to deal with. I almost regretted melting the other ones, putting Dabria in shackles was one thing, putting her in two shackles would be even better.

Diabolically twisted, but better.

"Now what are we going to do about Zoe and Drake," Killian began, rubbing his wrists and pulling me away from where I was staring longingly at the still glowing metal of Jarron's shackles.

"What about them?" Jarron asked, his swollen face twisting oddly as he pulled his brow together.

"They are still in Rydaim." My heart was pulling into a thunder of frustration. We should be in Rydaim, too. If the feather was a Travelers Mark we would be with Drake already, as Suvi had said. Nothing made sense, and my frustration made me want to follow the wind and soar out of the cave after him.

"That's the last place we saw them," Killian said. "But they are alive."

Or at least Drake is, I added internally, hating that I knew. Hating that it was possible that Zoe wasn't still okay.

"Callay is there, too." Jarron said, looking between us, his hope ringing right against mine. "They should be able to get out with her help. She must still have that map."

I wanted so bad to tell him yes, but seeing as I had blown up Killian's house, with Callay in it, I wasn't about to place a bet around that.

"Logically yes," Killian said, his voice hard, "But Callay does not know that they were with us. I only instructed her to protect Elliot."

"So, they are basically trapped in a city full of people who think they are dead." Ugh. Saying it aloud only made it worse. "With Dabria controlling minds, and Parris and his melty face," I stopped mid-sentence.

"Well shit. I pissed off a vampire and now they are stuck with him."

I needed to get them out of there, like three hours ago get them out of there. If only the burning feather thing had worked.

Maybe it still could.

It was a Traveler's Mark, I just needed to get it to work in the right way.

I jumped to standing, running over the events that had gotten us here. Ash-suit, creepy vampire, melty face, burny hands, boiling blood, feather.

That all seemed easy enough. I would roll my eyes if they wouldn't have noticed.

If I was going to try to replicate that, I needed to understand what happened, and how to call on the weird burny feeling when the feathers had erupted from my shift. I had seen my phoenix feathers multiple times before, but I had never seen them glitter and slide through the air like that. Creating that again was going to take some doing. Hopefully, this time, I wouldn't end up looking constipated and we could get to Drake and pull them out before something happened.

"Are you okay, Elliot," Jarron said, clearly trying to disguise a chuckle. "Are you trying to do magic, or do we need to find a bathroom?"

Okay, so I am not as good at calling on my super mystery powers as I would like.

I groaned, threw my hands in the air, and tried a different tactic. Jarron laughed more.

"What?" I was nearly shrieking.

"You just..." Jarron said, his battered face twisted beneath his smile. "What are you doing, darling?"

"I'm going to go back and get them." I was very aware that my voice sounded too grunty for the face I had been making, Jarron was now full on laughing now, which was awesome.

I really needed to get this under control, or I was going to end up farting fire again.

I had ruined my favorite pajama pants doing that. Not that that mattered now, my clothes were all long gone. Well, I mean, they were in Denver, but still.

Not here. Far away. Long gone.

I needed to focus on my magic.

Which brought me back to grunting.

"And how exactly do you think you are going to go back and save them?" Killian asked, his hands wrapped around mine, pulling me from my pseudo-constipation. He didn't even flinch at the heat of my hands.

"The same way I brought us here."

"And where are we exactly, Ellie girl?"

Well, that brought my magical adventure to a roaring halt. I stopped trying to call flame and magic to me, my grunting silencing as I straightened and looked around me, to the very boring, and very grey nondescript cave located somewhere in the wide, wide world.

"A cave." My false confidence reflected back at me in

Killian's disbelief, his smirk twisting over his face and pulling that dimple back into existence. My confidence had stayed intact, but my stomach was now tied up in happy little knots.

"And where is that cave Ellie?"

"It's all around us, Killian. That's what all this rock and stuff is. And that wind that's howling over there. That's the outside," I said back to him, mocking his condescending tone and giving him a look, luckily he got the point. Jarron however, was now reducing to a fit of deep booming laughter.

Neither was helping the bruise to Killian's ego, not that I cared, the guy was acting too much like a pompous prince. I didn't care if he was post-beating pissed, he needed to chill out.

"Alright. Point taken." His smirk was growing. "But either way, you don't know where you brought us, or how." I nodded, narrowing my eyes at him, it didn't take a rocket scientist to know where this was going. "So how do you plan to make it back to Drake, and then make it back to us."

My heart strings.

I wanted to give the answer, I opened my mouth to give the answer, but I closed it with a snap. It seemed legit, my heart said that it was legit, but when it all boiled down I wasn't sure it would work.

"I'm going to try to use the Travelers Mark. We need to get them Killian." I said instead, my voice soft as my hands dropped, Jarron slowly pushing himself up to join us.

"I agree," Killian said, squeezing my hands when I opened

my mouth, ready to fight him. "But we need to find a more sure-fire way to get there."

"And when you say we...?"

"You will come with us." I wasn't sure if the words hurt him to say, but he didn't seem too pleased even though he was the one who said it.

"Wow. Thanks."

"But first," he plowed on, ignoring my grumpy look while brushing his aside, "we need to find out where we are, and perhaps find you some flame-retardant clothes. Not that I don't mind seeing you like this..."

I quickly looked down, making sure that I wasn't showing off a little bit too much skin again, thankfully everything was covered. If not a little gross. Between the three of us there was a bit too much blood, and a bit too much ash and dirt.

"New clothes would be good," I admitted.

"And perhaps some food," Jarron added, "now that those damn shackles are gone my dragon can heal, yours too," he added with a nod to Killian, "but food will help that."

"Right," Killian said, his voice regrouping to that strong bossy leader. "Once I know where we are, and we all don't look like victims of a war..."

"We are victims of a war," I interrupted him.

"Then we can find a way to get back to Rydaim and save them." He continued on like I hadn't said anything. "I can go find that out now, should only take a few hours."

Tense knots wound in my stomach, the angry soul-gnawing fury screaming that there was no was in hell I was going to let this happen.

"Right now?" I gasped, "Killian, you are clearly still bleeding. I don't know what they did to you, but you are in no health to be trudging down a mountain, or over a desert..." I stopped. "Ugh. We really need to know where we are."

"Yes. Please do not worry about me, I have experienced much worse." Killian's voice had changed from the pompous, hot-headed roar of the last few minutes to the soft concern that I had heard a few times before. "I can still shift if there is trouble, and I know you will be safe with Jarron. Just wait here, it smells like there is water further down inside the cave, so take a moment to clean up, breathe, and I will be back before you can wash even half of that ash off. And I promise I will try to be in a better mood."

"Well if this includes a better mood then you have yourself a deal." I had to force the smile that time, not that he noticed, he pressed his lips to my forehead, the gentle touch warm and wet and sending a beautiful shiver through my bones, tightening in my back and in the pit of my stomach.

His arms wound around me as he held me against him, giving a nod, I assumed, to Jarron

"Please be safe," Killian said with that deep rumbling voice that always set me on fire, and yes, I shivered.

I didn't even get to nod before he was gone, practically running away from where Jarron and I stood in the middle of the grey expanse of rock.

"Thank you for letting me come with you," I called to

Killian, moments before he vanished into the dark tunnels of the cave, toward the biting wind that swirled from the opening. "Later, I mean. To Rydaim."

Killian turned, his face already twisting into a smug smile as he met my gaze, "Oh, it's more than that."

I waited, my mind twisting in concern as his smile stretched even wider. Oh, nefarious and sexy was such a good look for him.

"I don't want to miss whatever crazy bullshit you're going to pull off next."

Well, until he said that.

He smiled, my jaw dropped, and Jarron chuckled behind me as Killian walked into the dark.

"You're going to regret saying that!" I called after him, but I was only answered by a laugh.

Damn him.

16

KILLIAN

Killian hadn't even left the cave yet and he already knew where he was. Caves such as this only existed in a few places in the world, the size, the depth, the sheer number of stalactites that dropped from the roof and dripped their dampness over him. It requires a massive mountain, or an intense amount of magic, to create a cavern as big as this and not have it collapse on you.

He was sure Elliot had the magic needed to create such a cavern, but her control of it was limited, and certainly not powerful enough to create a cave for them to instantly travel to. So not magic.

They were clearly inside of a mountain, and the smell of ice and conifer trees that were drifting on the wind that was pushing in from the entrance cemented exactly which one. That combination of scents only occurred one place in the world, and he had been here enough to recognize it instantly.

The Himalayas.

One step outside of the cave and he had no question, although it didn't do much to help their situation. If anything, it made it much more confusing, if not a little horrifying.

Minutes ago, they had been deep inside the cave of Rydaim, along the coast of Spain. And now, they were thousands of feet above civilization, stowed away in a mountain between India and China. Nepal was a beautiful place, but they were miles away from anyone. Countries away from Rydaim.

"What are you, Ellie girl?" he whispered into the wind, staring at the expanse of mountains that cut into the sky like massive snow topped knives, slicing through the earth.

As beautiful as it was, it was impossible to wrap his head around what had happened. He had seen her grab one of the floating feathers, and then he had been sucked into a tube not unlike the ones Callay had transported him through.

The power may not be unique, but Callay had never transported him this far. It had always been to places nearby, places they had seen, not to unknown caves thousands of miles away.

It shouldn't be possible, and yet here he stood, staring over mountains that grew higher and more dangerous the farther away he looked. In the distance, the mountains that were nestled around Everest were clearly visible, and the peak of the girl herself poking above them.

It was amazing.

The mountain. Elliot. Her magic. All of it. It wasn't even the high-altitude that was taking his breath away.

Everest was glorious, even from miles away with hundreds of peaks stretching between them. As much as he loved that mountain, however, he was glad they weren't closer.

Scaling down one of the most popular mountain terrains in the world, wearing nothing but a tattered suit would not end well. Of course, being that far away also meant that they were farther away from most of the little villages that littered the range. Luckily, Killian had a built-in solution for that one.

Even if every other dragon alive would determine him a raging idiot for trying it. Perhaps he was. This would either work or he would end up injuring himself more. He would make sure it was the first, if only by his sheer stubborn will.

Shifting into his dragon had been second nature to him for a few hundred years, but shifting from one form to another with what would be considered life threatening injuries in either form was dangerous. Well, perhaps more deadly with the array of injuries he was sporting.

His ribs were still on fire from his beating, his hips ached with each step, the muscles pulling and twisting as though they had been detached. Every breath, every step, was close to agony. Muscles and bones were aching from the blade that had repeatedly pierced his side, the sharp edge of the dragon scale grinding against his ribs in an attempt to puncture whatever vital organ it could. He wasn't sure if that had been successful, but, he was fairly certain that a few of his ribs had been sliced in half. At least his lungs and kidneys seemed to be working well enough. Time would have to tell on the rest. The ribs were easy enough fixes for his dragon, but not when shackled, now that he was free of those the risk was minimal.

By the time he flew into the nearest village he should be well enough to reverse his shift.

Should.

It was going to take work enough to get into his dragon, he couldn't worry himself with what would happen at the end of that. He could heal faster in his dragon, he just had to make sure to land far enough away that if anything was to happen he would not attract attention. Seeing as he wasn't going anywhere in his now destroyed suit, walking into a village in his underwear was going to be distracting enough, he didn't want to see how his dragon would add to that.

It was just getting there.

The icy wind that swirled through the mountains tugged at his hair and at the strips of wool that hung from his once elegant suit. The breeze whipped everything around until it was in so much disarray that he could barely see the sun as it peeked behind the large puffy clouds that filled the sky in its attempt to dip back down beneath the mountains.

Weird.

They had made their trek into Rydaim at the break of dawn, they hadn't been in there long enough for a full day to have passed. Perhaps he was mis-remembering the time change between Spain and China. China was seven hours ahead of his home, even with all the bullshit they had escaped from, the sun should be rising, not setting.

She couldn't have moved them through time. That was not possible.

"I will figure you out, my princess," he whispered, turning around to take one last look into the depth of the cave, his dragon growling in his chest, trying to pull him back to her for possibly the sixth time since he had walked away.

He may have been a little foolhardy in his departure, but his temper had been getting the best of him. It was either stay there and explode, or come out here and do so. Out here was definitely safer, and seeing as they were miles from civilization it was also the perfect cover.

A scream of frustration, of failure, and of pain ripped through his chest as he tore the tattered suit from his body, ripping the already destroyed material until it fell around him in ribbons, useless bits of fabric that were picked up and carried away on the wind. Just like his plans for success, for his father's demise. For Parris's ruin. Just like the sound of his voice.

He screamed again, determined to expel the ridiculous emotions. Although this time, he let his dragon take control, the beast inside of him roaring to life as the howl of his dragon broke from his human jaw. The sound ripped through the air, bounced from mountain to mountain like thunder. The mountain range shook, the shimmering white surfaces falling away as his dragon's yell triggered avalanche after avalanche.

He watched them fall, the echoes of his dragon still ripping through the mountain range as he stood in the icy wind wearing nothing but dark green boxers, the tight fabric clinging to his muscles.

It had been decades since he had unleashed his dragon in these hills, and watching the snow fall from the mountain, the tiny flakes already drifting from the sky to replace it, he was sorry it had taken him so long to return.

Both dragon and man screamed again as the shift took hold, as his body stretched and ripped apart to become the beast within in. The process always hurt, it always ripped and roared through him. But this time was unlike any other. The pain was nearly unmanageable. He could feel the broken ribs crack deeper, feel his flesh tear apart where it was already cut.

This time he didn't try to restrain the scream of agony. Killian's voice rang out in a scream like which he had never heard, the pain transferring to his dragon as the beast took over and his roar ripped through the air in a storm of thunder.

Killian could only wonder what his dragon's call would sound like to the hundreds of adventurers that traversed these cliffs before he took off into the air, his dragon diving once before swooping into the clouds, relying on the heavy cloud cover to hide him.

The air was full of the aroma of conifers and elm, the nuts and dirt and snow that covered the ground below traveling right alongside. Even through its icy chill, the crisp air was like a baptism, a weight off his shoulders at everything that had happened, at how they had lost.

They had rescued Jarron, but that twisted vampire was still alive. Zoe and Drake were still inside, along with Callay. He had no interest in leaving any of them behind.

Not with that sadistic monster. Not with Dabria and her twisted manipulations. His rage bubbled up further and he let the fury stream from him in a line of solid black flame that rippled through the clouds in a desperate search of something to kill, or something to devour. Something to suck the life out of.

Even his soul was smiling at that hope, at the image of Parris drowning in his flame, of the billows of black smoke sucking away his life, while the flame burned away his flesh.

He should go there now, tear through the city and destroy the twisted little vampire and his henchmen, Dabria included. Then it would be over, the crown would be free. Ellie would be free.

The only problem was that he was sure he would be dead.

He had barely survived before, and while he would know more of what was going on inside of that dreadful city, it only gave him a bit more of an upper hand. There was no guarantee of survival. And damn it all, Ellie had gotten into his head. her laugh, her smile, but also her hyper logical request that we all stop trying to kill ourselves in her name.

He would not admit the truth in that, but it was certainly putting a damper on his need to protect her.

Protecting a mate was so much more difficult than you would think it to be. Especially when that mate was a headstrong and powerful phoenix shifter. Thinking about her was bringing more buoyancy to his heart, his wings soaring and spinning through the icy air as though he was in a dance.

Killian's dragon swooped wide before angling down, bee-lining right for the outskirts of a tiny village nestled in a low valley of the mountains. The place was small, but clearly touristy seeing as all the yurts and livestock were surrounding one permanent building, a two-story wood-paneled thing with very few windows.

A hotel, specially made so as to help keep the heat in.

It was perfect.

Killian folded in his wings, and dive-bombed toward a yurt on the outskirts, hoping that enough of the villagers were turning in for the night that they wouldn't see a massive black and green dragon drop from the sky. The darkness of twilight had already bathed the village, the animals were already penned, which meant little for a people where hard work was the backbone to life and stability.

Luckily there were no screams, no shouts because when he landed, he did so with a giant crash into the earth, tree's toppled, dirt and smoke kicked up in a giant plume of brown and black, and in the middle of it was massive dragon, stuck in the form of a monster.

In all the calm of flying, in all the thoughts of Ellie, Killian had forgotten one very big part of his current situation.

His ribs were cracked, and shifting back was going to take some work, work that he didn't have time for thanks to the asteroid level crash he had created, right next to the village.

Right where he shouldn't be.

He could already hear someone yelling not too far off.

Great, so he needed to shift out of his dragon before they reached him, and preferably do so silently. At least that part he could manage, he had no idea what these indigenous people would do if they stumbled upon a full-grown dragon, let alone hear one.

Worst case, he could fly away. But he doubted, at this point, that he could do so without risking more panic and problems.

Coming upon a dragon in the woods was one thing, watching one rip its way into the sky was another.

The not quite healed bones cracked as Killian worked to push his dragon away, the creature thrashing and dragging its claws through the soft dirt and leaving thick gouges behind. Another tree fell as Killian tried to re-break the bones that had already begun to fuse themselves back together in an attempt to force the shift to reverse, his tail swinging around to take the powerful conifer down.

The voices were growing louder, the shouts in a language he did not recognize only a few steps away now as his wings pushed back into him, his neck stretching high before recoiling.

This process had always been like a dance for Killian, his shifts so seamless that it looked like he was doing little more than flipping an expand and retract switch. This time he felt like he was fighting his beast, and the monster had no interest in losing.

Clamping his jaw shut, Killian fought the scream that wanted to break free, slamming the head of his beast into the dirt before bringing it back in, bones and skin and everything else rumbling back into him. Just like an accordion.

His human form snapped against his bones as a man with a torch and a boy with a rifle broke through the trees that surrounded him, looking over one of the massive trunks of the one he had felled. Killian was already standing to face them, every bone, muscle, and nerve ending on fire.

He was very clearly in trouble, not only was he not going to be able to attempt another shift until he was completely healed, but he had lost the soft boxers he had planned to wear into the village.

Now, he stood before the two men, naked, forcing himself to stay upright as they stared at him, their eyes and mouths wide and afraid.

Standing here was agony. Everything was starting to spin, the pain in his bones and muscles was starting to spread. He was sure two more identical villagers had joined the first.

Which was good, because he was going down, and he needed help.

Taking one last gulp of air, Killian said the only thing he knew in what he hoped was the native tongue of this region.

"Where is the bathroom."

Then, he hit the ground.

17

DRAKE

DRAKE AND THE OTHERS HAD MADE IT PAST THE RUINS OF THE Forgotten village when the caves were overrun with vampires. The nasty things rampaged through everything, ripping apart stone and any lone Forgotten encampment in search of anyone who had attempted escape. Every possible escape route was full of the things and Drake found himself wishing he had tried to memorize the map as Killian did.

No matter which way they turned they found their way blocked by either vampires, or a caved in tunnel, courtesy of Elliot's explosion. The magic that held Rydaim together was weaker down here, the caves having been carved by The Forgotten rather that the Dragons or the Fae. Those weakened walls couldn't withstand Ellie's blast, and had easily trapped them.

Everywhere Drake guided the girls, the air was full of dirt and sand from collapse after collapse, turning everything into a wall of brown and grey that they could barely see through, let alone move through. The four of them held onto hands, hems or anything else they could reach as they felt their way towards what they would hope was escape, and what Drake would hope included a fresh gulp of air.

Every few minutes the caves would fill with the sound of rocks as the stone continued to shift and crack, more tunnels collapsing, more caverns opening up.

The only saving grace was that the vampires wouldn't go near those sounds, they didn't venture too far into the dirt, seeing as the heavy plumes of the stuff restricted their sense of smell. It made for an interesting hunt, but also gave Drake and the others an easy option of going undetected.

With a hiss from Zoe, Drake had led them toward the groaning rock, the four of them cowering against the stone, hidden in a plume of dirt.

Vampires may be undead, but they could still be crushed. So could everyone else he was surrounded by, but they were going to have to risk it, they were out of other options.

Being in a cave collapse had seemed like such a cool adventure when he was a child, now it was a horrifying end that he had no interest in meeting.

"Do you think they are gone?" Callay hissed through the dust, her shape barely discernible through the wall of grey, her voice barely audible through the crunching groan of the rocks beside them.

"I think that if you keep talking they are going to find us either way," Zoe warned, the hard edge in her voice filled with a cool finality that Callay, fool that she was only scoffed at.

"If we keep fucking breathing in this air we are all going to die," Callay hissed back, the tiny spark of silver in her eyes blazing through the smoke like a homing beacon.

"I'd rather die from too much debris inhalation than those nasty creatures," Zoe snarled in return, more rocks shifting and threatening to drown out her voice.

"You won't die from either of them. I can take them," Fallon cut in, talking more at full voice than the other two and instantly earning herself a reaction from the suddenly snarling princess.

"You will die from me if you don't shut up." Her dragon was screaming from her voice now, the deep threat swirling through the dirt as both girls scooted away, presumably away from Zoe.

Between Zoe, Fallon, and Callay, there was too much domineering power in this corner of the cave. Well, too much for being around Zoe. Zoe could easily take them both down, and wasn't about to let them think otherwise.

Drake had been on the receiving end of that one too many times in his life as it was.

Drake sat with an entertained smile pulling around the corners of his mouth, he wasn't foolish enough to get into the middle of that anyway. He was more focused on trying to smell or listen for vampires, something that was proving impossible.

Their hiding place may be effective in repelling Vampires, but it was also making it impossible to detect when and if that one brave one would come along.

"It's been at least twenty minutes since the last one," Fallon hissed, her tiny shape shifting towards the cave they had come down, and what had once been an opening. At this point they could be completely closed in.

Drake had lived like a mortal for the past few years, but he hadn't felt more mortal, or more helpless than he did right there. Everything spelled danger, even shining his cell phones flashlight in a hope of cutting through the smoke, and he had considered it.

"We could move. Maybe go back to that hidden city of The Forgotten that you were talking about," Callay answered, it hadn't even been a full minute since Zoe's warning, and the two were clearly not taking the hint.

Zoe was back to snarling at them, the low growl of her dragon rumbling over the stone, they were pushing her patience past it's breaking point.

Drake leaned against the stone wall behind him, still determined to stay out of it, and carefully dispersed his weight lest he trigger another slide. The dust had only begun to clear enough that he could make out shapes, he wasn't willing to risk what little visibility that he had.

"That would be the first place they would look," Fallon hissed, "I'm sure that it is overrun by the freaking bloodsuckers."

"They can't stay there forever..."

"Will you two shut up?" Zoe snarled through clenched teeth, waving her hand through the air and clearing a bit of the dirt that was still lingering, revealing a very angry face, and very red and swollen eyes thanks to the dust.

The redness of her eyes made the fire in them look that

much more scary and the two girls, at least what he could see of them, scooted away, pure horror on their face.

She looked like a monster, which is exactly what he had related her to when he was very small. A big red eyed monster with horns and tail, of course that was before he had mastered his shift and the idea of the massive dragons hiding inside his family was still quite ominous.

Zoe the red eyed demon.

"You look just like Killian," Callay said, her voice shivering through the still clearing smoke.

That was only making it worse, but she did look like Killian. She was going to hate that.

The thought brought a chuckle to his lips, one he quickly silenced with a side-long glare from the demon herself. Zoe was already way too fired up to push that any further.

He laid his head back on the stone, feeling the vibrations, and focusing on staying out of it, and not laughing.

"Good, then you know I mean business." Zoe snarled and smiled, giving Drake a second warning glare.

Fine. He was more than ready to stay out of it and watch whatever showdown was about to unfold, when a voice that was pure ice dripped through the dust filled air, pulling everyone's attention.

"Good, because I mean business to."

Drake didn't have to see the man that was stepping through the heavy dirt to know what had found them. He knew from the low tone of the voice, the way it dripped with blood and death.

Only an undead vampire could turn his blood to ice so fast.

"I love business. I love the way the power behind it tastes on my tongue. Divine."

A pale face he didn't recognize broke through the last of the dust as all four of them jumped to their feet. He may not recognize the bloodsucker, but the thing clearly recognized them, and his eyes were growing wide in a hungry awe that they needed to stop.

Zoe gave him a look as she stepped forward, she knew the awe of recognition as well as he did. This one they weren't going to collect as they had with Fallon, however. This one they were going to destroy.

"Well, then you will love it when it tears you apart," Zoe sneered, red tinted smoke drifted from her mouth.

The threat was clear, but also useless, a ribbon of fire as powerful as hers was nearly as dangerous as the vampire that had found them. One burst of her fire and dozens of other vampires would be heading their way, ready to do them all in.

One they could take. Any more than that and they would be dragged right to his father, and then it would be all over.

They couldn't risk it.

The alternative was a gnawing right on his chest, the burning ash already coating Drake's tongue as his dragon pushed to the surface.

"Nice try, princess." The Vampire's smile spread as Zoe's did, both ready to lunge into a fight that would have far too much fire and screaming to be of any assistance to them.

This was bullshit. He hated it, but he didn't have another choice.

"Freeze. Don't move," the tone was clear, the command strong, and the Vampire quite literally froze mid lunge, his body looking as though it had been locked in place as he collapsed to the ground, his iron flesh hitting against the stone with a hollow thunk.

"Damn it, Drake," Zoe snapped, kicking the vampire's hand and twisting his frozen fingers until they looked like broken talons. "I was going to enjoy that."

"I'm impressed," Fallon said, hands over her waist as the vampire's eyes shifted between the three of them in clear horror.

"Well, I guess I can enjoy this too," Zoe said with a broad smile, squatting next to the frozen vamp and flicking at his still barren fang with her long, polished nails. "I'm proud of you, bro. Nicely done."

She meant it, but he wasn't going to go off beaming like a pig-tailed school girl just yet.

"I got him, now you get to finish him off. Get the job done and then we will move. I'm not sure how long this will hold." Killing vampires was probably his least favorite thing, all the dust and the screaming of a damned soul as it was dragged to hell. He hated it, and he would risk going further into the dust storm to get away from it if he had to.

Zoe on the other hand, "With pleasure."

She was looking like a kid with her very first lollipop.

Drake's stomach flip-flopped.

Smoke was already streaming from Zoe's mouth, her eyes glowing with her flame when Callay jumped forward, her hands up in a panic.

"Wait!" She screeched, earning herself another glare from Zoe.

"I'm not going to shield this from your precious sensibilities."

"Oh, fuck that," Callay said, the cursing sailor making a return. "You can rip his arms off and use them to play badminton for all I care. I do, however, care if your fire calls to more of his friends. At least let me shield you."

"Shield?" Drake was truly confused now, "Fae can't shield."

"Fae can't do much of anything here thanks to your bastard King," Fallon snarled, giving Zoe a look as if it was all her fault. Thankfully, Zoe rolled her eyes, she was too busy torturing the frozen vampire to really react anyway.

Drake nodded in pained agreement, but Callay stood with a giant smile of her face, holding her hands before her as they began to glow with the same silver light that always followed her around, the light twisting in a bulb of light.

The color was beautiful, the way it swelled and grew. But, it was also very similar to the light he had seen Elliot produce, and that had never ended well. Drake's stomach twisted, and he stepped away a tiny bit, eager to take any space he could.

"Well, the Fae that Ceres controls can't," she said, the light from the orb falling over her face in lines and ripples that twisted her smile into a wicked grin.

The look twisted through Drake's muscles, his heart pounding in expectation of some kind of bomb that he would have to fight off. Even if that was a thing. Even as he prepared for battle however, his dragon was calming inside of him.

"But I am not one of Ceres' Fae."

Drake might have actually swallowed a rock with how he was feeling. Everything was too heavy, the shock nearly too much to handle. Even the Vampire that remained frozen on the floor looked like he had been slapped upside the head.

Which he may have with how Zoe was pestering him.

Instead of exploding, the orb Callay held spread out from her like some kind of glittery rubber band, pulling around and through them in a grey balloon that thankfully took most of the dirt with it as it glued itself to the walls around them. They were in a bubble, a shimmery silver bubble. Under any other circumstances Drake might have been impressed by the magic, awed even.

But, instead, he was stuck staring at the girl who might as well have collapsed the cave with the bomb she just dropped.

"There," Callay said, wiping her dust covered hands on equally dust covered pants and sending a plume of the stuff back into the partially cleaned air. But no one moved, Drake didn't even try. "You can destroy the bloodsucker now."

That seemed to be the least important thing in the world right then.

"What do you mean you're not one of Ceres' Fae?" Drake

said all of them taking a step toward the silver haired Fae, all of them looking at her with differing levels of shock.

"I mean, he doesn't control me or my magic. I wasn't placed here for him." Callay was absolutely beaming now, but Drake couldn't have been more confused. Even Zoe was narrowing her eyes at the girl in confusion.

Confusion that got a whole lot worse.

"Did Parris create you, too?" Fallon whispered from beside him, and it was only then that Drake realized the girl didn't look nearly as stunned or confused as he and his sister did.

The vampire however, might have been ready to lose his shit. He had clearly stumbled in on a gold mine, and was incapable of sharing it.

This may have been the first time that Drake's gift didn't feel quite so wicked.

"Too?" Zoe said, accidentally kicking the Vampire in the face as she jumped to standing, the guy let out a weird smothered howl at the impact, the shape of his nose making it clear it had been broken. Without blood it was hard to tell, though, not that the bloodsucker would know either way. Undead monsters didn't really trouble themselves with broken noses, at least from what Drake understood.

Of course, the bastard vamps he knew weren't a very good base line.

"Parris created you?" Zoe turned on Fallon before twisting back to Callay, she was looking as if she was about ready to lose it. It was a good thing Callay had placed a shield around them, they were all getting too loud. "Both of you?"

This time the Fae did not shrink away from Zoe's hard glare, Fallon was slowly pulling into herself, however.

"He didn't create me," Callay said, a smug little smile on her lips as she popped her hips. "That damn..." she stopped giving the vampire that was still frozen on the ground a look. "Something else did. And sent me here to help you all. Killian knows."

"Killian knows?" Zoe was in full on growl, the sound of her dragon rippling through the cave in all its glory. Her confusion had melted into frustration and even Drake backed away from the sound, his beast withdrawing in submissive allegiance.

That sound alone was the reason he knew his sister was born to rule.

He was not the only one to hear it.

The vampire was clearly trying to break free of the bind now, although all he had been able to do was move one finger. It looked like a death twitch, well a death twitch for a cockroach, the guy was so curled up on himself he was a near perfect replica.

Fitting.

"Yeah, but I'm not going to spill-all until we take care of our friend here. So, chop-chop."

Zoe may have been better at taking commands from people than Killian, but the margin was slim, and only in the way that more times than not she didn't erupt into a tower of molten fire and burn down whoever was in front of her.

This was not one of these times.

"Breathe Zo," Drake grumbled from underneath his breath.

Now was not the place for an eruption, they may be inside of Callay's shield, but who knows how well the thing would hold up, and even if it would survive a tunnel collapse caused by a massive dragon and a pillar of fire.

That was not a risk Drake was willing to take.

He threw himself between the two women, shooting Zoe a warning look before turning on Callay.

"Once he's gone you will tell us everything." His voice was harsh, but he was careful not to push too much of his dragon into it.

"Both of you," he added, looking to the tag-a-long Fae with a commanding glare.

He was out of practice for that one, but it still seemed to work.

Fallon threw her hands up in false defeat, "Hey, I'll tell you all while you make the Vampire into a marionette. I'm pretty sure he already knows anyway. With what those things say while they bite into us, they all know about Parris and his little gourmet blood factory."

"Perfect. Talk," Zoe said as she leaned down, grabbing one of the elbows of the little cockroach and signaling Drake to do the same.

Great, so he wasn't going to get out of this.

Drake bit his tongue so hard that blood drizzled through his mouth, twisting his stomach into an even deeper pretzel. He really wanted nothing to do with this. But, unless he wanted to show himself as a weakling he didn't have a choice. It had been too many years away from fighting, too many years of feeling guilt for what he had done, and what had happened to so many of his friends. Now, to be thrust back into it.

In one massive explosion.

No wonder he had a rock in his stomach, it might possibly be the only thing that was keeping him from emptying the contents over everyone.

"Talk," Zoe said to Fallon as she lifted the now horrified Vampire up to Drake. The monster's body still frozen, even though his eyes were frantically pulling back and forth in a desperate plea for life.

Like that's going to happen.

The rock in Drake's stomach wiggled around like a living thing as he grabbed the monster's other arm, wrapping his fingers around the icy chill of his skin and prepared to pull the man apart.

Zoe smashed her fist against the forehead of the guy, sending a loud crack of bone against stone whizzing through the air. The rock that was his head cracked down the middle, the break somehow smashing through my bind and he began to gnash and kick in an attempt to escape. Too late, the crack was spreading, making the man look like an egg as Zoe and Drake pulled, the crack splitting further, right down the middle.

With one giant heave, the two pieces of him pulled away, a horrifying scream sending both of the Fae jerking back as his undead soul was pushed from this world and into the pit of hell.

It was a devastating sound, and one that had haunted

Drake's dreams for years. There was a reason he did not wish to be there. The scream was one. The ash was another.

A fountain of grey ash had begun spilling out of the two halves of the beast in a waterfall of rotted insides, covering the stone and piling over their feet.

Drake instantly regretted his choice of sandals. Dirt was one thing, the remains of an undead blood whore? That rock was struggling to keep the contents of his stomach from turning inside out.

He always enjoyed the air between his toes on mountain expeditions, but this was agony. Vile, disturbing, and disgustingly cold agony.

He wished that that would be the last time he had to do that, or the last time the Fae had to witness it. The two girls had been stunned into a stony silence.

"Talk," Zoe said again as Drake hit his shoe against the cave wall, hoping to clear out the last of the vampire guts from them and make them wearable again.

The sound of rubber against stone was a slap in their tiny bubble of the cave and both girls jumped, pulled out of the horror of having just watched a vampire being pulled apart. It only got worse, seeing as Zoe was now spitting streams of fire at different parts of the things, waiting for it to burn.

"Parris created about sixty of us," Fallon jumped into explanation, her eyes still wide with horror as Zoe continued to rip and burn the Vampire. "A few years ago, some punk kid burned down the facility where Parris had been keeping us all and sent shit to the wind."

"What facility?" Zoe asked between streams of fire,

becoming more and more frustrated as line after line of fire appeared to do nothing.

"This big old abandoned hospital where he made everyone. Eggs and babies and creepy nannies who raised and bit everyone," she stopped short and shivered before plowing on, each word sounding like a twisted horror movie Drake had seen once. "After one of Parris's pale faces defected and burned the place down, most of us went to this Orphanage in China with this kid with a superiority complex who showed up out of nowhere, acting like she owns the place. I'm not sure where the other ones got to. I ran away to find them..."

She faded away, the memories drowning in the silence as Drake tried to follow her story, something about it was nagging at him.

Zoe, however, no longer seemed to be paying attention. Drake gave her a look, but she only sneered at him, her lip curling up as she glared at the slightly singed pieces of vampire.

"Stacia was right," Zoe snarled letting the last stream of fire burn away the rest of his clothes before bending down and continuing to rip the thing into pieces. "These things don't burn anymore."

"Stacia?" Fallon interrupted, "The vampire?"

Drake took a hurried step forward, his shoes forgotten on the cave floor.

"Yes." The single world had far too much tension behind it.

"That's the kid who burned down our home. She's the one who used to bring us to Parris for feeding."

"Excuse me?" Drake was flabbergasted, he expected the same reaction from his sister, but she only shook her head.

"We knew that." Zoe was still focused on the vampire. "She ran away from the witch that was hiding her, about a week ago. Got spooked over something and splattered fake blood all over the place and was gone."

"Probably scared of that damn Phoenix." Fallon grumbled. "I barely survived the last time she attacked me. I would run away from that terror too."

18

JARRON

KILLIAN WAS RIGHT, THERE WAS WATER DOWN THE WAY. IF YOU could really call it that. It was more like a gentle trickle from all the congregated dew of the cave. Jarron had definitely seen a better-looking stream in the middle of the desert. It didn't run, it didn't rush. It just trickled, and every time Ellie smashed the shards of the balled-up shirt into it, they had to wait a few minutes for enough water to come back so they could keep cleaning his quickly healing wounds.

The only benefit was that the water was cold, and as far as they could tell clean-- well, before it got smashed with a blood-stained shirt. The damp wet chill felt amazing on the cuts, bruises, and still healing stab wounds that he was riddled with.

His muscles ached where that blade had cut through his skin, even days later. He had watched Killian get stabbed with the thing hours ago, there was no way he was in any position to get out of here in any other way than falling down the mountain.

The guy might be tough, but he wasn't that tough.

His brother was in pain. It was no wonder he had turned himself into a raging asshole.

He needed the space to calm down, thank god he could take care of himself.

Right now, however, Jarron had much bigger things on his mind, much colder, wetter, things on his mind.

He hissed as the cold water splashed over an especially large gash on his side, the sting both painful and deliciously comforting.

"Sorry," Ellie whispered, letting up the pressure of the shirt she was using to wash the blood from her. Or torn fragment of a shirt. It was a piece of the shirt she had stolen from him and was still trying to use to cover herself, which thanks to the now torn segment was doing an even worse job than it had been before.

He could see the rough curvature of her bottom as she kneeled next to him, the rip that had cut up the side pulling away enough that her belly was exposed. If he wasn't in so much pain he didn't think he would be able to control himself.

As it was... he hissed again, the fabric pressing against the inflamed flesh around the wound and sending a shock up his spine. His Dragon growled loudly, the sound echoing around the cave and right back to Ellie who was staring at him with wide eyes.

"I have to clean it," she was apologetic, Jarron wished she wouldn't be. This would go so much easier if she would just let him howl and scrub the shit off his skin, then his dragon could heal and she could start washing the ash from herself.

"It's okay, Darling. It needs to be cleaned. I can take the pain," he assured her, placing his hand over hers and pressing the sopping fabric into his skin. Trails of icy water ran down his side at the pressure, the ache moving deeper into his gut.

Water streamed from him, pooling around his stained jeans and soaking into the fabric. It was so dark in this part of the cave that he could barely make out colors, even with the low burning fire he had placed a few feet away to help Ellie see. The golden flames did little to help with the visibility, although the shadows that surrounded them seemed more defined. If not more haunting.

He was seeing Parris's face everywhere.

But that may be based more on trauma than shadow and delusion.

"Just because I'm cleaning it doesn't mean I need to subject you to more pain," she whispered, pressing more water into the fabric before gently placing it on his chest, cleaning away some of the dried blood from Dabria's icy lashings. Her appalling fire was some of the deadliest, he was still amazed he had survived her frozen temper tantrum.

Luckily the pain wasn't as bad here, he was sure his dragon had nearly healed the few ribs that had cracked and broken.

In another few hours he would be nearly as good as new. Well, except for where he had been stabbed, stabs from a dragon scale could take days to heal. They may not linger for eternity like his fire did to those he burned, but the added days in healing time was not something he was looking forward to.

"You don't have to be as gentle as a kitten either, darling."

She froze looking up at him with her wide eyes, the ridges of her pupils sparking with her flame just enough that they appeared to glow. "I don't want you to hurt Jarron. I'll be gentle."

Her eyes lingered on his, her soft smile pouring into him as the fire in his belly boiled. The flame in her eyes grew, and she bit her lower lip, pulling the flesh in such a way that made his stomach swoop, that made his need for her swell and grow. Such a simple act and he was suddenly finding it hard to control himself.

Everything was swirling and swelling, including his dragon, the creature nearly demanding that he reach out and grab her, wrap his hand around the perfect curvature of her bottom and pull her onto him.

Take her.

Mate her.

He gasped, the sound more of a moan as he leaned closer and she let out a shaky breath and dropped the lip, her mouth parting enough to welcome him in. Enough for him to taste her.

The kiss never made contact, although he was sure he could taste her on his lips. She pulled away quickly, rushing back to the rag and blood streaked trickles of water as if her life depended on it. He clearly wasn't the only one who was striving to control his need for connection.

"Thank you, Elliot," he whispered, his voice catching in his throat as he tried to push the desire away.

His control was vanishing at a dangerous rate. Watching her hand move over his chest, seeing the consuming fire in her eyes, was turning his dragon into a god-damned brass band. He was surprised Ellie hadn't said anything about the growling and purring that was coming from his chest. She clearly heard it, or she was just smiling at the blood.

He doubted it.

"Well, don't get upset if you are still covered with gunk after this. This isn't the most effective method of injury cleaning," she rambled, running the cloth over his chest, wiping away blood as she traced the deep grooves in his skin, letting trails of water run down his chest and over his abs.

"No, Elliot," He stopped her, placing his hand over hers and stopping her efforts. "Thank you for saving me. Thank you for being brave."

"I keep telling you all that I will always save you." She whispered, her free hand coming up beside the other, pressing against his other pectoral.

Her skin was hot against his chest, her fingers soft little branding irons as they traced the lines of his muscles, sending little shocks of electricity through him.

And he thought he was having trouble controlling his need for her before.

"You're my mate," she sighed, her fingers soft as they continued to trace the lines of his chest. "You're mine."

"Mine," he repeated, the sound full of the growl of his

dragon, his heart pulsing with need as his hand dropped from hers, the rag falling to his lap with a faint plop.

The rumble of his dragon continued as she traced his muscles, letting her fingers run over his chest, up his sides, over the lines in his neck, the flame in her eyes boring into him, drawing him into her. He threw his head back, staring into the dark abyss above him as he fought desperately for control.

He needed her to stop, he was very quickly reaching that point where he wouldn't be able to control himself, where his dragon would take control. Where he would mate with her and make her his.

Thinking the words as her fingers dragged over his chest, her hot breath rumbling over his skin, was only pushing himself closer to that line.

"Jarron?" She asked, her voice soft, her fingers coming to rest against his chest, her thumb resting against his nipple. Oh god. She was going to be the end of him.

"Hmmm?" He really couldn't manage more than that.

"What do you think will happen if I explode in here?" she whispered in a seductive lull that roared within him, the dangerous sound of his dragon filling the cave now. "I want to kiss you." His head snapped to her, as she licked her lower lip, as she leaned in. "I want you."

Mine, the growl of his dragon broke through the air, the rumbling roar swirling around them. The sound was horrendous, like stepping inside of thunder, being surrounded by a cave collapse, but she wasn't afraid, she just smiled.

"Mine." She responded, and closed the gap between them, pressing her lips to his.

A flood of warmth ran through him, his veins feeling as though they were trapped in an electrical storm, his dragon howling, his heart thundering. But all he felt was her against him, felt her lips, felt her hands as they trailed to his back, careful to avoid the still healing wounds that riddled him.

The soft pads of her finger pressed into his back, her tongue dragged over his lower lip, and he completely lost it. The sound of her moan in his ears, he grabbed the softness of her exposed bottom and pulled her onto him, laying himself down on the water-worn stone until she was over him, kissing him, her body pressing into him.

She rose above him, stripping off her shirt with a hungry flourish, the single article of clothing falling to the side as she collapsed back over him.

Jarron's lips crashed into hers, his eagerness for her growing as his hands pulled her into him, pressing her hips against his until she moaned in the same deep feral need he felt. Her voice rippled over him, the warmth between them growing until he heard what sounded like the boiling of water, the hiss of steam erupting around them as the dewy trickle of water sizzled into nothing.

Jarron pulled away from the kiss, leaving her heaving as he checked her skin, checked the stone, checked for any sign of explosion, but so far, so good, they were currently running at the same temperature of a nuclear reactor.

"Come back," she whispered, tugging at his frayed jeans as she coaxed his lips back to hers. "I've got this."

For a second, he thought she was talking about her magic, about the explosion that he was sure was minutes away. But instead she tugged at the button of his pants, her fingers fiddling with the zipper.

He groaned, the loud feral sound rippling over the cave.

"You little troublemaker," he whispered, the sound a rumble as he grabbed her, lifting her as he rolled and gently placed her beneath him, her naked body settling into the stone, heating it like she was a radiator.

Her hair fanned over the stone like flame, crowning her like the queen she was, like the queen she would be. Fire stretched through her, rippling over her skin in a flash that was gone before he could fully inhale. The flame stretched out from her, glimmering over the stone in snakes of gold and red, seeping into it.

Normally something like that would be terrifying with her, but she was so calm, the flame sparking around her with a power that reflected in her eyes. The fire, the power, a blazing heat that was beyond danger, beyond something he had ever seen before.

Power. Passion. It took his breath away.

"I love you, my Phoenix." He whispered, quickly removing his pants, and hovering over her, pressing his lips to hers, to her cheek, to her neck, her chest.

The moan that broke from her throat screamed in the pure note of her phoenix, the song lingering through the cave as he pulled away, and he breathed above her, his eyes locked with her.

"I love you, Jarron," she whispered in reply, and his soul burned and buzzed in an intense need.

He sat over her, her nakedness consuming him as he dragged his fingers over her boiling skin. Down her rib cage, over her stomach, the silky beauty of her nearly enough to destroy him. But not as much as her breasts, the alluring bits heaving with each ragged breath as he drove her wild, as his fingers moved from her abdomen, to her chest, to the soft circle of darkened skin.

"Ellie," he whispered, her eyes were all flame now, her skin smoked as though it was a moment away from erupting into flame. But she controlled it. He didn't want her too, he didn't want to control himself. This time it was worth the risk.

"Let me claim you." It was a question, a soft whisper as he caressed the tender mounds of skin, as she quivered beneath him. "Let me make you mine."

She exhaled again, moaning at the pressure of his hips against her and whispered the one word he needed to hear.

The word that instantly drove him wild.

"Yes." She heaved. "You're mine."

He didn't wait. He sighed, his hands tracing her hips to fan against her back, his lips pressing against hers and he pressed inside. As he took her for his own.

19

ELLIOT

I WAS LAYING ON STONE.

Buck naked.

My buck nakedness pressed against someone else's buck nakedness, who was also laying on cold hard stone.

Nothing about this situation said comfortable, and yet I was the most comfortable I had ever been.

I snuggled into Jarron's chest, his arms wrapping around me and pulling me into him with the gentlest of sighs. My legs instantly tangled with his, his hands drifting down the ashen skin of my back, his fingertip tracing over the curve of my bottom, to the side of my thigh, all the while leaving that trail of glittering passion behind.

Yes, I said passion.

Mother-fucking passion.

Waves of boiling, heated, totally forbidden passion were already raging through me. That soft touch of his fingers against my skin, as it drifted toward the secret places that were still rumbling in need of him, were turning me into a hungry passionate monster.

Wrapped in him, in pleasure, I moaned and lifted my chin to his, stealing a kiss as his eyes burned into mine. Burned was the operative word there. His eyes were completely on fire, there wasn't a scrap of black in the usual abyss of his gaze. He was pure light, every freaking bit of him.

Beautiful glowing eyes, and unnaturally glittery skin. I had seen the golden shimmer on his skin before, but this was like kicking it up into overdrive. Like if glitter had steroids, this is what it would look like. I ran my fingers over his chest, watching the color shimmer behind my touch as he shivered again and threw his head back, exposing his neck to me.

I couldn't help it, I kissed it, letting my teeth run over the tender base of his throat in a way that made his dragon purr. That was a little discovery I had made in the last few hours, and doing it again was as much of a reward. Feeling the purr of his dragon against my chest rippled through me in the deepest most pleasurable tickle.

Mmmm yes. I would take all of that to go, please.

"Are you wanting me to claim you again?" Jarron groaned, pulling away from my nibble to mumble in my ear. His breath was running over my neck in a wave and I shivered before his teeth pulled at the lobe of my ear with a little nip that made me jump. "Because I will."

How the fuck do you say no to that? I didn't think I could, I wanted him. I wanted him everywhere.

"Yes," I gasped, pushing him onto his back, my fingers digging into his shimmering skin as that same needy feeling that had overtaken me last night ripped and rolled its way through my bloodstream.

I was ready. My phoenix was ready. But I had one very, very big problem. I really, really had to pee. Like, I had to pee so bad my bladder hurt.

I don't think I had ever felt something so powerful before and now that I had acknowledged it, the thing was a force that I couldn't fight.

"Omg no!" I shrieked, frozen in place above him as his face fell into a look of pure confusion, his eyes darkening a touch.

"That's okay, darling," he whispered, "we can wait."

"No waiting. I mean yes." Holy hell, this was getting more embarrassing with each word that escaped. "I mean I really have to pee."

And there it was, the coup de grâce of embarrassment. Thank god that the cave was dark, or I am sure the strangely red color of my cheeks would be permanently burned into his mind.

"Figured as much," Jarron said, his voice full of light as he smacked my ass, the sound of flesh slapping concealed by my high-pitched shriek as I jumped to my feet, sending him a scowl as he chuckled.

"Go a little bit further down the cave, past the stream we used," he nodded once toward the dark end of the cave and my heart fell, freezing me in place as I wiggled into Jarron's blood streaked shirt.

No, I was not scared to go deeper into the cave, even as dark as it was it didn't scare me. It was more the 'pop-a-squat' scenario he had described that was making me question myself. I don't know what I had expected, the cave clearly did not have indoor plumbing.

I made a face, gave an even bigger sigh and Jarron chuckled, pushing himself to sitting as he grabbed me, pulling me back to him.

"Be back soon, darling," he whispered into my waist, lifting the shirt and planting a soft kiss on my hip bone. The soft touch ran through me in a shock.

Oh lord, maybe I could hold it.

No.

I needed to go before something more embarrassing happened.

I rushed away before I either jumped on him, or peed my pants. Well, not the pants part because I wasn't wearing any, but the peeing of myself was a frightening possibility.

Luckily, the floor of the cave was smoother than the one we had taken to get into Rydaim. I could walk on this floor without issue, which was good, because I still couldn't see hardly anything.

I don't know what it was about these caves, but they made me feel like a broken shifter. Weren't we all supposed to see in these things?

Jarron had checked the cave out before and assured me there were no drop offs, so given his instructions I needed to follow the sound of running water past where we were last night.

Which was great because following the sound of running water was the first thing I thought about doing when I had to pee.

Oh lord, the sound was making it so much worse. I picked up into a run, trying not to jiggle boobs and bladder too much in my attempt to reach some suitable stretch of cave in which I could relieve myself. The smell of blood flared in my nostrils as I passed the trickle of water we had been using to clean Jarron's wounds, surprised to see that it had picked up into a bit more of a running rivulet than the slightly damp stone from yesterday.

Well, just more water to help wash all my urine away.

Yeah, that might be the weirdest thing I had ever thought. I followed the water for a few more steps, trailing it around a slight bend when I froze.

There was a light up there. A softly glowing yellow light. It flickered like the light in a hotel room at midnight when you had left the TV on, before it faded away, only to come back stronger than before.

Well, that was not something you would normally find in a cave, well, at least to my knowledge. And I was well aware I knew next to nothing. I was still holding out hope that Jarron would show me a cave filled with thousands of diamonds or something. Diamonds to go with the gold of his eyes. It would be the perfect combination.

But that light ahead was clearly not a diamond, or even a pile of them.

Jarron and I had slept near the cave opening last night, so that we wouldn't miss Killian when he came back, and the light from the entrance was a dull blue glow, like the sky on a summer's day. Calm and beautiful, and also cold as shit.

This light however was warm, yellow and... unnatural.

The more I looked at it, the more I was sure someone was down there, turning the bathroom light on and off. Or any light really, bathroom just seemed more fitting seeing as I was currently squatting against a wall relieving myself and dreaming of toilets.

The light flickered again and I jumped up, doing my best to utilize the water and clean myself, even as I was staring into the dark at the flickering light.

On-off-on for a while - on.

A million, mostly terrifying, possibilities wrapped around my mind everything from aliens to cave trolls making an appearance. Not that I knew that either of those were real, but seeing that I was currently in a solid mating relationship with a dragon, bonded to his two brothers, hunted by a vampire, and also, I'm a Phoenix... cave trolls were clearly a thing.

Speaking of dragons, I turned around, staring through the dark toward where Jarron still lay waiting for my return. Waiting for me to come back not mauled by a cave troll.

I opened my mouth to yell for him, stopping myself before one squeak had made it out and swung back to the light second guessing my near yodel level scream. The flickering was still beating through the dark, calling to me.

What if it was a cave troll, what if I yelled and the thing

came running and I lost my head before I even reached them.

Yelling may not be a good idea.

I could go back and get him, I supposed, and our two naked asses could defeat whatever was down there. If it was still there by the time I got back.

Or, I could just go myself.

Check it out, get more info and then high tail it back to Jarron before anyone saw me. Besides, if things went south I could shift into my phoenix and breeze down the cave back to Jarron, probably shoot a few fire javelins at whatever monster was chasing me in the process.

Easy.

Plus, adding cave troll slayer to my supernatural resume was going to look so cool.

Careful to stay out of the water and make any more noise, I padded my way down the cave, toward the light that had stopped flickering and was now one big span of yellow-orange glow. The light spread over the stone, growing bigger, glowing brighter, the closer I got.

The light spread, and I wasn't walking in a dark cave so much anymore. The light was burning from inside a little alcove that looked as though it had been dug into the stone by a steam blower. The edges were smooth and shimmering, and from what I could tell, the inside was too. Before I got a good look, however, the light flicked off again and a loud voice ripped through the dark.

"If you don't stop doing that, Lilly, I am going to break your fingers off."

The troll. Well, kind of.

What he said sounded very Troll-like, but instead sounded more like some punk kid from London with very limited patience.

Heavy footsteps echoed through the cave and I plastered myself to the wall I had been walking against just as the light flicked back on and a little girl giggled.

"If you let me turn the TV on, Henry, then I'll stop destroying your work," a little girl's voice, I'm assuming Lilly, responded, the answering giggle and perfect British accent making me sure they were related.

Related British cave trolls. Okay, so cave trolls were seeming a little bit too far from a possibility now.

I scooted closer to the cave, I really needed to figure out what was going on here.

"No TV for a week, I told you that you couldn't go hunting until you finished your book work--"

"Book work is boring," the little girl interrupted and I took a very careful step forward, bringing myself closer to the light.

"And you didn't finish your book work."

I peeked around the corner of the cave trying to see into the brightly lit space, which was proving much too hard to do without burning my retinas. The light was everywhere, falling over what looked to be a kitchen space filled with what I could have sworn was a full science kit, complete with beakers and Bunsen burners, and a full living room, where a blonde-haired girl had parked herself in front of a massive television set.

Damn it. I bet they had a bathroom too. I was suddenly regretting peeing in the cave. Of course, just because they had a bathroom didn't mean I could get to it. I really needed to figure out what was going on here. Bathroom access was at stake.

Henry sighed and turned towards me, well not towards me, but toward the opening of the cave where I was no longer standing. I had already plastered myself back against the shadowed cave wall. I would have scaled the thing too if I needed, my heart was pounding enough that it probably wouldn't take too long.

"No TV until book work is done." Well, someone was in trouble.

"Who wants to do book work when I can snap my fingers and make things explode? I don't need to learn how to do that. I can think it and it happens. I can *think it* and make you explode."

Something slammed down, the girl giggled with a dark twisted sound that made my stomach curdle. Henry swore and I jumped so high I stubbed my toe, which sent me stumbling right into the beam of light and into where the two could see me.

Henry and Lilly looked up as one, their faces twisting in horror before they each moved into a fighting stance. I shrieked and jumped back, pulling the heat right to my hands, really hoping I didn't have to attack a little girl.

I was nowhere near ready for that.

The girl was younger than I thought, perhaps closer to eight than to ten. The boy, however, was quite a bit older. Late twenties, not that it mattered, I only noticed because he was staring right at me and his haggard look and few days growth made him look like a cross between a mountain man and a stressed-out housewife.

I was still trying to control my heat, to convince myself that I didn't need to attack these two, when their hands dropped and Henry's look shifted from fear to awe.

I didn't expect that look from stumbling into their secret cave, buck naked and covered in ash.

"Oh my god! Elliana!" The man, Henry, said, his face still frozen in shock as he rushed over to me, the little girl on the couch looking like she was about ready to jump out of her skin. "I thought you were dead."

I opened my mouth to ask, to find out who the hell he was, and what the fuck was going on, when his lips crashed against mine and my phoenix went absolutely fucking haywire.

She thrashed against my chest in a need to reach the man, to wrap around him, to pull him into me. The more she thrashed, the more my confusion left, the more the binds that wrapped around me broke, little bits of memory and magic finding their way to the surface.

"Henry," I gasped as I pulled away, my heart twisting, my soul flying away.

The Travelers Mark hadn't pulled me to Drake as I had thought it would, but it had pulled me to my mate. My soul.

"My husband."

20

KILLIAN

THE LAST TIME KILLIAN HAD A HEADACHE THIS BAD HE HAD been attempting to create a new tunnel using only his head.

He and Jarron were drunk on some wine they had stolen from the village and Jarron was mourning some girl that wouldn't let him take her to bed. He would like to blame the incident on youth, but seeing as Jarron was nearly one hundred, and Killian well over that, the only excuse he had was booze and women. Laying on this very pokey bed, thinking of Elliot and the danger he had left her in, neither of them felt like very good excuses.

He groaned and tried to roll over, to find a clock, or calendar, or some map of the region so that he could figure out where he was, and what was going on, but even the subtle attempt at movement wrapped pain around his head in a ribbon of spikes and murder. So instead, he growled, flopped back, and considered bursting into flames right then and forcing his dragon to fly him away.

Seeing as he had crash landed and ended up in some tiny

village, however, that wasn't going to happen. For all he knew he had been transferred to a large village and a doctor, meaning he had no idea where he was. Add to that, the tightly wound bandages around his abdomen, and he was going nowhere fast.

He settled for swearing loudly, smashing his fist into the straw mattress and staring into the dark abyss above him in an attempt to figure out where he was, and how much time had passed. He could only hope he hadn't wasted more time than needed foolishly crashing his dragon into rock-hard soil.

He needed to get back to her. Just the thought had him swearing again.

"Ah, you're awake," a low Italian voice said somewhere to his left, the crinkling of paper following right behind. "That's quite the record, with a fall like that we assumed you to be out for at least a week. Or dead."

He chuckled to himself and the low burn of a lantern spread over the ceiling of the room, the hand-crafted thatch absorbing the light in hauntingly dark lines.

So not a hospital then. With any luck he was still in the village, perfect. It would make it that much easier to get back to her.

"Many of us had our money on dead." He chuckled again, but this time the sound was forced and Killian let the muscles in his back tense, his mind systematically tensing and relaxing different muscles and joints in an attempt to find any injury.

Thankfully, it only seemed to be his torso that was on fire, the few ribs that were broken before still under agonizing pressure.

At least his dragon was doing his work correctly.

"You've got a few broken ribs, a concussion, and a little piggy tail that's growing out of your left hand." Killian jerked, pain ripping down his back as he turned toward the voice and towards the light that was instantly trying to burn a hole in his skull. His rib cage pulled painfully as his hand rushed to block out the light.

"Shit!" he swore again, the sound less slurred than it had been the last few times.

The man, or the shadow of him, as Killian's eyes were still trying to adjust past the blinding light, gave another chuckle, and Killian found himself wishing he could reach over and punch him.

"Sorry about the light. And I promise no pigs tail. I figured you were English, with the 'shit' and all, but figured it better to check."

The man dimmed the light, although it didn't do much to calm the pulsing jackhammer that was now assaulting Killian's head. He kept his hand over his eyes, blocking out most of the room. All except an end table, where the man was now squeezing water from a cloth in a china pot.

"This will help." The Italian continued, placing the still sopping rag over Killian's forehead and much of his eyes, blocking the light, and plunging him in to relative dark. The ache in his head instantly began to calm.

He couldn't help it, he let out a very loud sigh, which instigated another chuckle from the Italian. Rydaim may be close to Italy, but Killian had never met an Italian who laughed quite this much. It was getting on his nerves.

"My name is Mattia," the man continued after a moment, the guy was either desperate for communication or didn't understand the point of leaving injured people to rest.

Killian gave a grunt of acknowledgement, but neither moved or said anything. Thank goodness he now had this thing on his eyes so he didn't have to look at the guy.

Made it easier to pretend he was falling back asleep. He really didn't need some poor mortal getting tied up in this stuff.

"What's yours?"

Okay, so getting rid of this guy was going to be harder than he assumed. But he surely wasn't going to give his name. He had no clue how close Parris was to tracking them down. Or how much time had passed.

No clues. Or at least no more than he had accidentally dropped from the sky.

"Where am I?" Killian grunted, forgoing the man's question in hopes of getting a few of his questions answered.

"Priarty. Tiny village in Nepal, closer to India than China, near the northern tip of The Himalayas. Some come here to climb, others to meditate, others to learn, some to die. Which are you?"

This man and his questions, he was starting to get to Killian, but he wasn't going to let it show, the man had given him a near perfect explanation of where they were and when he combined that with his flight to get here, it wouldn't take him long to get back to Ellie and to get them all out of here. He would need a map first.

He would also need to be healed enough to shift, but he could start walking in that direction if it came to that.

It may only take one good night sleep for his ribs to heal, that was of course if his instant roommate would allow him that.

That and food.

"I came to learn," Mattia announced proudly. Getting some silence from this man was clearly building up into an impossibility. "There is ancient power in these hills that I wish to learn for myself. I have traveled through this region for much of my life, searching for it. Searching for the strength it will provide."

He clearly wanted Killian to ask what. Killian was not going to ask what. He was going to continue to focus on the cold water of the cloth as it trickled over his face and down his neck, willing his bones to heal faster.

He needed to get out of here, and the sooner the better, he may have already lost too much time as it was.

"What day is it?" Killian plowed on, his stomach twisting in a need to know.

"Tuesday." Mattia said, the scrape of glass and wood making it clear he was drinking something.

"This tells me nothing." The growl in his voice was clear to anyone else that he was losing his patience, but not to this man who continued to drink and chuckle.

Killian faintly wondered if he was drunk. It would make

sense. It would be irritating and force him to question all the information he had given him, but it would make sense.

"Tuesday the 12th, about 2 in the morning if I changed the time on my phone correctly."

Killian shot up like a light, pain radiating through his bones and pounding against his skull as he faced Mattia. The middle-aged Italian was frozen with what looked to be a glass of Absinthe millimeters from his lips. Drunk. Perfect. He could be wrong.

Please let him be wrong on this.

Mattia sat in stunned silence as Killian inhaled, trying to regain his bearing and force the pain from his skull, neither was working, so he chose to ignore it, heaving as he stared the man down.

"That's impossible. Show me a calendar." Killian's voice was a boulder of command, his voice rumbling around the room and causing what appeared to be a falcon on a perch in the corner to ruffle his feathers, its beady eyes staring at him. The creature was unhooded, which strengthened the chance of attack, any mortal would be scared.

Killian could bat the thing away like it was a drunk song bird.

"Now," Killian growled and the man jumped, catching up with what was happening.

Mattia set his glass down on the table with a clatter before reaching for his pocket, producing a cell phone with a fumble. His hands were shaking as he compressed the screen, swinging it around to a picture of a sunset and the time and date clearly visible in large print.

Tuesday August 12th, 1:18 am

Five days before they had raided Rydaim, the day he had left the circus with his father. The day those mortals had been tortured for Parris' gain and pleasure.

"How the fuck?" He stopped himself before he said anymore and collapsed back down on the bed, the stunned Mattia still staring at him.

"I believe you hit your head harder than you thought," Mattia said, his voice shaking as he picked his drink back up from the nightstand, the glass jingling against his rings.

"I didn't hit my head." His dragon was in full prowl now, and his voice was more growl than words.

"I'm not sure, you have quite the concussion, and I believe that was quite the fall." He paused, the unasked question heavy in the air and Killian felt his stomach twist.

Please let him leave this one be, please let that drunken fool just step away.

"Tell me what happened."

It was not a question, it was not slurred, and any hint of a laugh was gone. Killian's muscles stiffened and he turned his head slowly. He may be injured, but he wasn't foolish enough to avoid a threat. This man may be mortal, but he was going to look him in the eye.

"I fell from a plane," the excuse sounded ridiculous from the moment he said it, the corner of the man's smile twitching as he took a drink, and Killian quickly amended. "Skydiving accident."

"Is that where the flames were from?" It was clear that this man did not believe him, and Killian found himself quickly calculating the best way to end him, hopefully without anyone hearing as he still wasn't quite sure where in the village he was. How close anyone was to him.

"Parachute exploded."

The lie was ridiculous, it rattled against the hard edge of Killian's voice and Mattia's smile twisted again. At least they both knew how foolish he sounded.

"Yes, you could also tell me the truth you know, I saw the fall, and I must say, even in injury your dragon is glorious. My familiar here has been basking in the scent of your home all day."

The man nodded to the bird, but Killian had jumped up, pain and heat radiating over his skull and chest as injury and dragon battled for the front lines of his attention. His eyes were inflamed as he stared at Mattia, but instead of looking shocked as he had last time, the Italian sat calmly, legs crossed, sipping at the narcotic drink.

"Calm," Mattia said, waving a hand and sending him back to the bed. And not by choice, the bands that wrapped over Killian were strong, holding him so tightly he was sure he could not fight them. Not even without injury.

"What in the devil!" Killian growled, and the man smiled more.

"I believe you know my sister, Suvi."

The words should have been calming, except that the way he said her name was laced with enough malice and hatred to put him right back on guard. He should have killed the man from the moment he woke up.

"What about her?" He snarled, the olive skin of the man, who looked much too young to be Suvi's brother leaning over him and smiling.

"Oh nothing," he smiled, taking another drink and sitting back in his chair, thankfully releasing the bind he had put on Killian, his point sufficiently made. Killian was in no place to fight a Warlock. "We don't get along."

A pregnant pause filled the air and Killian found himself looking through the dimly lit room, desperate for weapons or escape, although he already had a feeling he would find none.

"She doesn't like dark magic. I, on the other hand, love it."

21

DRAKE

Drake still had vampire remains in his shoe.

The tiny icy particles were stuck between his toes, and wedged under the leather strap of his sandals. The cold pressed against his skin until he felt like he was standing in a cube of ice. It was uncomfortable, and made focusing on anything that was going on in the underground city of The Forgotten even worse.

What he wouldn't give for a shower, but the chances of finding any form of indoor plumbing or running water in this place was slim to none.

After the vampires had left, they had wandered through the tunnels, gathering injured and lost Fae as they all attempted escape. But every exit they found was blocked, every tunnel had collapsed, and the new winding paths they came upon threatened to swallow their haggard party. In the end, they were able to find their way back to the only safety they knew; the underground village. It was in ruin, even more than when they had made their way through it hours before.

Rocks had fallen from the ceiling and shattered what homes and buildings remained, crushing many of the bodies that were left behind from when Parris's men tried to clear out the place before.

Most of the entrances were clogged with rock, leaving the survivors to scuttle over the collapsed stone in fear of triggering another slide. A few other openings had appeared in the cave-in, each one leading to caves that at this point only spelled trouble.

It had been at least twelve hours from when Ellie had exploded over the main square in Rydaim, sending Parris, Ceres and all their men in a flurry of panic.

The Phoenix existed. It was real.

The Fae had overheard it from the Vampires as they hunted them. It was some sort of miracle, and it was all anyone had been able to talk about.

Well, perhaps not all. The arrival of Zoe and Drake had been screamed over the stone just as much. The miracle of their survival and existence like some form of beacon in the ruin. People still gathered around, many of the friends they remembered, crying over their return. Many others whispering to the children who may not remember.

Drake was trying to stay out of the twisted reunion, to stay back and allow Zoe to take the helm as she always had. It was her place, and she shone in it. Even if he had a knack for that kind of leadership, Drake would choose to step back and let her take the lead, if only to watch her skill.

So he stayed back, witnessing the reunion unfold, shuffling his feet in his sandals in an attempt to free some of the vampiric remains and staring at the slow trickle of water that moved through the cave, the former river having slowed after the collapse.

The cold mountain water had always been one of his favorites for drinking, but with the low stream the only source for such things he wasn't about to go and muck it up with Vampire dust, no matter how good he was sure it would feel on his feet. As it was, the survivors were already struggling to fill their buckets enough to clean the wounds and bites of those who still had a chance to live.

"You don't seem too happy," Fallon said as she plopped herself on the scrap of wood Drake had made his roost. The large slab was painted with dainty little flowers, he was sure it had been a wall at some point.

Perhaps to a child's room. The thought shifted his stomach.

"Excuse me?" Drake asked, turning from the river to the girl who was leaning back as though she was getting ready for a sporting event and not watching a race of people trickle in to survey the damage of their homes.

"Your face," she gestured toward him, her brow furrowed in confusion.

"Do I have something on my face?" The question seemed silly the moment he asked it, of course he had something on his face, they had emerged out of dirt covered tunnels and Vampire destruction piles.

He would be more concerned if he didn't have something on his face, seeing as water was in short supply. Come to that,

Fallon seemed a little too clean for what they had gone through, he certainly hoped that she wasn't so selfish as to use some of the precious water so she could look a bit cleaner.

"Well, yes. But that's not what I mean." She leaned back, twisting the end of her long brown hair around her finger.

Judging by the dirt on both finger and hair he would have to say his initial assumption had been incorrect. She was just as dirty as the rest of them, even the mud smears on her shirt were still present, the weird finger marks on her back making it look like she had rubbed it all there. Like a toddler after eating pudding.

"Then what is wrong with my face?" He was torn between laughing and grumbling at her. He was too on edge for whatever she was playing at, and he wished that she would just spit it out. Especially with the way she was twisting her hair around her oddly long fingers, the pale things looking like talons.

"You don't seem happy." She shrugged her shoulders as if it was nothing, and Drake found his face falling into a scowl, his temper and frustration rising as his dragon did.

"I'm sorry, am I supposed to be going to a beauty pageant?" He was full on growling now, and even worse, he didn't really feel bad about it.

It was really a show of how short Drake's patience was right then that an odd little girl was making his dragon growl. But they really didn't have a time or a place for games. He would have assumed that the hardened killer who had apparently survived Parris' child breeding factory would have caught on to that fact.

"In case you missed it, a whole race of people is being slaughtered, my siblings were just swept away and we are on the brink of a war," and a war we could not win. He kept that part to himself. He knew Zoe wouldn't admit it either. They had lost last time with thousands. They were doomed to be slaughtered with only hundreds on their side.

"I'm pretty sure that justifies not looking *happy*."

"True." She said, shrugging and clicking her tongue again. "Being kidnapped by that phoenix alone. I would be furious."

Drake was barely able to keep his anger restrained, although his dragon was rumbling loudly in his chest, the beast coating his tongue with ash. He was already struggling to keep his silver tongue restrained, but his dragon was becoming more and more desperate to make an appearance, something that she surely wasn't helping him avoid.

From the moment she had spoken so foul about Elliot in the cave he knew he couldn't say much, if anything, about his connection with her. Zoe's hissed demand as they had made their way back through the cave, and to The Forgotten's broken village had barely been needed. It was going to be hard to keep his tongue if she didn't stop going on the way she was.

"Who knows, maybe they will be lucky and destroy the monster before she destroys them."

Yes, she was quickly making his control an impossibility. The ash on his tongue was becoming a foul layer that he would give nothing more than to spit on her.

"What do you have against her, anyway?" Drake asked,

turning on the girl and sending the large slab of plywood they sat on swinging off balance. "You talk about her like she has tried to kill you or something."

"More like wronged us all," Fallon said with a scowl that was digging so intently into where Zoe and Callay were speaking with everyone that he found himself questioning exactly who that scowl was meant for. "She promised to save us, but instead she ended up running off into the night with one of the leaders."

Drake tweaked an eyebrow at her, nothing about what she said made sense. Yet, she was still scowling at Zoe and Callay, the latter of which was now making her way over to them.

"Would you care to elaborate?" Drake asked, sending the plywood shifting again as he made room for Callay.

Fallon's sour look was now directed at him, her lips pursed together as her beady brown eyes stared into him indecisively.

"She promised to save all of us from Parris and his minions. But instead she ran off with one of the minions and got herself killed."

She had said pretty much the exact same thing as before, just flipped the phrasing and filled it with a twisting dread. It wasn't the whole 'Phoenix running off with a minion' thing that was sending ice through his veins, and Callay's too with how she had stopped before them, she said the phoenix had gotten herself killed. Killed. Past tense.

"If she flew off with my brothers, then how can she be dead."

Fallon turned to him, fixing him with a condescending

smile that certainly wasn't helping him to shake the ice that was running through his veins. He had thought having his feet caught in vampire dust was cold enough. He was already shivering.

"She's a phoenix. They don't die," her response was even more condescending than the face she was giving him. "They just reemerge as ugly little babies and start again. I know some people at the factory had seen her do it a few times. There were rumors that her rebirth ash was used to make a few of us."

There were a million things wrong with that sentence and Drake really didn't want to dig into any of them. In fact, he would much rather parachute out of this conversation and swim back to the shore of sanity. He didn't want to hear anymore.

Callay, however, was plunging herself in feet first.

"Is that how you were made? From her ash?" Callay asked, her voice quivering.

The question was full of all sorts of visuals that he had no interest in visiting.

"Sure," Fallon said with a shrug. "It's why my magic is messed up. Vampire god up there just wants to make a million little phoenix bastards"

She gave a head nod to the city somewhere above or beside them, even she wasn't sure where. The collapsing cave had disoriented him enough that he had no idea where he was.

"Too bad he can't figure it out," she mused, that same twisted little grin he had seen stretch over her features before pulled on the lines of her face, twisting her smile in the creepy joy of having killed her master. " I'll just have to stop him for good."

"Who?" Callay asked, finally sitting down on the palate and sending us all swaying again. "You are going to stop Parris?"

Fallon gave a nod.

"Well, I am sure these dragons can use your help," Callay continued, the silver glint in her eyes growing into a spark.

The nervous rocks that had been invading him for the past little while were now jumbling around inside of Drake. He was stuck, sitting between two girls who were bathing the air with two different emotions. Fallon's determined fury was as strong as the pride and hope that was seeping out of Callay. Their faces were twisted to match, each of their looks were directed at the exact same woman.

Zoe.

She was covered in as much dirt and ash as the rest of them, but she stood with the Fae, crying, holding, promising. Just as she always had, just as amazingly powerful.

Fallon didn't seem to see that, her scowl was too deep, too haunted.

"Well, I'd love to help," Fallon said, a weird grate echoing with her voice. It took Drake a moment to recognize the sound.

He was so used to Dragons growling, Phoenixes singing, and Fae glowing that he had nearly forgotten about the very human sound of teeth grinding together in agitation.

The outcome of growing up in an orphanage, he supposed. Either that or it was the girl's furious agitation if he had to guess. It wasn't the first time he was glad she didn't have a knife.

"Parris is a very special kind of enemy," she continued, standing just as Zoe reached them. "He deserves the right adversary."

Drake had been so focused on the weird aggression that was seeping from the girl that he hadn't noticed his sister step up to them.

"I'm going to speak to them," Zoe announced the second they had all turned to her, clearly oblivious of their conversation. "There is so much pain, they need hope. They need to know we can fight this."

"I agree," Fallon said, shaking her head eagerly. "What can we do to help?"

"Probably move," Zoe said with the faintest of smiles, the tweak of her lips pulling her tear stained face. "I think you guys are sitting in the highest, flattest place in here."

"Anything else?" Drake asked as he and Callay jumped to their feet, Zoe already making her way onto the teetering piece of plywood. "A megaphone perhaps?"

She ignored him, which was good. He had seen his sister make these speeches enough in his life to know that there was nothing she needed. She had it all, something that was made clear as she stepped onto the plywood, the sheet barely shifting under her weight.

She was covered in dirt, her clothes were ripped, her hair was a mess, but yet she stood straight, tall, powerful and every eye in that place turned to her, the few that had lingered to the outskirts rushing over so that they could hear. There were only a little over a hundred who had survived, the number was heartbreaking knowing what they had gone through over the past few decades, how many there had been, and how many that were left.

They had already lost too many.

"My friends," Zoe called, gaining any stragglers attention, if there had been any. "I know I have spoken to you all individually, but I want you to know that I am with you, that Drake and I have never left you. And we are honored to be back here at this time of need. To help, to protect, and to come out stronger than before."

Her voice was as calm as the room, everyone holding onto each other and wiping tears from their eyes. Seeing them all there together was breaking Drake's heart all over again.

"We will survive this!" Zoe said with strength, the solemn faces of the Fae nodding along in agreement.

Well, all but one.

"No!" Fallon yelled, stepping right up to the raised platform and turning around to face everyone, the looks of agreement shifting to confusion. "No! We will not just survive! The time for surviving is over. The time for war and battles are over. I am done just "surviving" how about you?"

Zoe's calm speech was shattered with Fallon's yells, with murmurs of the crowd as she yelled, many of them beginning to nod in agreement, a few looking at Zoe in confusion. Drake could count himself among those. What happened to helping them? Who was this girl?

"I am done being led blindly into other people's wars! I want my own war! I want my own fight!" Fallon screamed louder, lifting her fist as shouts began to raise along with her, so many of the Fae beginning to scream alongside, to lift their fists in agreement.

Zoe looked over them in confusion. That was a look Drake had never seen in her, it was almost as disheartening as what was happening. Shock dripped over his skin, adding to the cold that was already assaulting him as he looked between the two women, trying to understand what was happening.

"Say something," Drake hissed, the two words jerking through her like a live wire.

"And we will!" Zoe yelled, easily lifting her voice above the screams. A few of them shouted in agreement to what she said, but there was more confusion than camaraderie now. "But now is not the time for fighting. We must heal before we can do anything."

"How can we heal when we are stuck underground. And by her father! What does she have that can help us?" Fallon continued to yell, gesturing to Zoe as one bats away a fly. Zoe's face didn't even fall, she continued to stare at the girl, arms at her side, fire in her eyes. The Fae didn't even seem to notice.

"She has nothing more than a bit of fire. We are Fae. We have been burned by fire for years, why would we follow that to our salvation. You know my story. You know what I have done, and what I have inside of me. I killed the dragon who enslaved me, I fought to keep my magic intact. You can do the same. We can do the same!"

The crowd began to murmur and nod as she continued, their eyes glistening with the shadow of light of their kind.

The light was so much dimmer than what he had seen in Callay, so much more dead. He didn't even know they could glow the same way, that there was still a shadow of magic left inside them.

Their rage was increasing, and Zoe calmly stepped down from the platform, a look of horror in her eyes. Drake could only stare at her, he had no idea what was happening.

"Let's follow our own magic, and our own kind. We do not need dragons to show us the way! Let's make our own future and strike down the vampires and the dragons with the power we have inside. My magic was ignited by a being that is very close to us, and we can use that power to ignite all of yours. We can make you strong again! We can ignite your magic."

Fallon held her hand forward then, her palm up as a stream of sparks flew from her skin, the multicolored lights rising only a few feet into the air before they sagged back down like heavy, and oddly colored, drops of rain. The second the colors appeared, the crowd lost it, screaming in both panic and fear as they jostled forward and back, these magical beings who had been denied their own powers in awe of what was barely more than a parlor trick.

Drake hadn't seen much of magic, and most of what he had seen were Elliot's terrifying explosions, but this was nothing compared to that. This is more like what he would see the climbers do on holidays, challenging each other to see who could hold the roman candles the longest.

"That's gross," Callay snarled under her breath, the complaint hidden by the growing cheers of The Forgotten.

"What did she do wipe a rainbow on some gryphon snot and set it on fire? I can do better."

"I am starting to question all that you can do," Zoe said, her calm pose now rumbling with tension as she folded her arms over her chest. "But now may not be the best place to talk about it."

"I can make a place to talk about it if that's what you need. I can do a lot of things you need, but you are right. Not here."

"Good, because this little girl is going to get them all killed. And we need to figure out a way to stop it."

Drake barely heard any of them, he only stared at Fallon and those weak little sparks as she continued to play the crowd, continued to make promises she couldn't keep. Not that any of them cared. Not that any of them knew.

He knew, however, and for once, he was glad that Elliot was not here with him, he knew exactly what Fallon was promising, and exactly what she thought she needed to deliver.

22

ELLIOT

ONE LITTLE WHISPER OF A KISS AND A MEMORY OF THIS GUY with his hands all over me and I was out of his arms and sprinting down the cave so fast I was leaving a blur of fire and smoke behind.

My skin had caught the moment he had touched me, rippling up my arms in bright purple waves that I hadn't seen before, and were so fucking scary I hoped I never saw again.

I looked like a broken Catherine wheel, sparking and flailing and falling over my own two feet.

I hadn't run away from my problems in a good long while, but yep, this time I totally ran away.

All I was missing was the shrieking.

I had never seen a color like that in fire, let alone in my fire, or on my skin and it was creepy as hell. All I needed was one eye and a horn and then I could fly around town and terrorize children.

But not the one behind me, because she could apparently make things explode.

Cave trolls would have been so much better.

First, my hair flies around me like I am caught in an invisible wind storm, and now I'm turning into a purple human torch.

At least I wasn't farting fire anymore.

"Elliana! Sweetheart, what's wrong?" Henry's voice echoed through the cave behind me, it ripped over the walls with a weird combination of panic and anger that only made me run faster.

Maybe I was farting fire, with how fast I was being propelled forward. I was officially freaking out enough for it to be a possibility.

"Come back, darling!" That whole frustrated freak out cranked up to an eleven.

No one was allowed to call me darling but Jarron, and he was still somewhere in the cave before me. I clearly should have gone to him first.

Of all the times for me to be a stupid, arrogant...

God, I'm an idiot.

"Elliana?" Henry's voice was an echo now, his sweet British accent rippling over the rock and pulling at my heart for reasons that I didn't understand.

Another string pulled at me, tugging at my soul and trying to drag me right back to him.

Oh hell no, that was certainly not going to happen.

I pushed away from it, my breath coming in ragged pants now, tears threatening to boil over and run down my cheeks as my phoenix went haywire and I was struck with another all too vivid memory that certainly couldn't be mine.

I thought the memory of some marriage and late-night innuendo that had smacked me upside the head when I had kissed him had been bad enough.

Henry flooded my memory again, looking a little more kempt and a little less frazzled as he laughed in what appeared to be a 1970s kitchen, cake batter lay forgotten on the counter, flour was everywhere, his hands were everywhere.

I shook my head to try and dislodge the image, and sent myself off balance and falling sideways in to a wall.

I barely caught myself against the cold stone, my palms flat against the uneven surface as I stared into the dark, trying to think of anything but that happy kitchen.

No, it wasn't happy. I needed to get that thought out of my mind.

Not a happy kitchen. It was an old, out of date, ugly kitchen, and didn't make any sense.

Why would I have memories of him? Why would I be an adult in those memories?

When I had found out that I had erased my memories and Suvi had warned me that my memories would be making a return, I had expected to be hit with memories of my father, of Elliot, laughing and making cakes with a toddler. Or of teaching a four-year-old me how to light fires or something.

Not of sexual interludes with some rugged mountain man.

As an adult.

Which, in case I needed to remind myself, wasn't fucking possible.

I was a child at the circus, I was rescued as a child. Not an adult. The guy was clearly some kind of Fae with a penchant for memory shifting - if that was a thing.

That memory wasn't real, and he certainly wasn't my husband.

The thought flip-flopped in my stomach, even as my Phoenix rose up as though she was doing the conga.

"I don't know him." I was firm, but neither Phoenix or heart were interested in believing me, they were all aching and screaming and making a racket that I was sure the guys on either end of the cave could hear.

Two guys, two strings, pulling me in the opposite directions.

I turned toward Jarron and continued my sprint to reach the end of the cave, desperately hoping that Killian had made a return, that he had brought clothes and food and even a blanket basket to get us all out of here.

We would need it this time.

We still had a chance to get out of here before the husband came back.

The husband.

Ugh. That was wrong on like a million different levels. Plus, if he was my husband then that little girl...?

Nope. Nope. Nope.

This could so not be happening.

I tumbled headlong into the stone again, this time smacking my panicking noggin' against the stone and sending another little flash from my supposed past into my mind. This time with me in a room before a tall mirror in a dress and boots that seemed too 'medieval assassin' for me. In fact, I probably wouldn't have recognized myself if it wasn't for the red hair. A hooded figure stood behind me, tucked into the corner of the reflection as if they weren't really there.

Even in memory I wasn't sure if they were there, they looked like they were too much shadow, a weirdly glimmering shadow.

"Will it work?" I said, my voice hitting against the stone of the cave as I spoke along with the memory.

"It will be quick, but act before he finds you. Then it will be too late."

The rumble of a voice that sounded far too feminine for the cloaked figure rattled against my bones and I jerked, both in the memory and in the now. I pulled myself back to the cold stone, to the trickle of water, and to the sound of feet that were coming ever closer.

And not from the direction I was headed.

Shit.

"Jarron," I gasped, hoping that whole heart string thing would still work. "I need you. I need Killian. Come."

I put as much force, and I hoped magic, into the words

before I continued my sprint through the cave, pulling myself as fast as I could as that faint purple light returned, although this time it didn't scare me quite so much.

This time it felt a little bit more familiar.

"Let's go," I whispered to the glow as it picked up and my feet left the ground, lifting into the air as they continued to run, paddling through air as though they were pedaling through water.

The purple grew, my hair started to do that whole flying thing and I was running through the air, watching my body hover in a purple glow.

Hovering. Soaring. No wings, no beak, no flames of red and gold. Just a purple glow that lifted me off the ground, as normal as if I had done this before. Which I very clearly had.

"Well fuck yeah," I gasped as I hovered in a purple glow, in the middle of the cave. "I'm a badass."

As familiar as it was, I had no clue what I was really doing. I knew I needed to move forward, I needed to get through the goddamned cave and reach Jarron, swoop him up and get out of here.

The thought had only barely hit my mind when I started to do just that, my awkward, still running, body propelling forward and zooming through the cave, around corners, along the trickle of water.

It was hard not to be amazed at this badassery I was displaying, even if I was also scared of said badassery.

As cool as this was, something was very clearly wrong.

I was picking up speed, my soaring tumbling flight quickly turning into some kind of rocket launcher. I was very clearly in trouble. If only because that tight little line that was pulling me to Jarron was getting closer, and I was moving faster.

I zoomed around the corner with all the speed of a bullet, my worry turning to absolute panic as the half-naked image of a gold-shimmering man burst into being. He was sprinting toward me nearly as fast as I was soaring toward him.

My heart beat faster at seeing him, my pulse echoing in my ears as my phoenix called in joy and damn it all, I sped up. Yeah, because that's what I needed when I was barreling toward someone like a freaking rocket. His panic drifted from confusion to shock to fear so quick that if I wasn't staring right at him, trying to figure out how to not crash land into his chest I would have missed it.

"Get out of the way," I shrieked, faintly wondering how much it would hurt if I barreled head first into the wall instead, when he intentionally placed himself in my path, his arms held wide.

Great, he thought he could catch a purple rocket when he had been repeatedly stabbed no less than a day ago. I hesitated to call him an idiot... nope, he's just an idiot.

"Get out of the way," I tried again, angling myself toward the wall, which he totally countered. Again.

Idiot.

"How the freak do you stop this thing!"

I was now looking for some kind of pulley or lever like a loon, because I was clearly driving an actual rocket, not a naked body covered by purple flame. Meanwhile, he was popping a squat like a football player, too bad I looked nothing like a football. Thank god he had put on pants, or this was going to be so much worse.

"I've got you." I didn't believe him, and sure enough when I hit into him, it was with a massive thundering impact that sent both of us into the wall.

I was pretty sure I heard the crack of a bone, although it could have been rock with the belly rumbling grunt and a few profanities that Jarron was letting off. I mean, he wasn't screaming, so there must not have been any spine breakage.

"Oh my god, Ellie," Jarron said with a grunt, having been clearly winded by my rocket power impact. "What in the world is going on."

"It's Blasting," I said, the name for whatever I had done smacking into the side of my head like I had been clubbed. "But none of that matters now. We need to get out of here."

I rolled over, putting as much of Killian's stubborn regality as I could into my voice, hating myself that I hadn't picked up more of it, while also simultaneously wishing I could channel him. Jarron was not moving.

"Move damn it," I growled, now pushing my shoulder into his back in an attempt to get him off me. Even with all my muscle he wasn't moving more than an inch at a time.

Damn it! I would have thought Killian would be the stubborn boulder. At least he was standing now.

"Blasting?" Jarron was confused, and I didn't blame him, the name made no sense, and I thought 'glowy hands' had been bad. I would have to address the whole 'naming magical abilities dumb things' later. "What is going on, darling? You look like you've seen a ghost."

"Nope, not a ghost," I hissed, impatiently pushing against the small of his back in an attempt to get him to walk. "But there is something down there, we need to get out of here, now."

Jarron continued to fight against me, only moving one painful inch at a time. Or maybe he was sprinting, it didn't matter, we weren't moving fast enough, or maybe this cave had become an endless tunnel of doom.

"Elliot, darling, what has happened?" Jarron ground his heels into the stone and turned to me with a scowl. "We can't leave without Killian. He should have been back by now, and we need to be here in case anything goes awry."

Oh god Killian. And even worse, Drake. They were all scattered to the wind. We needed to be together.

Ever since I drank that thing Killian and given me, that thought had been stronger than all the others, I had gone to Rydaim to make that happen.

Instead, everything had fallen apart, and my guys were nowhere near me, or each other.

My heart was pulling toward each one, their little lines guiding me in four different directions. Three forward, and one behind.

The one behind was suddenly feeling like a barb.

I hadn't meant him.

I didn't even know him.

I stopped my bulldozing, turning away from Jarron to stare down the tunnel, toward the faint yellow light that I could no longer see, right to where that damn barb was pulling me.

"Darling?" Every time he called me that the panic got a little bit worse, my phoenix got a little more indignantly needy of the other guys, and I got a little more upset. "What is it?"

"There is something here," I whispered, trying to ignore the buzzing that was now drifting over my skin, the little tugs in my heart that told me he was close. "We have to go. I can guide us to Killian. We need to be together."

Might take a few tries considering I had never actually followed those heart strings, but I was determined enough and I wouldn't give up until it worked. Then we could all go find Drake and vanish into some kind of cohabitating bliss.

Seemed legit.

I wrapped my hand around Jarron's, pulling him toward the opening Killian had left through, toward the aroma of pine and snow that was traveling on the back of the wind.

"We need to go," I repeated, ready to make my grand escape. Instead I was stopped in my tracks by a four-and-a-half-foot tall blonde-haired fury.

"Where are you going?"

"Oh shit!" Jarron yelped, jumping a good foot in the air and pushing me behind him, moving into instant protector mode and shooting a stream of fire at the girl from the cave, Lilly.

Well, at least I know that if I ever had a desire to go through a haunted house, Jarron could keep me safe. He would burn everything in sight, but I would be safe.

Burning this kid, however, I was not on board for.

"Stop!" I howled, going into instant protector mode and pulling him back, sending the liquid gold of his fire spraying all over the cave.

The thick liquid of the fire sprayed everywhere, burning through the dark stone and leaving a trail of gold behind. It would have been beautiful if it wasn't dripping to the ground in little golden puddles that was eating away the stone of the cave as though it had been carved by ice.

"That's not nice," Lilly shrieked as she stepped back from the puddle of golden fire that was now dripping from her dress and hands. "I really like this dress."

She shook the poufy red thing and sent Jarron's fire flying, like a dog who had shook water. The speck of flame hit against the wall, sizzling loudly as it ate away both water and stone.

But Lilly, Lilly stood there completely unscathed. There wasn't a burn on her overly pale skin, there wasn't a scorch mark on the poufy dress. Not even one of the long silver curls that fell down her back was out of place.

"What the fuck are you?" Jarron said, pulling me behind him as he stared the little girl down. "What did you do?"

Jarron was going into full blown protector mode, now. But I

was sidestepping him so fast that he couldn't stop me. Which, I mean, probably would have been easier if he wasn't still staring at the girl with his jaw on a hinge.

"I did nothing," Lilly said with a twisted grin, her pink polka-dot manicured fingers busily smoothing her dress. "It is not my fault that you doubt your powers. But I would step away from her before it happens again."

"I'm not going anywhere." Jarron's arm wrapped around me, as he stared at the girl, pinning me beside and slightly behind him.

He was ready to attack, which was good because I still wasn't a hundred percent sure that I could find it in me to attack a little girl.

Well, a frightening, possibly super-powered, little girl who liked to blow up things and watch TV. But still, a little girl.

"Clearly. You wouldn't be going anywhere with Elliana, anyway."

"Elliana?" Jarron asked, twisting toward me, but I didn't dare look away from her. The smile that had plastered her face had begun to fade, a strange darkness beginning to bleed through her eyes.

A darkness that was looking right into me and making the icy breeze that pushed in from the outside that much worse.

"Why are you leaving with him?" She continued, the last of her smile leaving as she gave Jarron a glance. "He doesn't even know who you are."

"I..." Words were failing me, thought was failing me.

Hell, everything but this overarching worry and the memory

of an old kitchen covered in flour was failing me. Could that image go away already? It wasn't true, and I didn't need it there, it was making it hard to focus.

"You don't even know who you are, do you?" I didn't think a child could ever sound more condescending.

The kitchen came back into my mind with one more spark of color before it changed, the laugh following in my mind as the vision shifted to a bright green hill, and me soaring down it right to a blonde man who was standing before a large metal building.

He looked familiar. As familiar as Lilly's silver eyes.

As familiar as her smile, as the dark that was taking over her features.

"You aren't my daughter, are you?" The words were out, the fear was free, and Jarron's gasp and shock was now directed between me and the girl. Luckily, the girl let out a giggle that was strangely comforting.

"No." That same stomach curdling laugh I had heard before rang over the cave, the girl laughing in a tone that was anything but 'playful child'. "You really don't know who you are, do you? Henry said that might happen. My being was brought by another dam, we do not even share the same sire."

She was talking about herself as though she was livestock, the twisted phrasing of her parentage barely making the fact that I was not even related to the girl any better.

"Then how do you know me?"

"I know of you. I know what you can do, and what you are supposed to do. I want to be just like you."

The words would have been ominous no matter how you sliced it, but it was so much worse when said by a child with perfect silver curls, who was wearing a poufy red dress, and had fixed me with a smile that was crafted by a demon.

Oh god, please don't let her be a demon.

I could totally take a cave troll, I would wrestle and burn the sucker to the ground.

But something told me this was more of a Demon thing.

Because, you know, I am a genius when it comes to all things supernatural.

This was right up there with the feeling that we had to stay together, and we all know how well that worked out.

Fuck. No wonder Jarron's fire hadn't worked, we were beyond doomed.

I was clearly getting ahead of myself.

Especially if we were facing not one demon, but...

"And him..." I quickly changed the subject, attempting to pull myself out of my demonic rambling, and nodding my head back toward the end of the cave, toward the dark that I was sure he was still moving through, coming closer.

"Your mate."

Jarron stood up a little taller at the word, his arm wrapping around me and pulling me into him, sure the kid was talking about him.

"He's not my mate." Yes, I was snarling, which only made what I had said that much worse, that much of a soul shattering heart grenade.

It had hit home. Just not the home I had hoped for.

Jarron tensed, his arms falling away.

I could practically feel the pain at what I had said rippling off him like a mirage.

"Jarron!" I turned toward him in a rush. I think my heart broke just as deeply with the look he had fixed me with.

The light that had shimmered from his eyes, that had run over his skin for the last few minutes had gone, reverted back to the dark abyss of pain, except this time I felt as though I was falling into it.

Somehow, he looked worse, he looked more defeated than when he had been chained at the edge of the fountain.

"I'm not talking about you, Jarron," I said, struggling to keep the shake of panic out of my voice. "I'm talking about Henry."

It didn't help to bring back the golden light in his eyes, the pain dripped from it as he stepped closer, his arm still around my waist, although not as tight.

"Thank you," The same smooth British accent called from behind me, Jarron's arm tightening as we turned as one, right to mountain man - slash - house wife who was stepping out of the shadows as though he had belonged there.

"I was beginning to think you would never say my name," Henry continued, giving me a smile as he stepped closer, the warmth in his eyes almost like a homing beacon against little miss ax-murderer behind me.

His smile burned into me, warming me and sending my phoenix into that same hungry tizzy I had felt before. I wanted to throw myself back into his arms, hell, I wanted to throw myself right back into his bed.

Which was as fucking irritating as everything, and the associated memories or mind infections, or whatever he was doing to me was sure not helping.

Instead, I clung to Jarron, watching Henry's eyes brighten before he turned to the golden dragon. I was stuck in between protecting Jarron and jumping Henry.

Because both of these seem like reasonable reactions to this situation.

"Hello there," Henry said, that same warm smile in place as he stuck his hand out to Jarron. Jarron didn't take it, but Henry didn't lower it either.

"Who the fuck are you, and what do you two want with my girl?" Jarron clutched me to him, his eyes rippling with gold again, although this gold wasn't the gold of happiness and joy that he had had before.

This one burned with the same angry light of his fire, the dripping bits still digging through the stone of the cave, oozing over the stone like acid.

Seeing the light, the fire, I could understand how someone would be terrified of him. Let's hope that would extend to whatever I had summoned.

"I'm Henry, Elliana and I were mated during her first life

cycle back in the late 1600s. It seems her memory was not intact for this regeneration, but no matter, it happens from time to time. If I know my phoenix she came back here of her own accord. You can't stop her from what she wants."

He winked then and I was hit with a very strong urge to slap him. Would have too if I wasn't so fucking dumbfounded over what he just said.

"The 1600s!" The cave rattled with my shriek and I stepped back, plastering myself against Jarron who thankfully welcomed me into him.

He didn't seem quite so freaked out about this. But then, I remembered with a scowl, he was three hundred years old or something. So to him, the sixteen hundreds was the stories his grandfather told him.

Well, maybe not his grandfather, more like his older sister.

Jeeze, how old is Zoe? My mind was officially swimming with ages and ancients and the fact that I was somehow part of them.

"Calm darling," Jarron whispered in my ear, his hand running over my back. "Don't take anything as gold until we have proof."

I liked the theory of proof.

I would like it a whole lot better if this guy would stop smiling at me, and if those little flashes of what I was still not convinced were memories would leave me alone.

This time it was a freaking wedding at what I was sure was a renaissance faire. With him, in some weird vest and me in white.

White and tomato red hair. That alone proved to me that it wasn't real. The chance of me being at a renaissance faire was the cherry on the top.

That so did not happen.

"I believe Elliana has all the proof you need." His smile was back on me again, I would like to say he was kind if everything in me wasn't screaming that this was super messed up and frightening.

You meet a guy in a cave who says he's your "original mate." Nothing about that sounded right.

"I can see your worry," Henry continued, his hand now extended toward me, yeah, I was going to ignore that too. "I know you are starting to remember. Do not be scared, darling."

"Don't call me that," I sure as shit let that snarl fly free. "Only he gets to call me that."

I clung to Jarron tighter, this would be that perfect movie scene where we look into each other's eyes lovingly.

I wasn't about to let the crown prince of smiles out of my sight, however.

"I understand, Elliana…"

"That's worse," I interrupted him, his face falling the tiniest of bits.

"It has been quite a while, I am honored to meet your new mate, however," Henry shook his hand, as if to get Jarron or I's attention, but Jarron was still scowling at him, holding me against him in what was probably the biggest show of ownership I had ever seen from the guy.

This time I totally welcomed it.

Henry could hold his hand between us forever for all I cared.

Henry's smile faltered at Jarron's scowl, his hand finally lowering as he cleared his throat and gave a tiny nod to Lilly.

Yes, giving a tiny code-like nod to a kid who likes to make things explode. We were totally safe.

It was time for me to head this off at the pass.

"What do you want from me?"

Henry stepped closer, his eyes wide, pleading. Kind. He looked so kind, and sweet.

I was suddenly questioning why I was second guessing him.

"I don't want anything," he whispered, his voice filled with that same calm, kind, tone, and my phoenix went back into that bristling purring rollercoaster she usually did when she wanted something. "I'm glad to have you back in my life. I can't wait to get to know you and..." he paused, turning to face Jarron who hadn't let down from his protector pose. "Jarron was it?"

"I'm not sure I trust you enough to know you," Jarron said.

"Normally it goes the other way doesn't it?" No one joined him in his laughing, well no one but Lilly and that was only because she was now poking at the still burning golden flames, watching them devour the stone.

"Well, why don't you come back with me. We can chat and get to know each other, maybe build that trust." With the way Jarron was still holding on to me, I didn't think it was possible to build anything.

It's unfortunate that Henry was persistent, and that he seemed to know my weakness.

"We have showers, bathrooms, and clothes. You can change, dress, and we can talk about the past, and all that we are doing to end this war, and destroy Parris's tirade on our kind."

Jarron and I exchanged a look, the same question melting in our eyes. *What the actual fuck?*

How is it that we somehow ended up in a cave, with some guy I used to know, who also is fighting Parris? My phoenix was playing at something, and the thing was bristling in a weird combination of anger and excitement that I couldn't tell up from down in.

That alone scared me, I had always felt like I was one with my beautiful bird. Now, I couldn't tell what was going on, or why.

Something about this stunk, and I wasn't sure if it was the good or bad kind yet.

"Come along," he said, everything about him full of smile and friendship, even though it was nothing of the sort.

We clearly didn't have a choice in the matter, especially with the way the tiny freaky kid was shifting herself behind us, herding us into the dark.

The sidelong glance that Jarron was giving me said the same thing.

We followed him slowly, letting Lilly slip ahead as Henry led us both further and further into the dark.

"I don't trust this," Jarron whispered, the same words echoing in my head in some kind of memory. But this time it was something that I couldn't grasp.

I could only nod, hold onto Jarron tighter and watch as he left a glittering trail of fire behind, hoping that Killian would follow it when he arrived.

I hated that I was questioning if that was really necessary.

23

CALLAY

"Who the fuck is fucking Fallon!"

I was irate, but I think I had every right to be.

Talk about a freaking bombshell. I had gone from feeling like I was one step away from success, to being trapped with the revolutionary twins, to staring into the face of what I wasn't convinced didn't belong to pure evil.

The little girl before me, however, only continued to throw rocks into the ocean, ignoring my sudden appearance and my outburst.

She stood with her back to me throwing rocks with a flick of the wrist and sending them skimming over the surface of the frolicking waves with what was surely magic. Not that it could be anything else. Rocks don't normally skip over eight-foot-high waves like they were dancing on pointe, yet hers seemed to be having no problem.

"I think you can fit a few more profanities in there," Xi said, skipping another rock, still not turning around to face me.

"Fine," I growled, my anger in a full-on tidal wave now. "Who is that damn brown-haired bitch that you sent into fucking Rydaim to fucking mess up all the damn work you have had me doing for the past two hundred years?"

"I sent no one," Xi said, skipping another rock, although the muscles in her back were becoming iron cords. I had never seen a little girl stand up so straight and rigid before.

"Don't lie to me, Xi. I need answers." I was doing my best not to grumble or glare, but it didn't matter, the tension in her back cracked anyway, and she spun around, still holding a perfectly flat, and perfectly glittering stone in the palm of her hand.

I knew it was magic, no stone shimmered that way. Of course, now I had other problems, because I had fucking pissed off a unicorn.

Fucking awesome.

"Well, if we are becoming in the habit of demanding answers, then I have a few that I would like addressed." I cringed, everything from the dark shade of green in her eyes, to the way her eyebrows were pulling together spelled trouble.

When would I learn that barging in on this chick and demanding answers was never going to end the way I wanted it to.

Never. I would never learn.

I wanted nothing more than to shake my head, plead forgiveness and run away. I would even do so with my tail between my legs. If I had a fucking tail. And I didn't, so instead I was trapped under the rainbow changing eyes of rage.

"For starters, what are you doing here?" She paused, bouncing the shimmering rock on her palm as she took a slow, and far too calculated step toward me. "Or, why did you use my hair when I explicitly told you not to come here unless the roof of Killian's house ceases to explode and you were needed to get the boys out."

"I know I..." she cut me off with a growl.

What was it with this girl that made me question my life choices so severely? A few hundred years ago I had just wanted to not to starve to death, and maybe to be in possession of a little bit of magic. This was not what I had in mind.

"What is your answer, Callay?"

I swallowed, hoping she wouldn't throw that rock at me or something. I had never seen her so mad.

"The roof exploded, but some chick with messed up Fae magic showed up, talking about Elliot like she is devil incarnate. I figured you needed an update."

"Where are the children?" Xi wasn't looking at me, she was staring at the rock as she continued to bounce it. I wasn't even sure she had heard me.

One track mind that one. At least this reaction didn't seem so bad. Especially after she didn't seem to care about the broken Fae with an ego complex.

Which fucking sucked if only because it would be awesome

to see Xi swoop in and stab her with her fucking horn or something.

"Zoe and Drake are trapped in Rydaim, starting a rebellion because that seems to be the only thing they know how to do," Yes, I totally rolled my eyes at that. "No matter how many times I try to convince them otherwise. Their answer for everything is 'let's start another revolution'."

Xi didn't seem entertained, she had probably seen too many revolutions in her time to really care. Hell, I wasn't completely convinced that the endlessness of Zoe's revolution wasn't what she was trying to do with this mess.

I had tried to figure it out about a hundred years ago, but when you are a pawn in a masochistic Unicorn's chess game, you'd be lucky to know if you are on a white square, or a black one.

Half the time I wasn't so sure.

"And Jarron?"

"With Killian." I swallowed, I had no idea how she was going to react to this next part. I thought she would be mad that some weird broken Fae was trying to undermine all of her work. But when I tell her I had lost the Phoenix. I was so fucking doomed.

"Elliot zapped the two of them out of Rydaim before anyone could stop them. One second, they were there, the next she was holding onto burning feathers like they were interdimensional elevators. And boom," I waved my hand in the air like some kind of deranged mime. "Gone."

I said it all very fast, because as far as I was concerned it was like a band aid, rip it off, hurts less.

As long as we are ripping off band aids and not arms or things. Xi had gone from looking impassive and she flipped and stared at her enchanted rock, to looking downright furious. "Good."

Wait. What? That was not a normal response for the level of fury that was radiating off her.

"Good?"

Xi's fury spread into a smile and she took another step toward me. I took another very large step back.

She was back to bouncing the rock, sending the bright reflections from the surface over me, over the sand, over the wall of rocks behind me.

"If she has mastered Traveling, then it should take her right back to Henry."

All those glittering lights from her rock picked it up into overdrive as my own magic rose to meet it, energy ripping from my bones and over my skin and sending everything into a kaleidoscope.

A kaleidoscope of hope.

And the heaviest mother-fucking dread I had ever felt.

"Henry? But that means..." My heart was pounding so fast it hurt, so fast I wasn't sure if I had really been able to get the words out.

"She does not know this, for if she did the danger she has been plunged into would be paramount. I am entrusting the phoenix to save your daughter from that vile man, but she has got to remember her past before he infiltrates her mind too deep. If she chooses not to remember, she will lose her chance to kill him. If that happens, then Lilly, and even Elliot, will be lost for good."

"No!" The cry shot out and I jerked forward, my heart shattering as though it had been hit by a mother fucking battering ram.

It felt like the day Parris had ripped the baby out of my arms all over again, that same soul crushing sadness.

Except this time, it was full of rage.

She was so close. I was starting to wish I knew how to Travel like Elliot, if only to rip that demon's face from his horns.

"What if Henry tells Parris of Elliot's arrival?"

Xi's lip twitched at my question and she stared at the palm of her hand, watching the glittering stone as if lines in the rock would tell her something about her future.

"I do not think he would be foolish enough to tell his former business partner that he has secured not only the lost phoenix, but the child they made in an attempt to replace her. Do you?"

I could only nod. No, he wouldn't be.

Xi had found out that Henry had double crossed Parris and stolen her daughter from some Vampire that was seeking refuge. I didn't know the details about her beyond the fact that Xi was hiding her.

But I knew about Henry, and just the idea that my precious baby was being raised by that monster was enough to incite copious amounts of rage.

The man was a monster, literally.

"I think we have a bigger concern in Henry eating the brothers, as he has with all of Ellie's other mates."

"What?" I guess a literal monster wasn't quite strong enough. "He wouldn't eat…"

"No, he wants Ellie for himself, Lilly is not in the way of that." She said quickly, filling in the gaps of my question before I had a chance to fully form it.

That was hardly comforting. My daughter would be okay, but I knew the state Killian and Jarron were in. Let's hope that Elliot got those cuffs off before the fucking demon showed up.

Fucking demon fit him better.

A fallen angel determined to cause as much havoc as he could. And he had, for centuries. He was like the god of mischief, if mischief was evil and liked to start wars and control people.

I had seen him do both, or heard of him doing both. I had never actually seen him, but I was okay with that.

I didn't make it a habit of searching out demons.

The idea that Killian, Jarron, and Elliot were there with him, however was a stomach twisting nightmare.

They better be on their toes.

"What do we do about Parris if we don't think Henry will return?" I asked, crossing my arms over my chest like I was some kind of tough guy.

I was really just trying to close the hole that was ripping

open in my chest from thinking about Lilly. And even worse, thinking about Lilly with a mate eating monster.

Luckily, Xi didn't see. She was headed back to the ocean, picking up pebbles from the rocky beach along the way.

"Let the revolutionaries handle him, Zoe's true path will be determined in that fight. It will be interesting to see what she chooses."

I couldn't think of a more Xi response than that. Ominous, vague, and made absolutely no sense.

I wanted to believe that all of that would go perfectly, if the variable in that equation wasn't a fucking thorn in my side.

"What about Fallon? If she keeps causing problems they may not get there."

Xi stopped gathering rocks, her eyes shimmering as she slowly pushed herself to standing, a perfectly flat stone pinched between her fingers.

"Fallon?"

"Yeah, the brown-haired bitch that you sent to mess everything up."

"As I said," Xi's voice was sharp, the rock in her fingers beginning to shimmer in a genuine rainbow of colors. "I didn't send anyone to 'mess everything up'."

"Well, that's fine, but she's doing it anyway." I took a deep breath, it was too late to gauge her mood, I was in it. And I was just as upset. "She's telling all The Forgotten that she is some kind of savior sent to save them. That because she has magic she is the one to save them all. But she doesn't have magic, she has ugly sparks that a mortal could make in their ugly shed in the woods."

Ugly shed magic.

Fallon wasn't doing magic, no matter how much she tried to paint it that way. They hadn't seen real magic in so long that they didn't know the difference. I could show them real magic, I could blow their minds with power and skill that they couldn't even think of. But no, doing so could easily lead to Xi adding a couple centuries onto whatever indentured servitude she had me under, so I was out.

I had already risked enough with that shield, and even more mentioning that I wasn't under Ceres control with fucking Fallon staring me down.

I could already be dead. Or mortal. Although I didn't know what would happen if she turned me back into a mortal. Instant aging seemed like a terrible punishment. The images alone were terrible.

"She is getting on my nerves and getting more Fae to follow her than are following Zoe. And I am pretty sure you want them to follow Zoe."

"That is what needs to happen. But it seems someone might be playing cards larger than mine. This Fae, is she taller than you?" I nodded, my frustration at the garage magic bitch fading.

It wasn't that hard to be taller than me, for Fae, it was unusual, but not impossible.

But Xi was looking like I had force fed her the worst news in the world. And there's the reaction I was looking for.

"Her magic, how did it look. Was it a bit..."

"Like a snake poking a badger who is holding a rocket?" I nodded, my face twisted, but Xi was already descending into an anger I had never seen before.

"Mattia." Xi swore, so loud and so vulgar I almost looked around to make sure no other adult had heard that.

Okay, so maybe this wasn't the reaction I had expected, it was worse. Xi swore again, throwing the rock right past my head and into the rock formations behind me, shattering the thing and sending magical sparks and enchanted rock shards all around us, most of it right into my back.

"What the hell is going on?"

"Listen to me. You are going to have to trust that Zoe and Drake can handle themselves. You may not have time to meddle or help anymore. You cannot let that girl out of your sight. You shouldn't even be here right now."

"Xi? What's going on? I thought Henry..."

"Henry is an irritating scoundrel and I hope to god the two of them never meet. But Mattia," She paused swore again and then turned, the little girl seeming to age before my eyes as she stepped forward and a beautiful woman emerged. She was completely naked and so beautiful that I was feeling solely responsible for having put my whole gender to shame.

Long hair fell over her back, curling into multicolored spirals that glimmered over her skin in the faintest sparkle, the same rainbow of lights shining in her fury-filled eyes.

Beautiful. Deadly.

I don't think I had ever seen Xi in her true human form, and could only stare, feeling like I needed to blubber or bow down, or something.

Instead, I stood with my jaw wagging around.

"If I am the light in this world, if I am the orchestrator of good and hope; then Mattia my opposite to that. Fallon is his pet, a shifter in her own right. I gave you the magic of the Fae in trade for your help. Mattia cursed his familiar with humanity and tethered her soul to his. You cannot trust her."

"So, he's the... devil?" The word struggled out me, but with the way she was talking it didn't seem to be strong enough.

Her answering chuckle only promised that.

"Not quite, I would say Henry more aligns himself with that degree of evil."

"He's more powerful than the devil?" I really didn't like where this was going. "If he's so powerful then why is he meddling with the dragons, why doesn't he go off and mess with the humans. They're fun."

And they were, I may not have had a lot of days off from my hundreds of years of servitude, but every day I got I spent it meddling with humans.

Or driving Killian crazy with old pieces of artwork.

They were both equally fun when it came down to it.

But this, this was not fun, Xi's fear was not fun.

The dread that was eeking up through my spine was not fun.

"He's not just messing with Dragons, he's messing with me."

That dread was quickly turning to panic. She was really starting to scare me. What kind of idiot messes with an all-powerful, scary as shit, fucking Unicorn.

Someone that's more powerful, that's who.

"You? But why?" The words shook as they ripped out of me, everything tensing as I waited for her answer.

"Because I was the one who created him."

"Well, Fuck."

ALSO BY REBECCA ETHINGTON

THE WORLD OF IMDALIND

THE CIRCUS OF SHIFTERS

Flame of the Phoenix, Book Four

Death of the Demon, Book Five

The Dragon Queen Series

Rising Flame (coming Late 2019)

THE OTHER WORLDS

The Through Glass Series

Book One: The Dark

Book Two: The Blue

Book Three: The Rose

Book Four: The Cut

Book Five: The Light (Coming 2019)

Book Six: The Ascended (Coming 2019)

Of River and Raynn, The Series

The Catalyst: Act One (Rereleases 2019)

The Requisite: Act Two (Coming 2019)

ABOUT THE AUTHOR

Rebecca Ethington is an internationally bestselling author with almost 700,000 books sold. Her breakout debut, The Imdalind Series, has been featured on bestseller lists since its debut in 2012, reaching thousands of adoring fans worldwide and cited as "Interesting and Intense" by *USA Today's Happily Ever After Blog.*

From writing horror to romance and creating every sort of magical creature in between, Rebecca's imagination weaves vibrant worlds that transport readers into the pages of her books. Her writing has been described as fresh, original, and groundbreaking, with stories that bend genres and create fantastical worlds.

Born and raised under the lights of a stage, Rebecca has written stories by the ghost light, told them in whispers in dark corridors, and never stopped creating within the pages of a notebook.

Find me online
www.rebeccaethington.com
contact@rebeccaethington.com

www.ingramcontent.com/pod-product-compliance
Lightning Source LLC
Chambersburg PA
CBHW032148190626
46814CB00005BA/1891